"I suggest we travel from here on as a family."

Charles glanced at the child before turning a steady gaze on her. "He has your eyes and all of my coloring. He could easily be our son."

"Yes, but…" Annabelle stammered.

"If we have to, we can make it official."

Annabelle's jaw gaped. "What?"

"Marry."

"You should not joke about such things."

"Believe me, I am not joking," Charles said flatly. "It would not have to be forever if you didn't want it to be. That way your reputation would be safe."

But what about my heart? She let her horse fall back behind the big bay so Charles could not see her if she failed to curtail the tears threatening to roll down her cheeks.

Why weep? she asked herself.

The answer was as clear as if it had been shouted in her ear. *Because I will soon be the wife of a man whose heart does not belong to me—and whom I already love.*

Valerie Hansen was thirty when she awoke to the presence of the Lord in her life and turned to Jesus. She now lives in a renovated farmhouse in the breathtakingly beautiful Ozark Mountains of Arkansas and is privileged to share her personal faith by telling the stories of her heart for Love Inspired. Life doesn't get much better than that!

Books by Valerie Hansen

Love Inspired Historical

Frontier Courtship
Wilderness Courtship
High Plains Bride
The Doctor's Newfound Family
Rescuing the Heiress
Her Cherokee Groom

Love Inspired Suspense

The Defenders

Nightwatch
Threat of Darkness
Standing Guard
A Trace of Memory
Small Town Justice

Visit the Author Profile page at Harlequin.com for more titles.

VALERIE HANSEN

Her Cherokee Groom

HARLEQUIN® LOVE INSPIRED® HISTORICAL

Recycling programs
for this product may
not exist in your area.

LOVE INSPIRED BOOKS

ISBN-13: 978-0-373-42523-5

Her Cherokee Groom

Copyright © 2017 by Valerie Whisenand

www.Harlequin.com

Printed in U.S.A.

He that delicately bringeth up his servant from a
child shall have him become his son at the length.
—*Proverbs* 29:21

Thanks to my Joe for taking me to North Carolina to see the Cherokee Museum and reenactments of tribal life. And thanks to the Cherokee clans who faithfully labor to keep their history and culture alive.

Chapter One

Washington, DC—1830

"What are *you* doing out here? Spying?"

Seventeen-year-old Annabelle Lang was so startled by the voice she nearly gasped aloud. Her guardian's new wife had caught her loitering in the hallway and peeking into the parlor to look at visiting dignitaries. How embarrassing.

Biting her lip, Annabelle shook her head enough to make her flaxen blond side curls swing against her rosy cheeks and replied, "No, ma'am. I just wanted to see the Indians."

"Well, you've seen them. Now stop wasting time, get back to the kitchen and help Lucy finish preparing the lemonade. I want both those new washtubs filled to the brim." With that, Margaret Eaton swept past, skirts and petticoats belling and swishing, long, dark side curls bobbing, to make a grand entrance into the parlor and join her husband, John.

Annabelle's heart pounded. Her feet were unwilling to carry her away. She had no clear recollection of her early years, before coming to live with the first Mrs. Eaton, yet the mere sight of the Cherokee delegation stirred her emotions and left her light-headed.

Little wonder! These men were tall and stately, some wearing the kind of tall hats, vests and coats she was familiar with. Others were garbed in turbans and long tunics with elaborately woven sashes at the waist. None was bearded, nor did they seem the downtrodden savages she had overheard Mrs. Eaton railing about. These men were regal looking to the point of inspiring awe.

Before she could turn away, John Eaton spied her peeking from behind the doorjamb.

He gestured. "Annabelle. Come here and take these gentlemen's hats and capes. We must make our guests comfortable."

Trembling and wondering if she was going to be able to walk steadily enough to do as instructed, she started forward. Everyone glanced at her except Margaret, an advantageous snub Annabelle prayed would continue.

Not all of these Indians had swarthy complexions and ebony eyes, she noted. Some were grayed with age, particularly the largest, most impressive old gentleman. His clothing was not only embellished with lace and gilding like that of nobility, his bearing befit royalty and inspired respect.

Several of the younger members of his party had the fairer hair and the blue or light-brown eyes of folks she saw every day. Perhaps that was because these men were the offspring of mixed marriages. She'd been told that was the way of many Cherokee, including prominent tribal leaders. They also spoke and read at least two languages, English and their own, a feat for which Annabelle admired them greatly.

One particularly stalwart young man whom she guessed to be in his twenties caught her eye. She chanced a surreptitious glance at him as she approached and found that he was studying her, too. It was as if she were a captive of his startling blue gaze, unable to break away, unable to consider anything or anyone but him.

His dark hair was fairly long, thick and slicked straight back, and he had his top hat in hand, having politely removed it when he'd entered the parlor. As Annabelle received it from him in passing she saw a tiny smile twitch one corner of his mouth. That simple acknowledgment made her insides quaver like dry leaves in a Potomac storm.

A much smaller version of that stately Cherokee emissary stood stoically by his side. The two were so similar, except for age, she wondered if they might be brothers.

She'd almost reached the doorway when Margaret let out an excited squeal. Annabelle stopped to look back. There was an expression of delight on the older woman's face.

One of the Indians, the one bedecked with all the lace and gilding, was speaking while a younger man who bore a strong resemblance to him translated his message into perfect English. Words and phrases of both languages flowed like the impressive political orations she had heard her foster father make.

"We have brought you a fine tea service as a token of our esteem." As his speech was repeated, the elder Cherokee gave a slight bow that was less than submissive but nevertheless did not lack gentility.

A member of the Cherokee party had first unwrapped a gleaming silver teapot. Now, her fan fluttering like the wings of a demented butterfly, Mrs. Eaton watched a matching silver tray and other accoutrements follow.

Annabelle knew little about such elaborate trappings, except that they needed constant polishing, but she could see that her new foster mother was clearly impressed with the gift. That, alone, was remarkable since Margaret was so terribly hard to please.

John Eaton offered his hand to the original spokesman and said, "Thank you, Major Ridge. As Secretary of War, I am honored to accept your exceptional gift on behalf of President Jackson."

The Indian leader then gestured to the rear of his entourage and the crowd parted like the waters of the Red Sea had for Moses. He was pointing toward the handsome young man and little boy who had taken Annabelle's fancy moments before.

"This child is the most valuable of our gifts, a presentation from Chief John Ross. You may call him after yourself, as well. From this day forward he is John H. Eaton Ross."

Annabelle's jaw dropped. The young man she had been watching so closely placed his hands on the boy's shoulders to guide him forward. The child's hair was almost ebony but his eyes were the color of a summer sky, just like those of his apparent supervisor.

The boy's expression was stoic, perhaps even tinged by hostility, yet he stepped boldly and stood tall in his tailored white-man's clothing. How brave he was. And how distressed he must be to have been given away like a stray cur's unwanted pup.

As Annabelle watched, Margaret's beseeching gaze focused on her statesman husband, silently begging him to refuse. Instead, he shook his head ever so slightly. Obviously, this was an offer they must accept graciously. To do otherwise would be to commit a grievous social and political error.

Annabelle's heart went out to the young child. She knew exactly what it was like to become someone's ward, especially when the adults involved were not happy about the situation. Yes, John Eaton had continued to care for her after his first wife's death but she had quickly learned that he did not consider her a daughter. And when he married widow Margaret Timberlake? Annabelle had quickly learned then what it was like to be truly ostracized.

She wanted to go to the Indian child now known as John and bestow the welcoming smile that the rest of the family was denying him. Naturally, she could not. Her place in the household was tenuous at best, and the less trouble she made, the more likely it would be that she would soon be sent to boarding school in Connecticut for a proper education, as she'd been promised.

The drawing room fell so silent that Annabelle was certain everyone could hear the rapid beating of her heart. No one moved. No one spoke.

Finally, because her armload of garments was so heavy and cumbersome, she began to edge toward the arched doorway nearest the hall.

One of the Cherokee wraps dragged just enough to tangle her ankles. She faltered. Staggered. Was about to fall and disgrace her guardian in front of all these important emissaries.

A strong hand grasped her billowy sleeve at the elbow. Stopped her fall. Righted and steadied her.

Preparing to thank her rescuer, she looked up straight

into the eyes of the Cherokee gentleman she had admired mere moments ago.

There was steadiness to his gaze, yes, but she imagined empathy, as well. He seemed to sense that she was held in little regard here.

It was hard to be certain of his age but she guessed him to be only a few years older than she. He was wiry yet muscular, strong yet gentle. There was a control within him that she admired and also envied.

A cautious smile lifted the corners of her mouth as she whispered, "Thank you, sir."

His answer was a brief nod, but in Annabelle's eyes he had just bestowed a most pleasing grin.

One meant only for her.

When he leaned closer to say, "Pleased to be of service, Miss Annabelle. My name is Charles," she was afraid the floor was going to fall away beneath her feet.

Charles McDonald couldn't get his mind off the afternoon's events. Leaving the boy behind in the Eaton house was the most difficult thing his chiefs had ever asked him to do. He and the child were kin through their mothers from the Wolf Clan, and as an uncle it was his job to help raise and teach the male children.

If it had not been for the presence of a clearly sympathetic soul in the person of the fair-haired young woman called Annabelle, he might have rebelled.

"No, I wouldn't have," Charles told himself. "I am not like some of the others. I obey my chiefs."

Even if they're wrong? Charles wondered. Cherokee history proved why leaders of opposing sects within the tribe didn't trust others to negotiate for them. Hence, the trip to Washington with Major Ridge, his son John

Ridge, Elias Boudinot and a half-dozen others to try to gain an audience with President Jackson and plead their case against forced relocation.

Placing the boy in the Eaton household was the strongest symbol of trust anyone could bestow. He hoped Eaton realized that, treated the child as the son he was meant to be and saw to it that he received a good education. A white man's education. The kind that would prepare him to one day speak for the Cherokee with the authority and intelligence that Charles's current companions exemplified.

Leaning on a lamppost across from the imposing Eaton residence on New York Avenue, Charles sighed. In a few more days he and his party would return to Georgia. How would the boy cope when he was left behind to fend for himself?

The grounds of the brick mansion he was observing were encircled by a wrought-iron fence. At the rear lay a vegetable and herb garden. As Charles watched, a familiar flaxen-haired figure, wearing a lacy cap that complemented the white collar of her darker dress, appeared in the kitchen garden. The handle of a shallow basket was looped over one arm. Her other hand held that of the Cherokee child.

Straightening, Charles shaded his eyes beneath the brim of his hat. The boy seemed to be instructing the young woman by pointing to various plants. Perhaps this new life was not going to be the ordeal for him that Charles had expected.

He adjusted his cravat and tugged on the points of his vest while dodging wagon traffic to cross the broad street. The young woman had seemed a bit timid when he'd originally encountered her but at the moment she was acting quite forthright. Another good sign. One he wanted to encourage.

She didn't seem to notice his approach but the child did. Not only did he begin to grin, he called to Charles, *"Siyo!"*

"In English," Charles replied firmly. He tipped his hat to Annabelle as he said, "Hello again, miss."

To his surprise, Little John ducked behind her skirt. Her hand rested against the child's cheek as if sheltering him while she smiled a greeting of her own. "Good afternoon, sir."

"You may call me Mr. McDonald or simply Charles, if you wish," he said pleasantly. "And you are Miss Annabelle…?"

"Annabelle Lang," she replied, blushing demurely.

"Have you worked for the Eatons long?"

"You are mistaken, sir. I was brought into the family long ago, the same way John just was, except I was less a gift than a charity case taken on by the first Mrs. Eaton."

"Please forgive me. Had I known you were not a servant I would not have spoken so boldly."

"You have not given offense. My grandmother raised me until a fever took her. Mrs. Myra Eaton took on the burden of my care when I was three years old."

"I cannot imagine you could ever be a burden," Charles said, growing more empathetic by the second. "Are you from Washington City, then?"

"No. Tennessee. I became a ward of the Eatons, stayed on there after Myra died and came to Washington when my foster father was elected to the senate." She cast a brief glance at the rear of the house. "The new Mrs. Eaton didn't take to me when she and the senator were wed last year, but she has promised to send me to a special school in Connecticut. The Cornwall Mission School."

"Cornwall?"

"Yes. You know of it?"

Charles wondered if he should be the one to deliver the bad news. It hardly seemed fair to let her continue to hope in vain.

"My condolences, Miss Annabelle. I must inform you that that school has closed."

"Surely not for good."

"I'm afraid so."

"But, why? It's said to be a wonderful school."

"Yes, it was. There was an unfortunate incident that caused its financial support to be withdrawn."

"What could have happened that was so bad? Was someone killed?"

Charles had to chuckle at her naïveté. "No, no. Let me simply say it was because of an affair of the heart."

"Oh, my. Was it very sad?"

"No, dear lady. Actually, Cherokee Elias Boudinot and a missionary's daughter Miss Harriet Gold not only married, they already have the beginnings of a lovely family. You saw him with me today in your parlor. He's the editor and publisher of *The Cherokee Phoenix*."

"I've heard of that amazing newspaper! So, something good did come out of the tragedy."

"That depends upon one's point of view," Charles said. He gestured at the child who remained hidden behind her full skirts. "Some things which are deemed best at the time may not prove to be prudent in the future. Like my nephew, Usdi Tsani."

"Is that his real name?"

"No. That simply means Little John."

"Tell me again. Let me learn it."

"Why would you want to do that?" Charles asked, genuinely puzzled.

"So I can speak to him in his own language and make him feel settled here. I know how hard it is to be thrust into a strange home the way he has been."

"Which is why you and he have already become friends," Charles observed. "That is a good thing."

"What about you and your companions? Will you be leaving Washington soon?"

"Yes." His gaze rested on the child as he answered and he saw John look away as if in pain. Although he would rather have died than show tender emotion, Charles yearned to embrace the child one last time, to bless him and wish him well.

Instead, he merely squared his hat on his head and nodded to Annabelle. "It has been a pleasure meeting you, miss. I know you'll look after the boy. If there is anything he needs, anything at all, send word to me at Plunkett's Boarding House before the end of the week and I shall see he gets it."

"All right."

The rosy glow of her cheeks reminded him of the blush on a peach and her eyes mirrored the bright, clear sky. He didn't know what her lineage was but the fact that she had been promised an education at the Cornwall School meant that she might very well have a part Indian heritage, whether she knew it or not.

Good thing this young woman resided in Washington and he lived down in Georgia, he mused, or he might seriously consider disappointing his mother by courting Annabelle Lang instead of choosing a full-blooded Cherokee bride the way his family wanted.

* * *

Annabelle wondered if her snug corset was the reason she could hardly draw in enough air to maintain her equilibrium. She gently stroked the hair of the little boy at her side. Perhaps someday she, too, would have such a beautiful son, although that dream was not likely to come true as long as the new Mrs. Eaton was in charge.

Being lied to about going to the Cornwall School did not sit well with Annabelle. All this time she had dutifully served the Eatons in the hope that her obedience and faithfulness would result in the education she had been promised.

And now? The mission school was gone. So where else could she study? What other institutions would accept an untutored, common girl like her? The Georgetown Academy for Young Ladies was far too elite for someone who had never been formally instructed, not to mention someone with questionable origins.

Charles had paused at the iron gate for a last word. "Perhaps the Eatons will provide you with a tutor since you are so determined to learn."

Annabelle smiled. "I have gleaned some basic skills on my own, including how to read and write. When young John is given a tutor I will copy those lessons, as well."

"Very wise." He touched the brim of his hat once again. "I bid you a good evening."

And good it is, thanks to your unexpected visit, she thought, blushing.

Adding sprigs of rosemary to her basket, she held out her hand to the boy. "Come. Let's go back inside and give these to Lucy, the cook. Then I'll show you around the house and point out your room."

The child stood staring after his departing kinsman as if made of marble.

"John? *Tsa-ni?* Is that how you pronounce it?"

A slight smile teased a corner of his mouth.

"I said it poorly, didn't I?" Annabelle asked with a benevolent grin. "Tell you what. Johnny sounds a lot like that so I'll call you Johnny. All right?"

A simple nod was his only reply but it was enough. Better communication would come later, once the child was more comfortable with her. She would do all she could to hurry that along, even if it meant slacking off on her household duties. Dusting and mending would wait. The little boy's broken heart would not.

"How old are you?" Annabelle asked as they entered the house and left the basket for the cook.

"Six summers."

"What a big boy you are. I've always wanted a brother just like you."

"Why?"

"Because I get lonely in this big old house. Mr. and Mrs. Eaton are not my parents, as you heard me say. The servants are nice to me but it's not the same as having a true family."

"You want blood kin," Johnny said wisely.

"I suppose you could put it that way." Annabelle bent closer to whisper. "I don't complain, though, and you shouldn't, either. It's very good of the Eatons to take us in and provide for us."

The boy tugged on her hand, then looked around as if making sure they were alone. "I will run away. You can come with me."

"What? Oh, no. We can't."

"Why not?"

"Because it's wrong. What would your uncle Charles say if you did something like that?"

"I am the son of a chief's son. I will go."

"Please, don't talk like that," she pleaded. "Think of all the trouble it would cause if you left."

She could tell by the child's stoic expression that he was beyond listening to the pleas of a mere girl.

There was only one thing to do. She would have to send word to Mr. McDonald to stop by again and have a stern word with the boy before he and the rest of the delegation left town. Until then she'd keep a close eye on Johnny. A very close eye.

"I think you and I should take our supper alone tonight and get to know each other," Annabelle suggested.

"Will they not miss you?"

"No," she admitted sadly. "The family usually insists I be present only for formal dinner parties."

She reached down to gently smooth his hair. "I'm certain they will want to present you to their Washington friends soon. Mr. Eaton is a very important man. Being secretary of war means he works closely with President Jackson."

The child did not look impressed. Smiling, she offered her hand. "Come. We'll explore the house together so you won't get lost."

"I never get lost," he insisted.

"Good for you."

Grinning, Annabelle started up the spiral staircase, explaining as she went. "Down the hall at the end is the guest room. You'll sleep there."

Before he could ask she added, "My room is right next to that one," and sensed him starting to relax.

Poor little thing. He acted so brave and put on such a grown-up front it was easy to forget how young he was.

No wonder he'd thought about running away. He had to be frightened nearly out of his mind.

Shivering, she realized she, too, was worried about his future. It was easy to put herself in his place because she shared it. Neither of them truly belonged in this stoic family and neither could depend on fair treatment from their so-called parents.

John Eaton had always acted preoccupied and distant toward her. His new wife, Margaret, was far worse because she paid attention to everything and could be very vindictive if displeased, which was most of the time. The older woman had had a sordid reputation in Washington before her marriage to Eaton. The more Margaret and Annabelle interacted, the more credence the rumors of perfidy gained. And the more trepidation they generated.

Margaret had already fired every young female servant in the Eaton household and had made it clear that Annabelle's presence was barely tolerable. There was no foundation for such jealousy but it nevertheless existed. Perhaps, because Johnny was a boy, he would not encounter so much of Margaret's malice.

Until the child got used to his new life here in Washington City, Annabelle vowed she would protect and guide him. It would be no chore to teach him city ways and household rules. Truth to tell, she was looking forward to the opportunity.

The fact that he was a smaller version of his uncle gave her heart an added prick and reminded her that she must contact Charles McDonald as soon as possible and entreat him to return and lecture the child about fidelity.

Annabelle's stomach clenched. If Margaret even suspected that Johnny was planning to run away, the whole household would suffer her fits of foul temper, probably for weeks on end.

Chapter Two

Moonlight gleamed on the rippling surface of the Potomac, making the water shimmer like molten silver. If not for the noise of the city behind him, Charles might have imagined that he was standing on the banks of the Chattahoochee, back home, listening to a cacophony of frogs and the calls of night birds.

How much longer would Georgia be home to the Cherokee? he wondered. Some of his people had already migrated of their own volition but until the tribal elders had the solemn promise of the current president that their claim to lands farther west would be honored, he and many others were reluctant to pack up and go.

A flock of white egrets took to the sky, startled by something near the river's edge. Charles instinctively slipped into a copse of trees.

"I seen him come this way," someone said. "High falutin he was, too. Real fancy dressed."

Another man chortled and spat. "Well, he can't have gone far. We'll get him. And then we'll teach 'em to stay where they belong."

"Don't forget, I get his stickpin."

Charles automatically reached for his pistol and grabbed empty air. The delegation had been instructed to exemplify peace. Consequently, he was unarmed.

Moving so slowly, so fluidly, that the roosting wild birds were not disturbed, he inched backward until his shoulders met the trunk of an enormous oak. Then he consciously calmed his mind and waited.

Leaves rustled. Nearby bushes shook.

The would-be assailants were nearly upon him.

Annabelle's supper with Johnny had been uneventful except that he had eaten little. She felt so sorry for him she didn't argue when he asked, "May I go up to my room?"

"Of course. I know you must be weary."

"Are you coming upstairs?"

"In a few minutes," she replied. "I have one errand to take care of first. Go ahead. I'll be up soon."

She watched him climb the stairs, then turned to check the empty hallway. There was pen and ink in a writing desk tucked into an alcove off the parlor. While the Eatons were dining, she could avail herself of the opportunity to write a short note to Charles—Mr. McDonald. The mere thought made her blush and hurry toward the desk. She must not be observed, nor did she dare let anyone see to whom her innocent letter was addressed. Not if she hoped to be able to carry out her plan and stop the child from fleeing.

She dipped the nib in the inkwell and began, "Dear Sir," ending with her signature and placing his name on the outside of the folded note paper. Her penmanship was not perfect because she'd had so little chance to practice and because her hands were trembling, but it would suffice. It would have to.

Replacing everything she had moved and used, she quietly closed the slanted lid of the desk and slipped the note into her pocket.

A quick, furtive check of her surroundings confirmed that she was still alone and she quietly headed for the carriage house to seek out one of the grooms and ask him to carry her missive to Plunkett's.

Although the sun had set, the moon was nearly full and there was plenty of reflected light from the lamp-posts lining the broad avenues of the capitol as she entered the rear garden. A few couples strolled arm in arm outside the iron fence while drays and coaches went about their business in the street.

Annabelle had swung a thin, gray cape around her shoulders as soon as she was outside. Now she lifted the hood, less for warmth than to hide her passage through the garden.

She patted her pocket. The sooner the note was delivered, the sooner she'd stop worrying.

In the street beyond the familiar garden path a teamster snapped his whip and shouted, "Out of my way!"

Curiosity caused her to look. Astonishment stopped her cold. Was that…? Could it be…? She'd left him only a few minutes ago, yet the young boy in the street looked terribly familiar. And with good reason.

Heart pounding, Annabelle almost called out, "Johnny!" before she thought better of it. So far, no harm had been done. If she could overtake him and get him back into the house before either of them was missed she might save everyone a lot of unnecessary grief.

She fumbled the gate latch in her nervousness,

thereby slowing her progress. By the time she reached the street the boy had vanished.

Where would he go? Washington was a big city and they were both on foot. If she were Johnny, what would she do?

"Go back to the boardinghouse where the Cherokees are staying," Annabelle guessed. She *had* to be right. If Johnny disappeared in a city this vast, his chances of being hurt or accosted were immense, particularly since he didn't blend in with the dirty street urchins who were out and about at this hour.

Nervous, she glanced back at the house. Few lamps were glowing. No one would miss her. Gathering a handful of her skirt and cape she hurried in the direction where she had last spied the runaway child.

Prayer was on her lips. "Please, God, please. Help me? Guide me?"

It was then that she realized her Heavenly Father already had. She already knew that the boardinghouse the Cherokees had chosen was only a block or so past the cathedral where the family worshipped every Sunday. She knew the way.

Circumventing trouble as best she could, she darted back and forth across the broad streets, dodging coaches and buggies while evading those individuals who might wish to do her harm. She had never ventured out alone at night and the face of the city was quite different than she had expected.

The boardinghouse Annabelle sought was built in the Federalist style with tall, narrow banks of windows facing the street and a small porch that led directly into the parlor. Seeing Plunkett's finely lettered sign gave her hope and renewed energy.

Before she'd taken two steps up the front stairs, however, Johnny burst out the door and ran past, snatching away what was left of her breath.

She lunged to grab his sleeve.

He struggled, twisting and kicking.

"Johnny! Stop. It's me." She pushed back her hood so he could better see her features.

"We have to go." Johnny pointed. "This way."

"No. I came to speak to your uncle."

"That is why we have to go," the boy insisted. "The man inside said he went to the river."

"He'll be back. We can stay here and wait."

The child tore himself from her grasp. "No! It is not good. We must find him."

Annabelle was unconvinced. Now that they had both made it to the boardinghouse the most sensible choice was to tarry there.

Unfortunately, Johnny was already running again.

"All right," she called, quickly recovering. "Wait for me. I'm coming."

They soon left the open streets for a parklike area and slowed to a walk because there was no artificial light. Patches of fog drifted in front of them as if clouds had sunk to earth, muting even the moon glow.

Johnny abruptly grasped her hand and tugged. "Stop."

Annabelle's breath caught. "Why? I thought you were in a hurry."

Rethinking their possibly tenuous safety, she pushed back the hood of her satin cape once again and bent over him to speak more softly. "What's wrong?"

"Men. Bad men. Fighting." He pointed.

She had barely made out shadowy shapes when there

was a muffled shout. The boy broke free and raced toward the altercation!

"Johnny, no!" Fisting her skirt she ran after him.

Someone yelled.

Annabelle drew closer. Her eyes widened. "Oh, no!"

A well-dressed gentleman was doing hand-to-hand battle with two ruffians and it was impossible to tell who had the upper hand. *Now* she understood the boy. Charles McDonald was being attacked and although he seemed to be holding his own at the moment, he was definitely outnumbered.

Charles threw a punch that sent one of the thugs reeling out of sight among some saplings, and dove after him. Bushes rustled and shook. A man grunted. Another shouted. The thug left in the open staggered and fell to his knees as if hurt or intoxicated. Perhaps both.

The seconds passed for Annabelle in slow motion. She heard another cry. Was that a splash? Were they that close to the Potomac?

The man she could see struggled to his feet and braced himself, ready for more fight. Charles reappeared and engaged him by circling, arms wide, ready for further attack. They locked arms and began grappling while Johnny beat the back of his uncle's foe with a broken branch and screeched unintelligibly in his native language.

The men fell together. Charles scrambled up first. His foe moved more slowly yet was far heavier and thus had the advantage of sheer weight when he threw himself back into the melee.

This was a new conundrum for Annabelle. She had never seen grown men fight, so she stood aside, gaping helplessly and standing clear. Her hands were clasped in front of her so tightly they ached.

Then she saw something metal flash in the stranger's hand and her attitude changed. "A knife! He has a knife."

Charles crouched and stepped sideways, keeping just out of the assailant's reach. "Stay back!"

The other man was slow and clumsy, carving harmless arcs in the night air, yet Annabelle knew it was only a matter of time until someone made a fatal misstep. What could she do? How could she possibly help the Cherokees?

Without warning, the attacker changed tactics and lunged for Johnny.

The child was too quick for him.

Charles grabbed a handful of dirt and threw it into the other man's face. "Hey! Over here."

The ploy worked. The burly man whirled, distracted, wiping at his eyes. But how long would that hold him off?

Annabelle had never in her life felt so powerless. So useless. As long as Charles's adversary was the only one armed, there was no way she could be certain the Cherokee would prevail. Unless…

Whipping off her cape she twirled it at arm's length and watched it billow out. The man with the knife was temporarily distracted and Charles darted in to try to disarm him. They wrestled until the attacker whipped one arm to the side and threw Charles to the dirt.

Annabelle could tell he was stunned when he landed. Johnny ran between his uncle and the knife-wielder, shouting and hitting him with the leafy branch.

The man roared and stood tall, facing both Cherokees. He was taller and much bulkier than she was but as long as his attention was so focused on Charles, Annabelle knew she had the element of surprise on her side.

With an unspoken prayer, she circled behind the big man, threw the cape over his head and yanked it down.

Blinded and surrounded, he flailed and slashed at the silky material, cutting portions of it to ribbons and opening gaps that were almost wide enough to let him see his opponents.

Annabelle screamed. Johnny rushed at the confused thug from one side, hitting him with a solid enough blow that he instinctively whirled to redirect his attack.

That gave Charles enough time to get to his feet, knock the other man off balance and disarm him. He threw him to the ground facedown and pinned him there. "Give up and I won't hurt you more."

Johnny was not so forgiving. "No! Hit him again!"

Annabelle sympathized with the child, even after the thug stopped struggling, and she had to admire Charles's self-control. She stood back, hands clenched once more, while he and Johnny tore strips from her ruined cape to truss up the would-be robber like a Christmas goose.

"Keep a sharp lookout," Charles warned, getting to his feet and taking a defensive stance with the other man's knife. "There were two of them. I knocked one into the river but he could have climbed out by now."

"If he has half a wit he's long gone," she said. "What in the world were you doing out here all alone?"

"I could ask you the same thing."

"I followed Johnny," she replied. "I'd written you a note asking you to visit and talk some sense into him before you left the city. I was on my way to the stables to ask someone to deliver it to you when I saw him running down the street. That changed everything."

Seeing the doubt reflected in his shadowed expression she said, "Here, I'll prove it to you." As she slipped her hand into her skirt pocket her self-assurance turned to chagrin. "Oh, dear, I don't know what became of my note."

"How big was the paper?" Charles was scanning the nearby ground.

Annabelle joined him. "Small. I had folded it so it would fit in my pocket. I doubt we'll find it without a torch."

"Then forget it." His brows arched. "I had thought the boy was in good company with you. Looks as though I'll have to rethink my conclusion."

"We had both expected to find you at the boarding-house, sir," Annabelle countered, spine stiff and eyes blazing from his scolding. "If you had been there, none of this would have happened."

"Sadly, true." He closed and pocketed the thug's knife, then dusted off his clothing and his hands. "All right. I'll escort you both home and then go report this fellow's crimes."

"But, what if he gets loose and escapes while we're gone? What if his friend comes back and frees him?"

"That can't be helped." Charles slipped off his coat and shook it, then draped it over her shoulders. "You're shivering. This will help."

"Thank you. My cape is ruined."

"Since you saved my life with it I will be delighted to replace it."

"I can't let you do that. What would people say?"

"That a gallant lady sacrificed her cape to rescue the victim of a mugging?"

"I hardly see my part as being gallant. I was merely trying to keep the fight fair."

That made him laugh. "Have it your way. Just please allow me to buy you a new cape."

Annabelle sighed. "I suppose that can be arranged, if you insist. The Eatons always use the same wonderful seamstress, a Miss Mills. Her shop is in Arlington, but…" Her eyes widened and she faltered, staring up at her stalwart companion. "Oh, dear. I hadn't thought of that."

"Of what?"

"No one knows I ventured out tonight. If Mrs. Eaton finds out from the dressmaker that I need a new cape, she will be furious with me. And perhaps with Johnny, too."

"Then we'll simply keep this incident to ourselves and I'll pay Miss Mills to do the same when I engage her," Charles promised. "Right now, I think I should see you home so you can go back inside as if nothing has happened."

"I never lie."

"Then you are a truly exemplary lady," he said, sounding amused. When he looked down at Johnny, however, his countenance sobered. "You will do as you've been told and stay out of trouble, Tsani. This is your home now and you will honor our tribe's promises. Understand?"

Annabelle saw the child nod and bow his head as if the weight of the world lay on his thin shoulders. Poor little thing. Truthfully, it would be just as well if she were not sent off to boarding school. Johnny needed her there.

Her thoughts whirled and danced like moths drawn to a glowing lantern. She had prayed for guidance, assuming the answer lay merely in the choice of an alternate school. Now it was beginning to look as if her answer to those prayers was a resounding *no,* but for a very good reason. One that certainly countered the disappointment.

Shivering as the excitement wore off and weariness lay heavy, she was thankful for many things. One was the Cherokee ambassador's strong arm around her shoulders and his strength to lean against.

Having been warned against allowing any grown man to touch her thus, she was terribly confused. Surely those admonitions did not apply to her current situation.

Nothing that felt this right, this perfect, could possibly be wrong.

Chapter Three

"Were so many lamps burning in the house when you left?" Charles asked, pausing with his little group before escorting them back across New York Avenue.

Annabelle shook her head. "No. Mrs. Eaton usually does needlework in the evenings and Mr. Eaton sometimes reads the newspaper or personal communications from the president, but the rest of the rooms are rarely lit."

"That's what I was afraid of. I suspect they have missed you already."

"Oh, no."

"It may not be as bad as it looks. I suggest you and the boy go back inside alone, though. Being seen with me will probably not be to your advantage."

"We did nothing wrong."

"You and I know that. Others may be harder to convince and I'm not looking forward to being lynched on my first diplomatic mission."

"Surely, if I tell the family you have assisted me they will understand."

"To do that you'd have to admit to having gone out after dark. Alone. Are you sure that's wise?"

She looked so crestfallen he had to smile. "I'll be fine. I'm going straight to my elders to report the attack by the river. You go inside and tell the Eatons you and the boy just stepped out into the garden. That won't be a lie."

"All right."

As he reclaimed his coat she tilted her face up to him and he could see moisture sparkling on her lashes. Against his better judgment he gently took her hands, noting that she was trembling. "Don't worry. I'll wait right here until you're safely inside."

"Thank you for seeing us home."

"I should be the one thanking you for saving my neck. I'm sorry about your cape. I'll send a messenger to the dressmaker for you first thing in the morning."

"A cape was a small price to pay for our victory over evil."

Let her go, his mind insisted. *Step away from her and forget you ever met Annabelle Lang.*

But he would not, could not, do so. Although he assumed that this goodbye would be their last, he also knew she would linger in his thoughts and in his dreams for a long, long time. Being so taken with this innocent beauty had not only been a surprise, it had left him questioning his future without her.

That notion was beyond ridiculous, of course. Even if he happened to be sent to Washington again, chances were good that Eaton would forbid them to court properly, meaning he would be fortunate to encounter her at all.

That was one way in which Cherokee courtships and marriages were better. All a couple basically had to do was share a meal and exchange blankets and they were considered wed. Many of his kinsmen partook of two ceremonies, the Christian one and the tribal one, thereby satisfying both factions.

What was he thinking! Charles asked himself, coming to his senses. He barely knew this girl.

I'm far from home and lonely, that's all, he insisted. *There's nothing wrong with me that being back in Georgia where I belong won't fix.*

He purposefully released Annabelle's hands and stepped away while donning his coat. To his chagrin the fabric retained her warmth and a trace of a sweet scent like roses. Just like Annabelle's hair.

"You'd better go in," Charles said, sounding more brusque than he'd intended.

She bowed her head demurely. "That's wise. Good night. And God bless you, sir."

"He did that when He sent you to my aid."

"Perhaps because in my prayers I had asked to be of help to you and the boy. Are you a Christian, then?"

"Yes. I went to the missionary school."

Her smile was so sweet, so tender, all Charles could do was stand there and watch her walk away. And with her went a tiny portion of his heart despite his firm decision to remain stoic.

Lucy, the heavyset, dusky-skinned cook, was in the kitchen poking the ashes of the stove to get them to ignite fresh fuel when Annabelle and Johnny entered. She wiped her hands on her apron. "Land sakes, girl. Where you been? Mr. John is tearin' his hair."

"I—we—stepped out into the garden to look at the stars."

"Then why didn't you come when he hollered for you?"

"I guess I didn't hear." Annabelle's guilty conscience nagged at her to explain further. If she hadn't had little Johnny to protect she would have confessed without delay.

"Well, get in there and let the mister know you're all right. After the trouble tonight he'll surely be glad to see you."

"Trouble? Because of me?"

"Mercy, no." The cook's coffee-colored forehead knit above graying brows. "Somebody done made off with that fancy silver tea set the missus got from them Indians." Her gaze darted to the boy, then quickly back to Annabelle. "He be with you all the time?"

"Yes. Of course he was."

"If you say so. But Mr. John, he was plum mad, 'specially when he couldn't find neither of you."

"Thank you, Lucy. We'll go right in and set his mind at ease." She reached for the boy's hand and held tight, urging him to follow as she admonished, "You let me do all the talking."

Both Eatons were in the parlor when Annabelle entered. Their expressions contrasted; John's being one mixing anger with relief while Margaret simply looked disgruntled.

"Where have you been?" John demanded.

"Out in the garden, looking at the stars."

Margaret pointed at the boy. "Him, too?"

"Of course."

Chewing the inside of her cheek to keep from breaking into tears of shame, Annabelle stood very still and waited to be dismissed. She had no idea what had become of the silver set but she was certain the Cherokees had had nothing to do with it. Washington was a bustling city, filled with all kinds of riffraff, as demonstrated by the incident at the river. Undoubtedly, a criminal element like that had robbed the Eatons.

"I have the servants checking the carriage house and the stables," John said. "Go upstairs to your rooms and stay there. Both of you."

"Yes, sir." Annabelle curtseyed politely.

She was more than delighted to take her leave. This current Mrs. Eaton might be a special friend of President Jackson but she wasn't kind and loving the way Annabelle's first foster mother, Myra, had been. Oh, how she had wept when that dear lady had gone to Glory at such a young age.

Climbing the spiral staircase with Johnny, Annabelle realized she was actually happier being ignored than being watched too closely. That revelation was a surprise. A welcome one. It not only helped her feel less unwanted, it gave her a sense of freedom she had never before sought or even imagined.

"A servant will assist you getting ready for bed," she told the child. "I'll call Adams. He helps our father."

"I have no father," Johnny said flatly. "And I can take care of myself."

"All right, whatever you say." Annabelle continued to hold his hand until she said, "Remember. You promised to be good and stay here."

"I remember."

She hated to leave him alone looking so small and forlorn, yet she knew she must. With a deep sigh she eased the door closed and walked away. It was bound to be a long night for the child, not to mention how hard it was going to be for her to stop thinking about Charles McDonald's narrow escape and her part in his rescue.

She smiled to herself and gave a little shiver, then headed for her own room. Many nights she had prayed for a cessation of dreams but tonight she was eagerly looking forward to seeing if the handsome Cherokee would appear in them.

Given a choice, she would definitely have wished to include him as a part of her nighttime imaginings.

Charles headed straight for the boardinghouse when he left Eaton's. Instead of a quiet atmosphere, he found the male guests gathered in the sitting room, smoking and talking while uniformed soldiers in blue and police officers moved among them.

"Where have you been?" Elias Boudinot asked Charles, speaking aside. "Tell me you weren't near the river."

"As a matter of fact, I was. Why?"

The shorter, slightly older man pulled him into a corner and spoke with a coarse whisper. "Don't admit it. These men are out for blood, preferably ours."

"What for? What happened?"

"Somebody got knifed tonight."

Charles felt the blade in his pocket, glad he hadn't been a victim of the same kind of mayhem. "I'm not surprised. A couple of toughs came after me. It was only by the grace of God I managed to escape."

"Good thing you didn't have a woman with you."

The hair on Charles's nape prickled. "What do you mean?"

"They say the dead man was all tangled up in a woman's outer garment. It looked as if whoever killed him had rendered him helpless before driving a knife blade between his ribs."

Charles plopped onto the brocade-upholstered, horse-hair sofa. "Say that again?"

"It wasn't a normal mugging. The victim was trussed up first, then murdered in cold blood. Worse, he was a soldier on leave."

There was nothing Charles could think to say or do other than sit there and stare. The man they had tied up had been alive and well when he, Annabelle and Johnny had left him. Charles knew she would swear to that—except she'd have to admit to having been on the scene if he asked for her support. And then what would happen to her already tenuous standing in the Eaton household?

There was only one real problem as Charles saw it. The cape. If anyone recognized the fabric remnants left behind and questioned Annabelle, she'd be honor bound to tell the truth.

As long as the police believed *all* her story, every-thing would be fine. If they chose to twist her words, however, his whole diplomatic mission could be in jeop-ardy, not to mention his neck. Murder was bad enough. The thought that a visiting Cherokee might have killed a Washington citizen, let alone a soldier, was far worse.

Charles's choices were poor on all counts. His tribe depended upon its ambassadors portraying an image of refinement and civility. So, what should he do? Tell the whole story and reveal the girl's name? Keep mum and pray that nobody knew Annabelle had come looking for him? And what about Johnny? Suppose he remained with Eaton while Annabelle was ostracized?

Agonizing over the unacceptable possibilities, Charles decided he could not sit there and let an innocent young woman suffer needlessly. He must slip out and return to warn her, even if it meant sneaking into the Eaton mansion and somehow using his nephew as a go-between. Then, if he and Annabelle could not see a solution to their dilemma, he would return to Plunkett's and confess his part in the altercation being investigated.

Leaving the sofa with the fluid movement of a skillful hunter, he was out of the room and headed for the back door without any of the soldiers noticing.

Elias watched him go without a word.

Annabelle tossed and turned as sleep eluded her. She'd opened the windows partway to ventilate her stuffy bedroom and could hear voices coming from the yard below as well as from the mansion's ground floor.

Was that *her* name? Had someone just called to her?

"Annabelle!"

There it was again. Curiosity drew her to the open window, made her lean out and look down. "Charles? What are you…?"

"Hush. There may be troops headed this way. I came to warn you."

"Why?"

"They're at Plunkett's now. Police, too. We must have been seen together in the park."

She drew her nightclothes around her more tightly and tried to still her trembling. Surely there was no way anyone could have found out about her unauthorized excursion.

"We didn't do anything wrong. You were the victim."

"The man we tied up is dead," Charles said.

"No! He can't be." Her head was starting to spin and

she leaned heavily on the smooth wooden windowsill. "You must be mistaken. He was fine when we left."

"Somebody killed him after we were gone." Charles's voice was barely audible over the noise beginning to arise from the front yard and portico.

And there she stood, in her nightdress, holding an inappropriate conversation with a man she barely knew. A man whose presence in the garden would be further damning evidence of her mistakes if they were observed.

"Annabelle!" John Eaton's voice boomed, echoing up the stairwell. "Annabelle!" Boots thudded. Her door was hit hard and slammed open against the wall.

She whirled, her back to the window, the collar of her long gown fisted at her throat. There was no mistaking her foster father's tone or his reddening face. Someone must have discovered her trespasses, as Charles had warned.

"Downstairs. Now. And cover yourself decently."

"Yes, sir." Threading her arms through the sleeves of a linen wrapper, she belted it over her gown and freed her long, heavy braid from the collar.

Eaton pushed past her to the open window and leaned out, giving Annabelle a terrible fright. It wasn't until he slammed down the sash and turned away that she was able to breathe. If he had spied Charles McDonald waiting below he would surely be shouting. At least one thing had gone her way this evening.

She followed, barefoot, to the upper landing.

John Eaton was descending to join a group of heavily armed men. The foremost one wore a constable's badge. The others were mostly scowling, uniformed soldiers bearing rifles.

For an instant she entertained the thought that Charles

had been wrong about the killing and someone had recovered the missing silver service. Then she realized there would be no reason to summon *her* if that was all that was wrong.

No. This all had to be happening because of what she'd done—or what they believed she'd done—earlier.

Frozen in place at the top of the staircase Annabelle stared at the angry crowd.

Eaton motioned to her. "Come down here. These gentlemen have some questions for you."

"May I dress first?"

"No. Come as you are. The sooner we get to the bottom of this the better."

Her bare feet on the carpeted steps made no sound. She slid one hand along the banister to steady herself and obeyed his command, not stopping until she'd reached the bottom.

"Yes, sir?"

"Where were you tonight?" Eaton demanded.

"I beg your pardon? I was with the family." Her nervous fingers found the loose braid hanging over her left shoulder and unconsciously worried the end of it.

"Not every second. I recall that you did not answer when I called to you. You told us you were out in the garden. Is that true?"

"Yes." Annabelle's stomach was churning and she wondered if she was going to be ill.

One of the soldiers nearest the front door held up a soiled, ruined garment for all to see. Eaton pointed to it. "Then how do you explain *this*?"

For the first time in her life, Annabelle wished she were the kind of frail female who fainted at the drop of a hat. Surely being unconscious would be preferable to having to admit that the shredded remnant was her cape.

"What a shame." She used the stair railing for support. "It was so pretty."

"Then you don't deny it's yours?"

"No. It's mine. How did they know?"

"There was a note found nearby with your name on it."

"I did nothing wrong. Truly." She fought to hold back tears.

Dismay and disappointment on her foster father's face was countered by the vehemence of Margaret Eaton's railing. "Do you see now? I warned you the girl was up to no good. Blood will tell and hers is tainted."

Eaton whirled on her. "She caused no distress while Myra was caring for her."

"That was years ago. She's nearly a grown woman and a wily one at that." Margaret dabbed at her eyes with a lace-edged handkerchief. "Your reputation in Washington will be ruined, John."

"We—I will stand by Annabelle," Eaton vowed.

Margaret clung to his arm, weeping. "You mustn't. Think of the scandal. She's not even kin."

"Nevertheless, I made a commitment." He faced the armed cadre to say, "Annabelle Lang will be secure in my care. Contact my office at the Capitol if you wish to speak with her further and I will make those arrangements."

All the men looked uneasy. The veteran constable who was clearly the spokesman cleared his throat. "I'm sorry, Mr. Secretary. The murder victim was from the president's old regiment and our orders are to apprehend and arrest the suspect."

"Tonight?"

Frozen in place, Annabelle held tight to the newel post at the bottom of the staircase, waiting for the final decision and wondering if she dared speak to defend herself. If she did, there was a very good chance that Little Johnny would also be blamed, not to mention his uncle. If no one believed *she* was innocent, how could she possibly convince anyone that others were blameless?

The constable nodded as he cast a glance over his shoulder at the military men. "Yes, sir. Tonight."

Annabelle quailed. This could not be happening. Not to her. She looked to her foster father, pleading with her gaze, and saw indecision. Was his influence so weak in Washington that he could not prevail?

Then she recalled how close Margaret had been to the president himself. Could this accusation be her doing? Had there been enough time to have influenced Jackson? No. Yet he must know how Margaret felt about sharing her home, even with her own three offspring, because as soon as she'd learned of her first husband's death she'd shipped the Timberlake children off to live with her late husband's relatives.

John Eaton's expression grew regretful and he stepped back before gesturing to the officers. "Do what you must, but rest assured I will engage an attorney on her behalf. She had better be treated with kid gloves or heads will roll, starting with yours."

Annabelle found her voice. "They're really arresting me?"

"I'm afraid so. You won't be held for long if I have anything to say about it."

She tried to fill her lungs with breathable air and failed.

Light flashed before her eyes as if she were staring directly at the summer sun and unable to look away.

A tingling on her soles and palms, coupled with the spinning of the room, made her light-headed.

Seconds later she closed her eyes, lost her grip on the banister and slumped to the floor.

Charles caught a passing cab and made it back to Plunkett's in time to hear Major Ridge, the graying patriarch of the Cherokee delegation, addressing the crowd in the parlor. He was speaking himself, instead of asking his adult son to translate.

"The Cherokee Nation is self-governing by order of your own President Jefferson. We will handle the matter."

"We got proof! A name wrote down," someone in the back shouted.

Another voice chided, "Since when can you read?"

"May I see your proof?" Ridge held out his hand.

"It's not here. Which one is McDonald?"

Charles stepped forward. "I had nothing to do with killing that man or any other."

"Can you prove it?" Ridge asked him.

"If I have to."

Grumblings grew to shouts and several men shook clenched fists and brandished weapons.

"Then we will hear your testimony when the time comes," Ridge said. Unwavering, he faced the gathering and raised one hand as if taking an oath. "All of you. Go. I will vouch for the carrying out of justice."

Slowly, begrudgingly, the venerable man's orders were heeded. As the room began to clear, some onlookers were still muttering but the Indian delegation stood united, shoulder to shoulder.

Charles didn't realize he'd been holding his breath until the door slammed behind the last accuser.

"All right," Ridge said. "I want to hear the whole story. From the beginning."

When Charles was through, the older man was shaking his head. "We must go and speak with the girl."

"Is that really necessary?"

"Yes." The old leader was adamant. "Is this woman truthful? Can she be trusted?"

Sighing, Charles nodded. "Yes. But if Eaton doesn't already know she was with me, asking questions could ruin her life."

"That is her problem, not ours. Those soldiers will be back. As soon as we have spoken with her, we will leave Washington."

"Before we've been granted an audience with President Jackson?"

"Eaton and Coffee say they speak for him. That will have to do. Our presence here is no longer wise."

"I am sorry," Charles said. "I truly did nothing wrong. The man was alive when I left him by the river. Here. See? I even took his knife."

Withdrawing the blade from his pocket he laid it across his palm and held it out.

It wasn't until then that he was surrounded by enough ambient light to notice the rusty color of dried blood on part of the blade.

Chapter Four

Annabelle took as long as she dared to dress and prepare to leave the house. Part of her mind was spinning while another part felt numb. There had to be some way out of this dilemma, yet no answers came to her.

Worse, she mused, if the authorities had recovered her note they not only knew her name, they knew to whom it had been addressed. That put Charles McDonald in jeopardy and made her hope he had not returned to the boardinghouse after leaving the Eaton garden.

Everything, all their troubles, pointed back to the boy, didn't they? Too bad the opinions of children were not given credence, even under normal circumstances. Certainly Johnny would not be listened to in a Washington court. He might, however, make a good emissary to his uncle's group.

Annabelle rapped on the wall between their rooms. An answering tap came quickly. All she said was "come" and he appeared at her door in seconds.

"Did you hear?" she asked.

The child nodded.

"I need you to go to the Cherokees, tell them what has happened here tonight and warn your uncle. Will you?"

Another nod.

"Good. Be sure you do it secretly. Don't run up the street the way you did when I was chasing you. You must be very, very careful. No one must see you or catch you. Can you do that and sneak back into this house later?"

"Y-yes."

Johnny's lower lip was quivering so she bent to give him a hug of encouragement before adding, "God be with you."

Placing a kiss on his cheek she straightened, tossed her braid to hang behind her and stepped into the hallway, knowing she was in the right and prepared to prove it somehow.

By the time she was halfway down the stairs, however, most of her courage had evaporated like a drop of water on a hot day. She was determined to hide her fear, though. The less she looked and acted helpless, the braver she felt, so she did her best to stand tall, to face whatever awaited.

"I have to go *now*, to make sure she's all right," Charles insisted after he had listened to the boy's story and sent him back to Eaton's with another member of their group acting as guardian.

Ridge shook his gray head. "You will stay here until morning when we will go together."

"I'm sorry, sir. I can't. I'm afraid it may already be too late."

"If you disobey you will cease to be under my protection," Ridge warned.

Charles had not anticipated that severe a reaction but

he accepted it. "So be it. The woman would not be in trouble if she had not come to my aid. She saved my life."

"And now you will lose it by foolishness?" Ridge countered. "I had thought better of you."

That was the last comment Charles heard as he left the boardinghouse and hailed a cab. The horse seemed to sense his urgency because it was prancing as he boarded. "The Eaton house," he shouted to the driver. "Fast."

He had to arrive, to intercede, before Annabelle was taken away. He had little doubt that she would be, given the attitude of the soldiers who had confronted his delegation, and his people were important diplomats. The young woman, by her own admission, was merely a ward, and one who was not wanted by the new mistress of the household. What chance would she have if the Secretary of War did not stand up for her?

Perhaps Johnny had misjudged Eaton. Charles hoped so, because otherwise Annabelle's chances of escaping unjust punishment were slim.

If the party of lawmen and soldiers had not called his name and mentioned Annabelle's lost note he wouldn't have worried so much. Since they had, however, he assumed they had not only read his name but her signature, as well. They were both in trouble up to their necks.

Yes, *necks*, he affirmed. The part of a criminal where the hangman put the noose.

When Annabelle felt cold shackles close around her wrists she nearly fainted for the second time. Only pride and an immense desire to present herself blameless before her foster father and Margaret kept her on her feet.

The constable led her onto the porch by the short chain between her wrists, making her feel as if they considered her a dangerous animal rather than an innocent girl. Reality dimmed. If this was a nightmare it was the worst she had ever experienced.

Pausing to get her balance on the top step she lifted her gaze. A curious crowd had gathered and most were craning to get a good look. Some onlookers actually pointed at her and called out insults.

From the east, a cab was approaching at speed. The driver pulled hard on the reins. The horse reared. Women screamed. Men cursed and jumped out of the way.

The door of the cab swung open. Annabelle gasped. *Charles! No, no, he mustn't be here.*

She saw him start to push his way through the crowd. There was no way he could hope to rescue her from all these armed men. However, he might be a good witness to her innocence in the future, if he survived and kept himself out of prison. John Eaton had promised to hire legal representation, yes, but she doubted he would be amenable to adding a Cherokee client to the venture.

Given so little time and so few options she took a deep breath, looked directly into the crowd where Charles was and screamed, "No!"

The instant he faltered and met her gaze with his, she shook her head and mouthed another, "No," praying he'd take heed. She sensed his indecision and resisted being pulled down the steps.

Once more she spoke, this time calmly. "No. Not now."

And this time he gave a brief nod in response.

Heartened, she stood tall and descended until she stopped in the midst of the cadre of soldiers and civilians. The best thing, truly the only good thing, was that Charles McDonald had not rushed into the fray and joined her in chains.

As soon as Johnny explained to his kinsmen and they understood her dilemma, she would somehow assure them she would not testify against any of them. After all, they were innocent, as was she. This was Washington City, where the law of the land stood strong. She would be fine. This was a mere glitch brought on by a mob. People who were not guilty did not end up staying in prison.

Charles considered going back to the boardinghouse but could not make himself give that order to the cabbie. Instead, they slowly followed the group walking alongside the wagon carrying Annabelle to the closest jail.

He had to clench his fists and grit his teeth to keep from jumping out again and rushing to her rescue. He huffed, disgusted with himself. She had been right to stop him. Such a rash act would have been too stupid to be heroic. And it would have accomplished nothing worthwhile.

Instead, he disembarked near the jail, paid the cabbie and sent him away while he infiltrated the milling crowd to listen to rumors. Clearly, a Cherokee presence at the river altercation was known and he was thankful his clothing fit city life. The only way he'd be identified was if somebody besides Annabelle happened to recognize him.

Knowing she was held inside those barred doors made him want to pound on them with both fists. The more irrational claims he overheard about her character, the harder it was to control his temper, so he slipped away and circled the stone building, hoping to calm down enough to think clearly.

Shadows absorbed him the way a placid lake smoothly

covers her sunken secrets, and he easily reverted to instinctive oneness with nature.

His shiny black boots sank in mud and fetid odors assailed his nostrils. He ignored everything. Barred windows set high in the walls permitted sound to escape while denying direct sight. Since all the noise was concentrated at the front of the building where the soldiers were busy congratulating themselves, Charles took a chance and softly called, "Annabelle?"

All he heard was street chatter. He moved on to another window. Then another. Wait! Was that sobbing? "Annabelle?"

The weeping stopped.

Charles came closer. "Annabelle?"

"Y-yes."

"It's me."

She sniffled. "Go away."

"I can't. I have to help you somehow."

"That is the worst thing you can do. Secretary Eaton has promised to hire an attorney and have me released as soon as possible."

"Why didn't he stop them from taking you in the first place?"

Although her voice kept breaking, he heard her explain about the victim's relationship with the president's regiment and her suspicion that Margaret's wishes had also prevailed.

"Then I will stay here until you are free."

"And be caught? I would weep forever."

"But you saved my life." As he spoke he was casting around for something to climb up on. A wooden barrel provided a prop.

"I had to act for the sake of the child. He was counting on both of us," she said.

Charles assumed that was her way of covering her revealing admission that she would weep if anything bad happened to him. So, she felt their emotional attachment, too. That was heartening—and worrisome.

One booted foot on the barrel, he pulled himself up until he could reach through the barred window. He still could not see her but perhaps he could take her hand and convey moral support.

Hearing her gasp he said, "You see my hand?"

"Yes. But I can't reach it." She paused. "Wait!"

The sound of metal scraping against stone echoed and Charles thanked God for background noise to cover it.

First he felt her touch his hand. He closed his fingers around hers. Willed her to draw strength from him. And then her damp cheek and wisps of her beautiful hair brushed the back of his wrist. Their connection was tenuous yet deeply moving as she held tight to the lifeline of his presence.

The words that came to him were in Cherokee and he whispered them tenderly, knowing she would not understand yet needing to express affection. Perhaps no translation was necessary, he mused, because when he spoke, Annabelle's grasp tightened and her cheek pressed more firmly.

Then, suddenly, she broke away and was gone. Metal clanked and someone shouted, "Get away from that window."

Charles jumped off the barrel.

His hand felt cool and he glanced down. It was glistening with Annabelle's tears.

* * *

Annabelle did not even try to sleep. The cot she had moved under the window was so dingy she couldn't bear to lie upon it, let alone unfold the blanket. Her eyes often drifted back to the tiny window Charles had reached through and she gave thanks he had escaped unseen. That he had tried to comfort her at all was a conundrum. After all, they hardly knew each other and any involvement with her while she was incarcerated was taking a terrible chance.

She sighed and leaned back against the cold wall, crossing her arms. The authorities had her note. Therefore, they also had his name. Although it didn't sound Cherokee it might nevertheless lead back to him, partly because the whole delegation had attracted so much attention when visiting her father. Perhaps that was why soldiers had been sent to Plunkett's so quickly.

Although she didn't know how much time had passed, she had watched the movement of the sun across the sky. What was taking her foster father so long to come for her? Surely he would act. At least she hoped so. Given Margaret's animosity and obvious bias against her, she was beginning to wonder if John was going to help her, after all.

It was late the next day when Annabelle heard the approach of footsteps. Her spirits rose the instant she recognized John Eaton's voice. The sight of him brought her to tears again and she fought to stay stoic as the jailer unlocked the cell door.

The deepest urge was to shout, "Father!" but she refrained. There was nothing about his somber countenance that was encouraging. When he merely nodded to her and turned away from the open door, she wasn't sure if she was free to follow. The jailer guffawed and gestured, "Well, go, girlie, or do you like it here?"

That lit a fire under Annabelle's feet and she hurried after John Eaton. He had a carriage waiting. For a moment she thought he might climb in ahead of her as if she were unworthy of gallantry but he did pause and allow her to board first. He even offered a hand, which reminded Annabelle of the much more tender touch of another man through the bars of her window.

"Thank you," she ventured as the carriage started off.

Eaton made a guttural noise that sounded like a growl. "There is only so much I can do when the president is set against you. You do realize that?"

"Yes, but I didn't do anything wrong."

"That is not what the evidence shows. There is a very good chance that you will be arrested again and tried for murder. If I could stop it, I would."

"Can't Margaret... I mean, she and President Jackson are friends. Isn't there something she can do?"

"Ha! You will be fortunate to get her to tolerate you at home, let alone expect her to speak on your behalf. My wife can be headstrong, as you well know."

"Even if you plead my case?"

The expression on her foster father's face was stern and seemed almost wily. When he answered, Annabelle understood why.

"I had to fight other suitors to win Margaret Timberlake's hand and I will not give her up, nor will I choose you over her. That should go without saying. I suppose, if you were older, affairs of the heart would not puzzle you so."

The carriage had slowed and entered the Eaton yard before Annabelle was ready to ask, "What shall I do?"

"I haven't decided. If I send you away, I will be abetting an escape. If I let you stay here and vouch for you, it will look as if I support what you have done. Either choice may pose a risk to my career. Since one of the Cherokee delegates seems to also be involved and is technically untouchable by our laws, you will take full blame." He disembarked with a sharp, "You have shamed me."

Annabelle was less concerned for herself than for Johnny as she followed. "What about the little boy? What will become of him?"

Eaton grimaced. "As if I didn't have enough troubles with Indian affairs. I suppose I shall have to keep him for the sake of a temporary peace. As soon as the President and Congress decide against the treaty, however, I won't care what becomes of him."

"How can you be so cruel?"

"Self-preservation, my dear girl. Politics is a cutthroat business and it's time I treated it as such."

"You sound just like your wife."

That finally brought a slight smile. "She will be delighted to hear that."

"Should—should I come in?"

"Of course. You still live here. But I suggest you and the boy make yourselves scarce, particularly when Margaret is around."

Watching the man she had once thought of as a father walk away, Annabelle felt so downtrodden she was dazed. Had he really changed so much? It was hard to fathom that the once mellow man had hardened his heart but his words backed up that painful conclusion. Perhaps the best parts of him had passed away with Myra and his marriage to Margaret had brought out his sterner side.

To put it that way was to simplify, of course, but she was fast losing hope for her future. Any future. Anywhere.

Starting for the kitchen she took time to admire the flowerbeds and smell a pinch of fresh basil while she thought of the servants and how so many of her former friends and allies had been let go. She still had Lucy, the cook, and Adams, her father's valet, but no one else had known her for long. No one else could be counted on to provide solace while she resided in the Eaton home.

That was where she would start, Annabelle decided. If she could find Lucy she would ask her for advice. If not, she'd turn to Adams. Truth to tell, the grandfatherly man had bounced her on his knee when she was small far more often than John Eaton had.

Thoughts of her friends brought a smile. She was still smiling when she sensed someone nearby. The whispered *"Siyo"* told her who.

"Johnny!" Crouching, she opened her arms for the child's embrace.

"You are back." His shrill voice was muffled against her shoulder.

She set him away and grinned. "Yes, I am. Are you all right?"

The child nodded. His sky-blue eyes glittered. "I took your message to my uncle."

"I know. What did he say?"

"He was mad."

"I am sorry for asking you to disobey. I just didn't know who else I could trust."

Johnny stood taller, proud. "Will you run away with me now?"

A tiny part of her conscience wanted to set aside responsibility and tell him yes, but she refrained. Knowing that Eaton didn't plan to make a permanent home for the Cherokee child had changed things. What she wasn't sure of was how she should behave and how much she should reveal from then on. If he did decide to leave she certainly could not allow him to travel alone, yet if she accompanied him she would be considered a fugitive.

"I need to speak with your uncle again," Annabelle finally said, "but I don't want you to get in more trouble by going to get him for me. Do you know when the delegation is planning to leave? Is it today?"

His ebony hair swung against his shoulders as he rapidly shook his head. "It was tomorrow."

She sensed more to the story. "And?"

"They are gone."

"What? Now? Already?"

The boy looked ready to cry. "Yes. All gone."

"Are you certain?"

With a slow nod he assured her before beginning to sniffle and pointing to the uppermost dormer of the elaborate home. "I saw them pass. From up there."

Bereft, Annabelle sank to her knees in the garden and embraced the child while they both silently mourned and the setting sun cast their shadows among the fragrant blooms.

Chapter Five

A trip back to the jail where Annabelle had been held had proved fruitless, so Charles had returned to the Eaton estate and stationed himself across the street to watch, as before.

Now that Major Ridge had released him as a diplomat, he had to be even more cautious. Ridge had kept him out of jail once. That would not happen again.

And now? Although he had sent most of his belongings home with Elias, he had kept enough provisions to sustain him a few more days or weeks, if need be. And he had rented a saddle horse rather than keep hiring cabs and take the chance there might not be one available when he next needed it.

What he wanted to do was spirit Annabelle away to safety in Georgia. To do so, however, would not only be dangerous, it would be insane, and he was no fool. How their lives had become so entangled in such a short time was an unsolvable puzzle. Perhaps, if his assumption were correct and she did have Indian blood, that was part of the reason they'd been so drawn to each other.

A bigger question was, what did *Annabelle* want? He

knew she had aspirations of an education but there had
to be more to her future plans than that. Most young
woman her age were already thinking of marriage, yet
she had never mentioned suitors, probably because she
was trapped between the servant class and the snob-
bish elite of Washington City and didn't fit into any social strata.

Charles swung a leg over the horse's neck and slid
to the ground beside it the moment he saw activity in
the Eaton garden.

He was about to call "Annabelle!" when she spotted
him. He made it across the street just in time to receive
her headlong rush through the gate and fold her into his
arms. To do so in broad daylight was to muddy her already sullied reputation, yet he could not stop himself.

"What happened?" He set her away and feasted his
eyes on her natural beauty. "How did you get out of jail?"

"John Eaton came for me. The things he said on our
ride home were frightening. It was awful. He said I had
shamed him and, and…" Tears began to brighten her
eyes and she sniffled. "I thought you were gone. Johnny
said your party went home."

"They did."

"What about you? Aren't you in danger of arrest,
too?"

"No. Since I'm a Cherokee and an emissary to President Jackson, Major Ridge convinced them that the tribe
would mete out my justice."

"But, they all left. Why did you stay?"

Charles gazed deeply into her eyes. "I had to stay
after I saw them taking you away in shackles. We know
we are not guilty of killing anyone but if we cannot prove

it, I will pay a visit to the powers that be, tell them the whole story and throw myself on their mercy."

"No! What if they don't believe you?"

"All I care about is convincing them that you are innocent. After that it doesn't matter."

"Yes, it does. You mustn't do that." She sobered even more and glanced toward the house. "There is more to tell. Secretary Eaton was very angry when he came to get me out of jail. He admitted some terrifying things."

"What things?"

"For one, he's not going to keep Johnny as a son, the way you thought. He'll only let him stay until the treaties with your tribe are finalized in some way. I don't know the whole story but I fear there will be nothing of benefit to the Cherokees when all is said and done."

"As many of us have suspected," Charles murmured. "Was there anything else? Any details you can give me?"

"Only that President Jackson is not to be fully trusted."

"What do *you* want to do now?" Charles asked, unsure of anything other than his concern for the young woman.

Annabelle shook her head and sighed. "I wish I knew. I had thought to escape unhappiness by being sent off to boarding school but with Margaret having such a strong influence on my future, I do not see that happening. Not even if we manage to prove our innocence."

"Then rethink everything. Start from the beginning. Let yourself dream."

"What possible good can that do?"

When she lowered her head in despair, Charles lifted it with one finger under her chin. Tears were trickling down her cheeks and he brushed them away with a gentle touch. "Don't give up."

"But...I have no hope."

He placed a light kiss on her forehead as he said, "You have me."

"For how long?" she asked in a shuddering whisper.

Because he had no idea when he would have to follow the rest of his party back to Georgia, he didn't answer.

Given a choice, Annabelle realized she would just as soon remain right where she was, in the company of Charles McDonald. That, of course, was unacceptable no matter how much she wished otherwise.

His suggestion about her dreams for the future made her pull herself together, step back and look up at him. "There was a time, when I was much younger, that I used to imagine returning to see my grandmother and finding the happiness I once enjoyed. The only way I will ever do that, of course, is when she and I are together again in Heaven."

"You were living in Tennessee, you said?"

"Yes. Sometimes I recall little pieces of those times. They come and go like the flash of a firefly. When I try to remember details, I fail."

"Did you bring any possessions with you when you came to live with the Eatons?"

She paused to think. "There was an old doll I named Rosie. And of course my clothes, although Myra insisted on having a new wardrobe made for me."

"No papers? Letters? Anything like that?"

"No. I have asked. Why?"

"Because they might tell us who your people are."

"I have no one. I told you."

Charles's brow knit. "No, you told me exactly what you have been told all your life. As you recently noted, that does not mean it's the truth."

"If John Eaton is hiding secrets, he will never reveal them at this point. He's furious with me. I think he almost hopes I'll be convicted and sent to prison so he won't have to deal with me anymore." She made a face. "At least Margaret does, and she has the ear of the president."

"How is that possible? She can't be that influential."

"Yes, she can." Annabelle was nodding. "Before she was widowed she ran a boardinghouse here in the city. John Eaton used to stay there. A lot of politicians did, including Andrew Jackson. Margaret is supposedly the reason why Emily Donelson, the president's niece, moved out of the White House and he has no hostess in residence. Emily refused to entertain the Eatons."

"The president sided with Margaret against his own family?"

"Yes. So you see my dilemma."

"That I do."

Annabelle cast a surreptitious glance at the rear door of the mansion. "I should go back in."

"Why did you come out in the first place?"

"I don't know." She shrugged. "I have always preferred to be outside, and this morning I was particularly loath to encounter anyone other than Johnny."

"The authorities are no longer bothering you?"

"Not at present. My freedom is legal, although that could change in a heartbeat." The instant Annabelle mentioned hearts, she felt hers leap and placed her fingertips at the base of her throat. Such an intense fear of the unknown was new to her and gave her palpitations.

"If it would not cause tongues to wag, I would invite you and the boy to join me for a picnic lunch."

"There is no way I dare ride out with you, sir, especially now," Annabelle said. "Surely you understand."

"Of course. It was a foolish notion."

"I am sorry. Breaking bread together can be a good way to get better acquainted and I would like that. Diplomats share sumptuous dinners to help facilitate conversation."

He eyed the house. "I hope you are not suggesting that I publicly darken the halls of Secretary Eaton's home without being asked."

"No, of course not. We will just have to hope a suitable opportunity arises someday. If your party was still in the city, perhaps they would be invited for lemonade and sweets again and we could spend a little time together without raising eyebrows."

Johnny appeared, seemingly from nowhere, and ran up to them. Charles scowled at him. "Where have you been?"

"Exploring. I found another garden. Much better than here." He started to tug on his uncle's hand. "Come see."

Giving Annabelle a questioning glance he resisted. "Do you have any idea what he's talking about?"

"I think so. I'm told an old retainer and his wife used to live in an apartment of sorts at the rear of the carriage house. When the Eatons moved in, they filled it with stored possessions. The yard is not much to look at but you can tell they enjoyed their privacy."

"Privacy? Can it be seen from the street?"

Annabelle shook her head. "I don't think so. I really didn't pay much attention when I first looked."

He bowed slightly and swept an arm in the direction the boy was going. "After you."

Raising her skirts above her shoe tops, she circled the far end of the carriage house and stable, pushing aside bushes as she went. She paused in a tiny garden surrounded by overgrown foliage and pointed to the remains of a small corral beyond. "I had forgotten this was even here."

She could tell he was thinking because he was half frowning, half smiling. "It can't be seen from the street. Do you realize what this means?"

"Not really."

"We could meet here later for the picnic we dare not have in a park." He hesitated. "That is, if you are willing."

"With Johnny, of course," she added, blushing.

"Of course. I would not have suggested otherwise. The boy will chaperone us and we will be meeting in broad daylight. Nothing could be more socially acceptable." He grinned. "At least in our peculiar circumstances."

"All right. I'll ask Lucy to pack us a basket lunch. She does not have to know where Johnny and I have gone or who else will share our meal."

"When shall I return?"

"Margaret meets with a sewing circle for tea today and John will be leaving for the Capitol earlier than that." Annabelle grinned. "Will you wait until Margaret's gone?"

"It would be my pleasure."

He tipped his hat and gave another bow. On most men such actions might have looked effeminate, but not when Charles McDonald made them. The strength and power of his physique were impressive indeed, enough to warm her cheeks all the more.

Annabelle rested her hand beneath her throat and felt her heartbeat accelerating. And this time it was not due to trepidation. It was definitely a result of watching the Cherokee emissary walking away.

The only thing better was going to be his return.

Charles knew that every additional hour he spent in the city after the departure of his kinsmen increased his risk. Nevertheless, he was not going to just ride off and leave Annabelle. Nor Johnny. If what Eaton had told her was true, the boy's days of good care in that household were numbered. In that case, it might behoove him to allow the child to flee as he'd wanted all along.

Unfortunately, the timing was off. If Johnny stayed until the treaty disagreements were settled, one way or the other, many months could pass. By then, chances were good that Annabelle would have been tried and probably wrongly convicted due to outside influences.

Charles grimaced. She wasn't the only one who could end up in prison. He was in the same boat. With Ridge and the rest of the diplomats gone, there was no one to assure Washington authorities that Cherokee justice would be carried out. Charles had lost his primary defense.

He saw to the needs of his rented horse, loosening the saddle girth and watering the animal at one of the livestock troughs shaded by poplars along Connecticut Avenue. Grass there was thick and kept trimmed by sheep. Too bad he couldn't bring Annabelle here for a picnic instead of lurking in an overgrown, abandoned garden, but he could see the problem of being seen together in public. Word would surely get back to Margaret Eaton, one way or another, and she was a force to be reckoned with.

It was not hard for Charles to accept that a woman could be in charge because that was the way his tribe functioned. His own mother ran a successful plantation. Inheritance and authority passed down through women and so did clanship. It was because of her that he was numbered among the Wolf clan.

Rows of soldiers marched by in the street, rifles on their shoulders. Uneasy, Charles tightened the saddle girth, mounted up and headed back toward New York Avenue. He didn't know why he kept imagining that he and Annabelle Lang belonged together, he simply did, and mental arguments against such feelings failed repeatedly. Truth to tell, the closer he got to the secret garden, the more anxious he was to see her again.

He left his horse hitched to a rear portion of the wrought-iron railings that surrounded the entire property rather than bring it through one of the distant gates. As soon as no one was watching, he vaulted over the fence and ducked into thick shrubbery. It was debasing to have to skulk around. His pride would not have allowed it under other circumstances. But this time? This time was different.

Pushing through the leafy branches, he spied her. Ringlets of her hair reflected the sun's glow as they peeked from beneath a small bonnet and she was waving boldly, a far cry from the shy way she had behaved when they had first met.

"I am so glad you didn't change your mind," she said as soon as he was closer.

"Never. Margaret's gone?"

"Yes."

"You had no problems?"

"None worth mentioning." She tugged Johnny out from behind her. "I did have difficulty convincing this little man that we weren't going to get into trouble by doing this."

"I pray you are right." Charles laughed and tousled the boy's dark hair.

"Where did you leave your horse?"

"I tied him out behind. It's a lot easier to hide myself than a full grown mount." He eyed the basket. "The servants didn't suspect anything?"

"No. Lucy has been the family cook for longer than I can remember and nobody else saw me leaving."

"Good. Where shall we set the food?"

"I brought a cloth and swept the ground a little while I was waiting for you," Annabelle said. "There is a lovely place over there beneath the honeysuckle."

"Perfect." Charles helped her lay the cloth, then recruited the boy to keep watch for a bit, just in case.

Johnny pouted. "I'm hungry."

"We will call you when it's time to eat. I know Miss Annabelle will not let you starve."

As soon as the child walked away she began to speak quietly to Charles. "I tried to listen in as John was discussing Indian affairs with Margaret this morning but I'm afraid I wasn't able to learn anything new. It is clear the president and his cabinet do not value treaties. Especially not since gold has been discovered in Georgia."

"We have known about the gold for many generations. It is unfortunate that word has gotten out," Charles said.

"Is that why the powers that be want the Cherokees to move west?"

He nodded. "That, and coveting the land. It's not just us. Have you ever heard of the Five Civilized Tribes? We are the Cherokee, Choctaw, Chickasaw, Creek and Seminole."

"I think so. It seems unfair to expect you to uproot and leave the farms that you have worked for so many generations."

He managed a smile for her benefit even though his heart was hardened. "It is more than unfair. It is criminal. And unless we can solve our tribal differences and learn to work and stand together, we will lose."

Turning her sky-blue eyes to him and growing somber, she offered, "Sadly, I believe the same can be said of you and me, Mr. McDonald."

Spreading her skirts gracefully, Annabelle settled at the edge of the cloth and began to take food from the basket. There was fresh bread and cold meat and Lucy's delicious sweet pickles, plus part of a pound cake for dessert. A clay jug held lemonade which she poured into small tin cups.

Yet she hardly tasted the meal. Ideas kept whirling through her mind and being rejected by the logical side of her personality. She felt she would burst if she did not share her concerns, so the moment Johnny finished stuffing himself and resumed his guard post she opened a fresh conversation. "I need to ask you a question."

"Fine." Charles was seated with his back against a poplar trunk and looked far more relaxed than she felt.

"You wanted to know about my dreams? Well, I have given that a lot of thought and I know what I want."

He sat forward, legs crossed, and studied her. "Go ahead."

"I want to find my family, whatever is left of it. I have no idea where to start or how to proceed but I think, if I could just learn who I am and where I come from, I'd be happy."

"Even if the story is a sad one?"

"Yes. Even then."

She could tell he was weighing his words carefully. Finally, he spoke. "What if there is Indian blood in your line? How will you feel then?"

"Oh!" Taking a moment to think it over, Annabelle said, "Probably the same way you felt when you were old enough to realize your last name came from a Scot." She began to smile at him. "We are what we are. God made us in His image. Who are we to complain?"

"Nevertheless, it will change the way you are viewed and accepted. It will make you someone else."

She disagreed. "No. It will change nothing other than the perceptions of others. I will still be Annabelle Lang. I will still be a foundling without roots or history. If you could choose, which would you prefer, knowing the truth or wondering for the rest of your life?"

Charles stood, approached and offered a hand to help her up. "I would take you to Tennessee tomorrow if not for the damage it would do to your reputation. You would not only be branded a loose woman, everyone would think we were running away because we killed that man."

"I know. I haven't worked out any details yet." She glanced in the direction the boy had gone. "Or decided what we should do about him." Lowering her voice further she added, "We can't leave him behind."

The lack of a definitive reply from her companion

bothered her so much she said, "I am far more worried about Johnny than I am about myself."

Charles bent to help her gather their leftovers and put them back into the basket. "Then you must understand why my concern is more for the both of you than for my personal safety."

It did not surprise her to hear him add, "That is why I stayed in Washington."

At that moment she knew she should try to dissuade him, to make him leave for his own sake. Instead, she disappointed herself by remaining silent.

Chapter Six

They refreshed themselves with the clean water from a pump used to refill the horse troughs, then prepared to part. It was not an easy parting. "I think you and the boy should go back to the house and act as normal as possible," Charles said firmly.

"But…"

He shushed her. "Hear me out. While you're there you will be in a perfect position to glean information that may help my people. I'll continue to pose as a gentleman and listen to rumors as I move around town."

"You *are* a gentleman," Annabelle insisted.

"Thank you. As I was saying, there is no way a stranger would know who or what I am. I'll take lodging in a different boardinghouse each night and try to lose myself in the city until we know more about Eaton's plans." Pausing to observe her reaction he continued, "Keep in mind that you have no assurance the secretary will continue to provide legal counsel or even speak up for you if asked. Consider his position in the White House and the murdered man's army allegiances."

"Do you really believe he would be that cruel?"

"I think he already told you as much."

"That is so unfair."

"And very human," Charles countered. "Eaton rose to power early in life. He was a younger senator than most and he will want to continue to be important to President Jackson, as he is now."

Annabelle sighed. "You are probably right."

"Tell me more about Margaret," Charles urged. "Does she have no Achilles' heel?"

"I don't think so. She has withstood alienation from some of the most powerful people in Washington, even Floride Calhoun, the vice president's wife. They call Margaret and John Eaton's marriage the 'Petticoat Affair.' I overheard the servants talking about it."

"Very well. Put all that out of your mind for the time being and concentrate on learning what we need to know before taking any action."

"Where should I begin?"

"With Adams, I think, since he knew you as a child. Perhaps, now that he knows you are in serious trouble, he will speak more openly. But you must take care to engage him where your conversation will remain private."

"What about John Eaton? Should I inquire about his plans for me?"

"Only if he broaches the subject," Charles warned. "We need to face one lion at a time, not take on a whole den of them at once."

Dancing along in front of them like a spring lamb enjoying life in a lush pasture, the Cherokee boy whirled and grinned back at the adults as they pushed through to the usual yard and stood together for a moment rather than part.

"I shot a bear once!" Johnny spread his short arms. "It was this big."

"It was also already made into a lap robe," Charles told Annabelle, laughing.

She shared in the merriment. "That's the best kind."

Annabelle felt an odd sensation standing there looking at the Eaton house. It was as if she were a stranger, not a resident, and she said so. "It is very odd, is it not, that since my incarceration I have felt like an outcast?"

"Not really. A lot has changed for you recently."

"And for you." The expression on his face revealed no secrets, yet she sensed enough to know he agreed.

"Yes."

Resting her hands on his broad shoulders despite their visibility in front of the carriage house, she said, "I wonder if I will ever belong here again."

"Would it pain you if you did not?"

"It already does," she confessed, stepping back with more difficulty than expected. "I don't want to go inside."

Johnny echoed, "I don't want to go inside."

"Well, you'd both better change your minds because we need more information before we can make any plans. As tempting as it may be to just mount up and ride off, we'd be considered criminals if we left the city and be pursued relentlessly. When we do go, it has to be done sensibly."

"Yes, sir," Annabelle told him. It pleased her to hear faint agreement from the child. She held out her hand to him and he grasped it.

"You carry the picnic basket." Charles offered it to Johnny, scowling when the boy merely scuffed the toe of his shoe in the dirt and avoided eye contact. "Take it."

It seemed best to redirect everyone's attention, so Annabelle smiled at Charles and gave a little curtsy. "Thank you for a lovely afternoon. It was the best I have had in longer than I can recall."

He tipped his hat. "My pleasure, Miss Annabelle."

A wiry groom appeared at the door to the carriage house. "Sorry. I heard voices and thought you was Mrs. Eaton come home."

Annabelle's pulse sped. "Oh, dear, is it that late?"

The groom nodded and cast a furtive glance toward the street, perhaps in an effort to warn her.

She clasped Charles's warm hand and was instantly reminded of the way she had clung to him when he had reached through the bars into her cell. "You must go. Hurry. If Margaret sees you here, there is no telling what she may do."

Nodding, he leaped the side fence easily and strode away, heading for his waiting horse. The sight of him stalking off made Annabelle light-headed.

Truth to tell, watching that man do anything had the same effect and she relished its repetition.

Washington City was, as usual, busy as a beehive in a honey tree. Charles reined in as soon as he'd ridden a fair distance from the estate.

It distressed him that he and Annabelle had not thought to make plans for future contact while they were together. Yes, she was used to looking for him lurking across the street. Unfortunately, she might not be the only one who had noticed his repeated presence and he wasn't positive they had a reliable ally in the groom. One warning was not sufficient proof of fidelity. He might have mentioned expecting Mrs. Eaton's arrival without realizing how important it was to Annabelle to avoid her.

Charles slowed his horse to a walk and dismounted at Fourteenth Street and Pennsylvania Avenue. Several frame houses there had apparently been joined to form a hotel that looked large enough to afford anonymity. The bed roll tied to his saddle was hardly the kind of luggage a well-dressed man would be expected to carry but he made the best of it.

"The rest of my bags are to arrive soon," he told the disinterested young clerk. "I wish a room and a meal."

"We got a place to eat next door," the younger man said. "No shootin', no drinkin' in the room, and use the chamber pot and the spittoon or my ma'll have your guts fer garters."

"Agreed." Charles signed the register and accepted his room key. Given the rules of the house he could tell he'd chosen well. "Do you have any famous folk staying here?"

"Such as?"

"Oh, I don't know. Senators or judges, maybe?"

"Not if we can help it. They're the worst."

Laughing to himself, Charles shouldered his blanket roll and climbed the stairs. The room left a lot to be desired but it did have one invaluable feature. It looked down on the street corner. If he needed to keep an eye out for unusual activity, he could not have chosen a better vantage point.

The only thing he wished was that he could see as far as the house where Annabelle and Johnny were staying.

Slipping in through the kitchen, Annabelle left the basket and hurried the boy upstairs with her.

"Remember, you must never breathe a word of what we did today or who we were with."

Nodding sagely, Johnny pulled crumbling bread from his pocket, dropping crumbs on the carpet in the hallway by his room.

"What are you doing?" She tried to catch tiny pieces as they fell. "Why did you keep that?"

"To eat on the trail. When we go home."

"It's way too soon to be worrying about that." Carrying a palmful of crumbs and broken crusts, she went to the nearest window and tossed them out. "There, food for the birds. Now go get washed up so you don't look as if you spent the afternoon outside."

Although he was muttering and making faces, the boy complied. Were all small boys so obstinate? she wondered, as she followed him into his room and poured water from the ewer into the washbasin.

"I'm hungry," Johnny said as soon as he had finished scrubbing and dried his hands.

"I suppose Lucy can find something for you if you ask her nicely."

To Annabelle's surprise he grasped her hand. "You come, too."

"I was planning to do a bit of needlework. Mrs. Eaton asked me to embroider some handkerchiefs for her." And it was not the time to vex her, Annabelle added to herself.

"Can't you do that downstairs?"

His logic was inescapable. She picked up her wicker sewing basket and followed him down, pausing at the doorway to the kitchen.

"I will sit right out here while you eat so I don't accidentally soil this linen," Annabelle said kindly. "Go ahead." She stuck her head through the opening and smiled. "We have a hungry young man here. I told him you could help fill him up."

"Mercy, yes," jovial Lucy said. "Come in, come in. Sit you right down at the table and I'll get you a big glass of milk to start with. Do you like biscuits and gravy?"

Grinning broadly at Lucy's predictable reaction, Annabelle backed around the corner and seated herself in a small side chair. The light there wasn't ideal but it would do until Johnny finished eating.

She had just fitted another handkerchief into her embroidery hoop when she heard the back door slam. Fear that it might be Margaret took her breath away until she heard the familiar voice of one of the stable hands. If it had been the same man who had recently warned her she might have gone to thank him. Instead, she went back to her needle and floss, bristling when she heard the man ask, "That the Injun kid?"

Lucy answered, "Yes. And a sweet young'n he is, so you mind your manners, Caleb."

"Long as I can have some of your biscuits and gravy and be on my way, I'll be as mild as a lamb." A chair scraped the floor.

"Take your cap off. Where do you think you are, the barn?"

"Yes'm. Sorry. Boy looks a bit puny if you ask me. But I suppose he'll fill out as soon as he gets more of your fine cookin'."

Lucy set crockery bowls on the table with heavy clunks. Cutlery tinkled. "What's your hurry?"

"I got a reward to claim."

Annabelle's ears perked up. She rose slowly and approached the open door, taking care to remain hidden as she peeked around the edge of the opening.

She could tell that Johnny had spotted her but he continued to devote his full attention to buttering his biscuit while acting as if he didn't comprehend what was being said.

"Reward?" Lucy asked. "You meaning to find Mrs. Eaton's missing pretties?"

"Naw. I'll leave the woman stuff to you and the house maids. I'm off to collect me a bounty on a murderer."

Lucy leaned closer to the man but Annabelle's keen hearing picked up enough.

"A bounty on *who*? The law come for Miss Annabelle last night but Mr. Eaton, he got her out of jail already."

"Not her, one of them fancy Indians. I've got me a cousin at the arsenal. He says the word is out. There's a big reward for the Cherokee what brought the boy here, dead or alive."

A flash of understanding almost caused Annabelle to gasp aloud. She chanced a second look. The cook's eyes met hers and held a warning as Lucy edged her substantial body between Caleb and the doorway, blocking his view.

"More, please?" Johnny asked with an innocence that belied the fright Annabelle knew he must be feeling.

"'Course. How 'bout some jam to go with it?"

"For my room?"

"Sure enough," Lucy said. "I'll wrap some food in a cloth for you. Just be careful you don't spill anything, you hear? And don't eat so much you spoil your supper."

"Yes, ma'am."

Annabelle stepped back and flattened herself against the wall, her sewing forgotten. They had learned far more than anyone had expected. The problem was, she didn't know where Charles had gone or how to warn him.

If he wasn't made aware of the new danger, he would be a sitting duck. If he *was* told, however, he would probably flee, and then what would become of her dream to go back to Tennessee or Johnny's desire to return to Georgia?

The dark-haired child stepped out of the kitchen carrying a checkered cloth bundle. Although he never looked over at her, Annabelle knew he was aware of her presence.

"I am going up to my room now," he called back to the cook. "Thank you for the biscuits."

Without another word he began to climb the stairs, getting halfway up before the back door slammed and he froze in place to look back. "You heard?"

She hurried to join him. "Yes. Everything."

"Now we will leave?"

"We can't. Suppose it's a false rumor and we run for nothing?"

"Suppose it is true."

"There is that." She hustled him the rest of the way to his room and shut the door behind them, then began to pace and wring her hands. "I don't know what to do."

"Then leave with me. We will find my uncle and warn him."

"I guess you didn't hear everything we discussed this afternoon," Annabelle told him. "Charles didn't go back to Plunkett's. He said he was going to find another place to stay. A place where he wasn't known. Washington is a big city. I wouldn't know where to even start looking for him."

"How will his hunters know, then?"

"They won't. But there are a lot more of them than there are of us. And they're men, so they can go places that are forbidden to me—and to children."

The boy seemed to be considering their dilemma. Finally he began to smile at her. "You will ask John Eaton."

"He won't know, either."

"What if he is the one who ordered the hunt?"

"He can't be. He wouldn't." Yet even as she was offering excuses, she knew she could be wrong.

Dead wrong.

Chapter Seven

Approaching the Eaton house via the kitchen garden as he had before, Charles moved silently from shadow to shadow. Clouds drifted across the moon at irregular intervals, making cautious progress essential.

He'd overheard enough gossip in the hotel dining room and several saloons to know that sympathies had turned against him even more. And since his standing had changed, there was a good chance that Annabelle's had, too. Because he could no longer safely wait in public for her to notice him, he was going to do the next best thing. He was going to enter the Eaton estate and seek her out.

A guttural shout from inside the house stopped him cold. Instead of approaching Annabelle's window he circled, following the sound. John Eaton was in the dining room, arguing with Margaret, who was screaming at him like a demented old crone. "Do you see now? Do you, John? What have I been telling you?"

Charles closed the distance and used the edge of the velvet draperies to hide a discrete peek inside. The two people he had expected to see were present. So were

Annabelle and Johnny. The boy had stepped forward as if to shield her instead of hiding behind her full skirts. Annabelle appeared stalwart and in control but a slight trembling of her clasped hands gave her away.

John Eaton spoke. "How could you accuse me of such an evil deed? Do you think so little of me?"

Although Annabelle opened her mouth, Margaret gave her no chance to reply. "She just accused you of setting bounty hunters on her beau. What do you think?" the older woman yelled.

"I think it is time you let the girl speak for herself," John countered, his face reddening in anger. He faced Annabelle. "Well? Explain yourself."

"Yes, sir. There is word about that someone has placed a bounty on the head of one of the Cherokees and I could not think of anyone else to ask about it."

"You mean Charles McDonald, I take it."

She nodded. "Yes. I—I—as you know, I was at the park with him the night the man was tied up with strips torn from my cape. I promise you, the thug was alive when we left him. He and another man had beset Charles, and..."

Interrupting, Margaret said, "You and that Indian are on a first-name basis? I should have known."

"We are friends, that's all." Annabelle knew she spoke the truth even if she wished there could be more to their relationship someday.

"Friends, ha!"

John intervened. "Please, Peggy. Let me think."

"There is nothing to think about," the matron countered. "Your precious ward has chosen sides and made herself quite clear. She cares nothing for your position in the president's cabinet or your reputation in Washington. It's time she left. Even you must be able to see that now."

"Where would she go? How would she manage? She's never been on her own for even a day."

At this juncture, Charles wanted to show himself and offer to look after Annabelle but thought better of it. There was no reason to inform the Eatons of his plans, or of the conversation he'd had with Annabelle during lunch. Once John Eaton released her she should be free to travel as long as he explained the situation to the proper authorities and personally vouched for her innocence. The question was, would he do so?

"I will give you traveling money if you choose to go," John said. "I think it's for the best that you leave Washington. I don't know who placed the bounty on McDonald but it's possible there may be one on you, too. If that happens I may not be able to shield you."

As Charles watched, Annabelle straightened and nodded. "I would like a chance to bid Lucy and Adams goodbye before I leave."

"Why should John grant you anything?" Margaret said, her voice once again raised. "You and your Indian friend probably made off with my jewelry and the silver service."

"Denial doesn't seem to do me any good but I will try one more time." Annabelle faced John rather than Margaret. "I have done nothing wrong in any way, nor would I, given the opportunity. I may not understand politics but I do know right from wrong." She began to back toward the hallway. "If you will excuse me, I will begin packing."

"It's best, for all of us," John called after her as she and the boy left the room.

Charles was easing away from the window when he

overheard Margaret say, "See? I told you she was in league with those crafty Indians. You should thank me."

"For what?"

"For—for seeing to it that she showed her true colors, of course."

Though Charles was no longer watching the Eatons he saw shadows join in the room, heard a woman's gasp and suspected that John had accosted his wife. "What have you done? Tell me."

"What any honest citizen would do. See that the law is upheld and the guilty punished. You should be on your knees, thanking me and begging my forgiveness," Margaret told him.

Had she just confessed? Charles suspected so. Given what he had learned about her from Annabelle and others, there was a very good chance that she had had something to do with offering the bounty for his capture or death.

Was Margaret acting on behalf of her husband as she claimed? Charles doubted it. Assuming she had figured out a way to rid herself of Annabelle by bringing about her banishment, he could see how his continued interest had played right into her hands.

Starting back around the house he smiled to himself. Margaret might think she had arranged for Annabelle to suffer when the opposite was true.

All they had to do was get out of the city before bounty hunters caught up to him. To the three of them. Given what he had just overheard, there was no way he was going to leave his nephew behind.

Annabelle ducked into her room while the boy went to his to pack. She leaned against the door after quietly closing it.

This small area and the furnishings she'd brought to Washington from Tennessee were her sanctuary. Now she stood in the middle of the bedroom and prepared to part with the familiar. There was a small, thin, quilted comforter on the bed. Propped against a pillow was Rosie, the only doll she'd ever had. Rosie's porcelain cheeks were shiny pink but her fingers and toes showed chipping and cracks. Beneath a yellow bonnet was a dark, curly wig that had been combed so much—by Annabelle—the poor doll was nearly bald.

The thought of leaving little Rosie behind caused such a pang of sorrow she decided to stuff the toy into the bottom of her traveling bag. Then she would have one item from her childhood. Myra had repaired the doll and even embroidered her name on its cloth tummy to remind her of happier times.

Annabelle pulled her bag from beneath the bed and opened it just as someone rapped on her door.

She froze. The soft sound of her name being called from the other side of the closed door was so familiar and such an intense relief she called, "Come in," without thinking.

Charles eased the door open and stuck his head through to tell her, "Nobody saw me. We need to go."

"I know. John just..."

He crossed the space in two strides and took her hand. "I was listening outside the window. I heard everything. The faster we leave, the better."

"A lot of men are looking for you. I wanted to warn you but I didn't know where you'd gone."

"I understand. I'm sure they still are." He eyed the sparse contents of her armoire, reached in and withdrew a long, heavy, woolen coat. "You'd better take this, too."

"Why?"

"The mountains can get cold at night, even in summer."

"Mountains?"

"Yes," Charles said flatly. "I am going to give you a letter of introduction to my family and put you on the next stage going south to the Blue Ridge."

"I beg your pardon? I never agreed to any such thing."

Charles pointed to the half-filled case. "Stop arguing and pack. We're running out of time."

Cautiously opening the door leading into the upstairs hallway, Charles peered both ways. "So far, so good." He hefted Annabelle's bulging valise and motioned to her. "Come. Quickly. And bring that coat."

She took one last, longing look around the room, then sidled past him. "I'll get Johnny."

In seconds she was back. Alone. "He's not there."

"Where could he be?"

"I don't know. I told him to pack his clothes. Surely he understood that I wasn't going to leave him behind."

"Where would he hide? Did you search his room?" Charles pushed past her to do the same.

"Yes. I even looked under the bed. He's not here."

"His clothes are gone. All of them."

That was a relief but left unanswered questions. "Maybe he went to the stable." Annabelle led the way back into the hall and went directly to a white-painted door in an alcove at the far end of the corridor. "This is the only way out that will give us an advantage. It's a servant's passage."

She turned the knob. Hinges squeaked just enough

to make them both stand very still. Listening. Waiting to be discovered.

When no one else appeared, Annabelle finished opening the door and started down the steep stairway while Charles secured the door behind them.

Pressure of his hand on her shoulder startled her, causing her to glance back. "What?"

"Hush."

"Why? Is someone coming?"

He had turned, put down the suitcase and was looking up the stairway, past the entrance they had just used. "Wait here. I'll be right back."

The man was exasperating. *Let him go?* Not on her life. If he thought she was just going to stand there and blindly follow his orders while he went off without her, he was sadly mistaken.

A faint peeping sound echoed. Ahead, Charles paused, giving her time to catch up. "Why are you bothering with a bird when a posse is out to get you?" she asked in a near whisper.

The Cherokee's hand swept back toward her, his unspoken instruction clear. He wanted her to keep still and wait. Fine. Silence she would grant him. Forward progress without her was altogether different.

A riser creaked beneath his weight.

She saw him lift his boot and reposition it. The action was carried out so quietly she was amazed. How could such a big man move so noiselessly?

Annabelle stuck as close as she could without crowding him. What she wanted most was to grab his hand, to feel the strength and warmth that had previously imparted such comfort.

That was unfortunately impossible because Charles

had just raised both hands in front of him as if preparing to snatch a darting firefly out of a summer night's sky.

Pausing because he had, she was caught unawares when he suddenly sprang into action, took the final two steps as one and whirled to one side before he lunged out of sight.

She saw his leap. Heard a scuffle. A muted cry.

Afraid to follow too closely, she hesitated. Her breathing was ragged, her heartbeats thundering in her ears, throbbing in her temples. Annabelle desperately wanted to call out to Charles.

Was that wise? she asked herself. The man had obviously tangled with someone or something beyond her field of vision. If she spoke now, would she be putting them both in jeopardy?

Before she could decide what to do she heard the rumble of his voice bidding her to join him.

"It's safe?" she whispered back.

He stepped into view. One hand was grasping the back of Johnny's shirt and lifting him off the ground the way a mother cat carried her kitten by its scruff. The other hand reached out to her.

Annabelle was glad for the assistance because the welcome sight of the child, coming on the heels of the fright of hearing Charles grappling with an unseen foe, had left her weak in the knees.

She let Charles pull her the last few steps, then asked, "How did you know?"

Grinning, he released both her and the child. "Wrong bird."

Little Johnny looked angry and embarrassed as he straightened his clothing and glared at the man who had treated him so unceremoniously.

Bending over so she'd be eye to eye with the child, Annabelle touched his arm. "Are you all right? We were very worried when we couldn't find you."

His chin jutted, his stature stiff. "I am fine."

"Wait here," Charles told her. "I'm going down to fetch your traveling case."

"I thought you were in a hurry to leave?"

"I was, until I saw this place. We can wait here, rest and watch below. It will be safer to ride out just before dawn, if we can, than to travel in the middle of the night."

"Safer like it was when you walked by the river?" Annabelle countered.

"No. Safer armed and on horseback."

"So, you've given up stuffing me into a coach and sending me south like a Christmas package?"

"One move at a time," he said, quirking a smile at her. "My first plan was to put you both on the rented horse with me. If we delay our departure until everyone is asleep, I can turn him loose and we can borrow a couple of Eaton's horses, instead."

She was appalled. "*Steal* them?"

"No," Charles countered. "Borrow. They're used to being stabled here. Horses love to eat. They'll head home for a good meal as soon as we release them."

He was right, of course. The bothersome element was that they were planning another crime that could also land them in jail. And this time they'd really be guilty.

It was a long night. Although Annabelle did doze, she noted Charles's shadowed form at the dormer window every time she opened her eyes.

Johnny was so excited about their pending trip, his

exuberance almost gave them away several times before they'd even reached the door leading outside, let alone made it as far as the carriage house. A glow was beginning to peek over the trees to the east, making the morning mist seem like fog.

Evidently, one of the stable hands was already at work, mucking out the stalls, because there was a lantern burning in the barn. He had fortuitously hitched both the Eaton horses in the courtyard while he worked.

As Annabelle saw it, the only problem remaining was how to get her hands on suitable saddles and bridles. The gentlemen in her escape party might be fine riding bareback but she knew she needed a saddle if she hoped to stay on the horse for long.

"I'll go scout inside the stable and see about getting bridles, first," Annabelle said in a coarse whisper. "You two wait out here."

"No. We're coming with you." At Charles's side, the boy was nodding vigorous agreement.

"Johnny might get away with it but you won't," she countered. "If I'm spotted, it won't really matter since I live here—used to live here."

"I can go," the child insisted. "I am like *tsula*, the fox."

Charles's chuckle was little more than a rumble. His smile was cynical. "If you were a fox, you would starve to death. You make so much noise, your prey would be gone before you got close enough to pounce."

The boy made a face and crossed his arms, looking for all the world like a tiny Napoleon. His pose was so amusing she almost laughed aloud despite the tense situation.

"All right," Annabelle said. "Johnny, come with me.

If we are seen, I want you to distract the groom and keep him busy while I pick out proper tack."

"I can do that, too," the boy insisted. "I know all about horses."

"I'm sure you do. But the bridles are hung on high pegs and the saddles are too heavy for you."

"I am strong."

Charles interrupted. "I have an even better idea. You two can both distract the groom and I will steal—I mean borrow—the saddles."

His common sense was irrefutable. Annabelle grasped the eager child's hand. "All right. Johnny and I will go in first and keep the groom busy while you get what we need."

"A horse for me!" the boy added.

She held tight to his smaller fingers, afraid he might bolt when she told him, "The Eatons have only two horses here in Washington. They left the others behind in Tennessee and brought their favorites, so unless your uncle chooses to keep his horse, we'll have to share."

"I might, if the bay were half the mount that these are," Charles said flatly. "The boy will ride with me on one of these. I'll fetch my bed roll, then turn loose the rented bay and send him home so they don't think I stole him, too."

"Where did you leave him? I'd think someone would have seen him by now and figured out you were nearby."

"I left him hidden behind this building in the old corral we found. I needed a place to give him hay and water and let him rest. He should not have drawn interest by being there unless one of the grooms stumbled upon him."

"That's why you kept looking out the window."

"One of the reasons." He canted his head toward the carriage house door. "You had better get going before that groom finishes and comes for these horses."

"All right. The tack room is on the far right, just inside these double doors." She touched his sleeve. "Be careful."

"The same to you."

Annabelle could tell how apprehensive he was. That was understandable, particularly since the Cherokee child was staying with her. Still, she had no trouble imagining that the concern in the man's piercing blue gaze extended to her, personally. They had been acquainted for a mere few days, yet their lives already seemed inexorably entwined.

And they are about to become more so, Annabelle realized, expecting her heart to grow heavy with the portent of doom. Yet it did not.

On the contrary, she was looking forward to their journey, no matter how difficult it might prove.

The reason was clear, although she was loath to admit it, even to herself. Her elation and sense of adventure came directly from her traveling companions—particularly the tall, handsome one on whom she had come to rely.

There was no one, anywhere, who meant as much to her as Charles McDonald.

Without a backward glance she stood tall, lifted her chin and strode boldly into the carriage house with the child at her side.

Chapter Eight

Charles hid next to the wide, wooden doors, thankful they'd been left propped open. If he could not have watched Annabelle—and Johnny—from there as they entered the stable, he would have found another vantage point. Neither of them was going to get out of his sight for an instant, if he could help it. Not until he was certain all danger was past.

Consciously slowing his breathing and heartbeat the way he had just before the attack at the river, he waited.

There was plenty of lantern light inside the modest structure. He would have no trouble choosing the proper tack. As soon as he got a clear signal from either Annabelle or the boy he would make his move.

She was pausing at one of the stalls and standing on tiptoe to peer over the walled-in front.

Charles judged that that enclosure was empty because she quickly moved on to the next, skirting the straw-and-refuse-filled pushcart that sat next to its gate.

Her lilting voice carried well as she greeted the male servant who had been tending to the stable.

"Ah, *there* you are," Annabelle said as her hand

waved a signal behind her back. "I wondered why the horses were tied to the hitching post."

Charles made his move. In three long strides he was through the exterior doors, across the straw-strewn floor and had entered the tack room. It was well kept and sensibly arranged, facilitating his task.

He chose two bridles and the most useful of the saddles to carry out first, draping it over his forearm. One quick look told him the coast was still clear and he made his escape unseen.

Rather than take the time to ready one of the horses, he dropped the bridles and flung the first saddle over the hitching rail.

One down, one to go.

Furtive and cautious, he rechecked his access. Annabelle moved to bodily block the stall's open door and Johnny, who had been too short to peek over the solid, lower walls of the enclosure, was stepping up beside her.

Suddenly, the boy gave a whoop that sounded like a coyote with its leg caught in the jaws of a steel trap.

Charles froze. He couldn't make out everything the child was shouting but there was no mistaking his alarm. He was wildly waving one arm and had Annabelle by the hand, trying to drag her away in spite of her resistance.

Johnny kept pointing at whoever was inside the stall. Charles thought he heard the Cherokee word for bad, *uyoi*, but could not be sure.

Abandoning his quest for the second saddle, Charles ran across the carriage house to confront who or what had frightened the child.

He was almost there when Johnny spotted him and began to jump up and down, screaming warnings.

"It's him! The man who wants to kill you. Run!"

Annabelle was forcibly restraining the boy.

Charles swept them aside, out of danger, and boldly faced his foe.

Instead of drawing a gun, Caleb raised the four-pronged iron pitchfork he'd been using to clean the stalls, held it waist high and charged at Charles like an angry bull.

Annabelle screamed.

Johnny continued to shout.

Charles dropped into a crouch, arms extended, and dodged the thrusts of the lethal tines.

His goal was not merely to avoid injury. He had the others to worry about, too. If the ruckus drew more servants or even the master of the house, someone was bound to get hurt. He just didn't want it to be either of the two souls he was looking after. They mattered too much. *Both of them.*

That momentary diversion of thought caused a slight hesitation. A deadly error.

Caleb's next jab caught a piece of Charles's coat. Threw him off balance. Made him stagger.

By the time he had regained his defensive stance the other man was almost on top of him, the newest thrust of the pitchfork aiming for his neck.

Annabelle was desperately casting around for a weapon. She could see the boy doing the same. The stable was simply too clean, too neat.

"Please, God, help me. Show me what to do?"

She considered throwing herself between Caleb and Charles, but quickly decided against it. The groom was very likely to stab her as well, particularly if he'd heard gossip that she'd been ostracized. Besides, she had Johnny to protect.

Johnny! Oh, no!

He had clambered up onto the refuse in the manure cart and was crouched as if ready to leap at Caleb. Waving both arms she yelled, "No!"

In the few moments it took him to process her order and decide to ignore it, Annabelle had reached the piled-high cart where he was poised. An idea hit her like a bolt of lightning. "That's it!"

Her triumphant shout stopped Johnny in his tracks, caused him to stare.

Struggling to overcome natural loathing, Annabelle reached into the piles of straw in the cart, plucked out a stinking missile—of horse dung—and flung it at Caleb's back.

The plop against his homespun shirt was audible but not enough to stop him from trying to spear Charles.

Rolling, the Cherokee avoided another wild jab.

Johnny followed Annabelle's example, aiming for the back of the man's neck with far more accuracy and effectiveness than she had shown.

Roaring, Caleb ducked and wheeled, raising his weapon.

Johnny's next effort caught him in the center of his forehead, spilled over into his eyes and began to drip down his ruddy cheeks.

Screaming, spitting and clawing at his face, the stable hand dropped the pitchfork.

Charles scooped it up and held him at bay with it while the boy continued to lob handful after handful of gooey, green manure.

"All right," Charles said with a chuckle. "That's enough.

You're already so filthy, yourself, I may not want you in the same camp with me."

Annabelle was holding her hands out as far from her burgundy traveling dress as possible. "We can wash in the horse trough."

She pointed at the now subdued groom who was still sputtering and trying to clear the mess from his eyes. "What are we going to do with him?"

"I saw a rope in the tack room. Get that stuff off your hands and fetch it for me. We'll tie him up to buy time. Hopefully, nobody heard the ruckus."

Her overwhelming sense of relief brought thankfulness and a smile. Although she was still uneasy, the sight of their nemesis sitting in a pile of horse leavings and whimpering about his face being dirty struck her as delightfully amusing.

The weapon the Lord had provided was certainly unusual, yet it had worked flawlessly.

The next time she prayed for divine assistance, however, she hoped God was not in quite such a playful mood.

It had been Charles's decision to bring the horses inside the stable and saddle them there, out of sight, while the only member of their party who was not wanted by the law went back into the house to fetch their meager belongings.

"What about the rest of your things?" Annabelle asked Charles when Johnny returned.

"There's nothing left at the hotel." He pointed to the rolled blanket he'd retrieved when he'd released the rented bay. "I sent most of my clothes home with Elias. Getting safely out of the city was more important."

"I suppose you're right."

Knowing that his companion was still on edge Charles decided to tease her. "I may want that in writing. I believe that is the first time you have admitted that my choices are best."

"It is not." She began to smile. "Well, not entirely, anyway."

"Thank you for that concession." He returned her grin. "With Caleb bound and gagged we've bought ourselves a little time. Anyone who looks out from the main house and sees that the horses have been taken back inside will think he's finished his chores and put them away."

Charles tightened the final cinch. "You'll have to ride astride like the boy and me." He paused, concerned. "Are you sure you're able or do you want me to harness a horse to the carriage."

She set her jaw. "No. The only way we can safely send these horses home is if they're unencumbered. A carriage would get in their way."

Charles almost laughed. She still believed it would be possible to return Eaton's property? Well, maybe it would be. But he wasn't going to count on it. Nor did it bother him much. Until a few hours ago Annabelle had been a part of the Eaton family and therefore entitled to use of the animals. Besides, the rich, powerful politician was not going to be left afoot. Not when he had so many connections and such great influence among his peers.

The way Charles saw it, their main goal had to be getting out of Washington and losing themselves in the countryside. That would mean traveling byways and even forging their own trails from time to time. A carriage would have seriously complicated their escape.

"All right," he said. "I've fastened the traveling bags behind one saddle and your coat and my roll behind the other. You will ride the smaller horse."

Annabelle had been stroking the velvety soft nose of the dappled gray mare. "I'm glad. This one has always been gentle and friendly."

Before boosting her aboard he handed her a leather pouch jingling with coins. "Take this."

"Why?"

"In case we are separated. You will need money."

"But…"

"Don't waste time arguing." He waited until she put the sack of coins into her pocket, then bent and laced his fingers to make a step, lifting as soon as her foot was in place. Although she sat the horse well she failed to pick up the reins as he had expected.

"It is a help if you can tell the horse which way you want to go," he said. "I thought you had ridden before?"

"I have, but I usually just stood on a fence and hopped on an old mare that was out to pasture. She went wherever she pleased."

"We don't have enough time to make you a proficient horsewoman." He motioned to the boy. "Come here. You'll ride up front and handle the reins. Miss Annabelle will sit behind you."

The look of triumph on the boy's impish face caused Charles to add, "And remember what I have told you. No tricks. You will be responsible for her well-being. See that you take your job seriously."

"Yes, sir!" Johnny said, grinning. Clambering aboard the mare by way of the stirrup leathers, with a little help from Annabelle to keep him from kicking her, he was ready in mere moments.

Charles kept one eye on the mare and the other on the kitchen door while Annabelle slipped her feet into the stirrups and arranged her skirts for modesty.

As he turned to mount the other horse he froze. Heard a distant shout. Then another.

The hair prickled at his nape, his instincts keen.

"Go!" he shouted to her and the boy. "Now!"

Johnny was expertly wheeling the mare to face the stable exit. The normally docile animal had apparently sensed everyone's high anxiety because she was prancing and side stepping.

Angry-sounding raised voices came closer and closer.

"Kick her," Charles commanded, hoping Annabelle would understand because the boy's heels were hanging too high to have much effect through the saddle leather.

Doors banged. Shadows loomed closer. Man-size shadows.

Charles was out of options. Shouting, "Hang on!" he slapped the mare on the rump with the ends of his own reins. She leaped forward and cleared the doorway before breaking into a canter.

At first, he feared the horse's rapid acceleration might unseat Annabelle but she leaned forward to successfully make the transition to a breakneck pace. Arching over Johnny she looked far more capable than she had until then.

Charles barely had time to thank the good Lord before he heard a shot and ducked.

There was no time to flee. The crowd was nearly upon him.

Frantic, Annabelle clung to the child and hoped to shield him with her own body if need be. She didn't know where they were headed, nor did she care, except for the fact that Charles had not followed.

"We have to wait for your uncle," she yelled to Johnny. "He will come."

She had serious doubts, particularly because she had caught a glimpse of the mob approaching the carriage house. John Eaton's valet, Adams, led a pack of armed men who were in a clearly agitated state. That made them dangerous. So did being part of a cadre with a single goal—to thwart their escape. How could Charles, or any man, hope to prevail against such numbers?

"No!" Annabelle insisted. "We have to help him."

Still, Johnny did not rein the horse in or make any attempt to turn it. Annabelle was at a loss as to what was best. If she tried to wrest the reins from the boy they might both be unseated.

As it was, she kept bouncing from one side of the slick saddle to the other. Her feet in the stirrups were the only things that kept her from slipping all the way off.

That, and Johnny's uncanny balance. He had no foothold, no handhold, yet he was in such unity with the galloping animal they moved as one.

Finally, still on the south side of the Capitol complex, he allowed the mare to slow to a walk, much to Annabelle's relief. She straightened, stretched cautiously and felt the taut muscles of her back spasm.

"Thank you for slowing down," she said with a sigh. "I didn't know how much longer I could hang on."

"We rest the horse. She will need her strength."

"How do you know? Where are we going? How will your uncle find us?" If she'd had a handkerchief in hand she would have worried it.

"He has told me what to do. Take you across the river."

"How? The Potomac is deep and wide. This horse can't possibly swim that far with both of us on her back."

"I know."

His replies were so stoic and brief she wanted to scream in frustration.

"Then we should wait for Charles."

"He will come."

"Don't keep saying that. No one but God can see the future."

"I know Tsali. He will come."

"Charlie? Charles? Is that how it sounds in Cherokee?"

The boy nodded. Turning down a side street that led south he slowed the mare even more.

Many of the houses they were now passing were tiny shacks, clustered on dirt lots overgrown with grass and weeds. Little smoke rose from morning cooking fires and the windows were nothing but gaps in the walls rather than being glassed the way the Eaton homes had always been.

Cur dogs yapped as she and the child rode past. If someone had asked her to describe the city before today, she would have told them that such poverty did not exist in Washington.

One thing, however, was familiar—the smell of the river and its environs. They must be getting near a section of the Potomac. Therefore, they were also close to being trapped between whoever might come after them and the cold, rushing waters.

Annabelle shivered at the thought. Patting the bag of

coins to make sure it was still deep in her skirt pocket, she felt bereft.

What good was a sack full of money if the person you cherished the most in all the world was lost to you?

Chapter Nine

The first man who had lunged at Charles fell with a blow to his chin. Adams kept yelling instructions to the others, trying to make himself heard above the cacophony of shouting, while John Eaton lagged behind and kept his distance, obviously willing to let others fight his battles for him.

Charles had been in challenging altercations and had triumphed handily. This time was different. He was outnumbered six or seven to one. His situation was not impossible but success was far from guaranteed.

One at a time. Easy does it, he told himself. As long as they came at him singly or even in twos he figured he'd be able to hold his own.

Suddenly, the sleeve of his coat was slashed, the knife wielded by a small, wiry man he had not noticed before the cut.

Charles could have countered with the blade he had taken from the dead man at the river but chose not to. If no one else died here, there was less chance that he and his little group would be pursued as avidly. Above all, he must see that no harm came to John Eaton if he hoped to keep President Jackson from being drawn into the conflict more than he already was.

Adams raised a silver-headed cane and brought it down across the forearm of the knife-wielder with a crack. The man shrieked. The weapon fell to the straw-strewn ground.

Astonished, Charles hesitated. Met the valet's hard gaze. Saw…what? Compassion?

"There will be no killing today," Adams said, his voice pitched so low it was almost inaudible. He eyed the remaining saddled horse. "Go. Keep her safe."

Charles needed no engraved invitation. Nor was he too surprised to hear the elderly valet allude to Anna-belle. She might not think she had friends within the Eaton household but she obviously had at least one be-sides the cook.

Without bothering to foot a stirrup, the Cherokee swung aboard the sturdy chestnut gelding and gave it a hard kick.

Men scattered. Yelled. Menaced. The horse never faltered. It charged out the open doorway and down the drive, its shod hooves clattering on gravel.

Another shot echoed.

Charles ducked, clinging close to the horse's neck, but not enough to keep a bullet from clipping his hat and sending it flying as he reached New York Avenue.

Shouting blended into an undecipherable din behind him.

In the street, freight wagon teamsters fought to con-trol mules frightened by the melee.

Cabbies laid whips to their horses' backs and sped away, out of danger.

Charles became one with his galloping mount. He

knew Johnny would do his best to get Annabelle to the river and find a way across, as he'd instructed. He just wondered how long it was going to take him to track them down and how much time he'd have to search before Eaton organized a real posse and started in pursuit.

In his mind he could still see Annabelle as she rode away. Beneath the ethereal beauty that had originally caught his eye lay a heart of pure courage. Of kindness and gentleness supported with the solid strength of an oak. No matter how many times she was disappointed she rose to her feet and stood tall.

In missionary school he had been taught to know and love a Christian God, as did Annabelle. Their childhoods and customs had differed, yet their faith provided a tie that was unbreakable. She might not have an earthly father. Neither did he. But they shared a heavenly one.

Charles prayed continually as he rode out of the city. And while he was at it, he realized he needed to thank God for turning a terrible situation into a chance to save an innocent young woman. Might there be more to the seemingly divine plan? Perhaps. Time would tell. First, he had to find her again.

The sun was rising, casting light on the moving river water and making it shimmer.

"I don't understand," Annabelle said as she leaned forward to whisper to the boy who shared the saddle. "What are we doing down here with all these farm animals?"

A raised hand signal was all the reply she got before he pulled a coin from his breeches pocket and urged the horse forward.

Annabelle did not care for the party they were approaching, nor was she certain doing so was wise. If Johnny had not seemed so sure of himself she might have put up an argument.

Johnny displayed the coin prominently. "This. To cross with you," he said to a burly, nearly toothless man who was standing beside a ramp leading to a moored transport barge.

The riverman guffawed. "Now why would a lovely lady want to keep company with the likes of these critters?" He gestured toward a small herd of cattle milling nervously on the barge's rear deck.

"Do we cross with you or do we find another boat?" Johnny asked flatly.

Annabelle's mouth was dry, her palms damp. The Indian child sounded so competent and so in charge, she was awed.

"Eh, I guess you can come aboard," the man agreed with a shrug. "But you're on yer own with them cows. If they shove yer horse into the water, I ain't fishin' nobody out."

"Agreed." Johnny tossed the coin and the boatman caught it deftly. "How soon do we leave?"

"Soon as my men get that last muley cow to take the ramp. You can follow her on. Don't be slow or we'll cast off without ya."

Annabelle could barely speak. She cupped her hand to mute words meant only for the boy's ears. "We're going across on that contraption? Why don't we just stay here and wait for your uncle?"

"Because he told me to do this," Johnny countered.

"To take this boat?" She was incredulous.

"No. Join a large party and cross quickly. He will meet us in Virginia."

"But how will he find us? Where will we go?" The momentary look of confusion and indecision on the Indian boy's face was fleeting. But she had seen it. That was not a good sign.

"You haven't really talked about this with Charles, have you?"

Johnny's nod was sure. "He said to go north, then stay near the river. When I saw a party about to cross with livestock, I was to join it."

"He told you to ride a *cattle* boat?"

"If you were the law, where would you look for a runaway lady like you?"

"On a passenger ferry. You're absolutely right." Sighing, she scooted back in preparation for dismounting.

"You stay on the horse, Miss Annabelle," Johnny said. "I will lead it up the ramp. You will be safe with me."

"I believe you," she said. "I just wish…"

"You wish to see my uncle again. You will. Soon. He will come to us."

"How can you be so positive?"

"Because he gave his word," the child said with a quirk of a smile as he swung a leg over the mare's mane and slid effortlessly from the saddle. "He is Cherokee. He will come."

Charles wasn't sure how difficult it would be for Eaton to muster a cadre of troops and give chase but he didn't imagine it would take long.

He slowed Eaton's big chestnut gelding to an easy lope and left New York Avenue. Johnny was a good rider and an even better student. All Charles had to do was follow his own instructions and he'd overtake Annabelle and the boy soon.

Worries about success became another fervent prayer. "Father in Heaven, help me find them? Guide and direct me? Please?"

There was regular boat traffic across the east branch of the Potomac. The best place to hide an animal the size of a horse was among other large animals, he'd reasoned, which was why he had instructed the boy to cross on a flatboat that was also transporting livestock.

Given those parameters, choices were thankfully limited. Smaller craft were anchored to the riverbanks by stout ropes while white, brown and black laborers unloaded all manner of supplies intended for the growing city.

Charles shaded his eyes, scanning the bank and bobbing boats, then checking behind him to make sure he had not been followed. Helping Annabelle get away would be for naught if he led the authorities straight to her.

Yes, she was innocent. And, yes, she should have been able to remain in Washington and eventually obtain justice, as should he. But they could trust no one. More factions than they dreamed of were probably at play behind the scenes. Margaret Eaton was simply the only one they had unmasked, thus far.

Ahead, near a bend in the river, a large flatboat was leaving the shore. Its side sweeps were extended like oars and there were two stout figures manning the rear tiller to counter the sideways push of the current.

Charles stood in his stirrups. Eaton's gray mare was aboard! He wanted to wave and shout and celebrate but held his emotions in check.

"God's speed, dear lady," he whispered. "Are you watching? Can you see me?"

As if answering, the slim rider aboard the mare raised an arm and waved.

In seconds, Johnny was clambering up onto the low rail that enclosed the milling herd and waving both arms. The actions were so wildly exuberant they almost caused the boy to tumble overboard.

Laughing to himself and praising the Lord, Charles reined his horse and started to follow along the bank. Now that he knew they were safe, he could take his time finding his own way across the river.

And in the meantime, he'd watch their crossing and continue to give thanks.

"We need to go back," Annabelle told the oarsman they had paid for transport.

His cynical chuckle was not comforting in the least. "You must be daft, woman. Once the boat is in the current there's only one way she can go."

"Then how do you get back across?" It seemed like a sensible question so she was dumbfounded when he guffawed even louder.

"We drag her upstream and start from there," he explained. "Now go back where you belong and let me do my job so's I don't get in trouble with the boss. I don't wanna fling you in the drink to shut you up but I will if I have to."

Annabelle believed him. Passing beneath a narrow staircase that led to the roof of the cabin in the center of the rectangular barge, she returned to Johnny.

He was holding the mare's reins and comforting it.

"Is she still trembling?" Annabelle asked.

"Not so much now. I told her that a boat is nothing to

be scared of." He began to grin. "I said a horse like her should be braver than any old *waga*."

"I take it that means cow?"

He nodded with obvious delight. "You speak Cherokee."

"I'm just a good guesser." Annabelle grinned. Now that they had seen Charles was alive and well—and knew they were safely on their way to Virginia—she felt a lot more like smiling.

"The man won't turn back?" the boy asked.

"No." Annabelle sobered. "He says they can't."

"Did you offer a bribe?"

"I never even thought of it," she admitted ruefully. "It wouldn't have done any good. He told me they have to start farther up river to get back to the place where we saw your uncle."

Johnny laid his small hand on hers. "It will be fine, Miss Annabelle. Tsali will cross and meet us."

She peered back at the last place she had seen the handsome Cherokee, hoping for one final moment of connection.

Instead, she saw a group of mounted men sweeping along the grassy banks at full gallop.

Their progress led her gaze to the right. To the evident object of their mad dash.

Charles was at least seventy-five yards ahead of them, bending low in the saddle and whipping the gelding with the ends of the reins, asking it for more speed.

The others were not gaining on him. Not yet, anyway. But how long could the horse keep up such a feverish pace? And how could Charles hope to find a way across the river to join them when he was running for his life?

* * *

He had seen the first riders top the ridge and pause there. That hesitation had given him a head start. Unfortunately, his rapid departure had also made him stand out from the rest of the individuals doing business along the river and had marked him as their quarry.

Shouts of "There he goes. Get him!" rose above the normal din.

No one had taken a shot at him yet but he had no doubt they soon would, even though the chances of hitting anything at that distance, particularly from astride a galloping horse, were slim.

He considered abandoning the stalwart gelding, and might have done so already, if Annabelle's possessions had not been tied to its saddle. She must value her personal belongings or she would not have bothered to pack them.

His eyes caught an anomaly in the terrain and his heart leaped. "Aha. Thank the Lord!"

Veering suddenly onto a barely discernible trail, he disappeared into a copse of trees.

The land opened up only slightly on the opposite side of that grove. Charles kept to the tree line. Watching. Waiting to be rediscovered. Praying he would not be.

As soon as he rounded another large clump of trees and knew he was once again hidden, he stopped the gelding and dismounted.

The animal was still in a frenzy from their wild flight, lathered at the neck and foaming where the bit bridged its mouth.

He held tight to the reins, using his free hand to pat the horse's quivering neck while speaking softly. "Easy, boy. Easy. That's it. Settle down."

The horse blew, snorted and pranced for a few more moments, then trusted him enough to stand. Its hide twitched beneath his touch when he slid his left hand down the withers and freed up his right.

So far, so good. "Easy. That's it. Almost done."

As soon as Annabelle's and the boy's traveling bags were loose from their tethers Charles stepped back. She had wanted to return Eaton's horses. Now he would send this one home—and hopefully fool the posse at the same time.

Knotting the long, loose reins together so the animal would not get tangled in them as it ran, he gave it one last friendly pat before shouting, "Yah!" and slapping it on the rump.

The horse jumped and headed in the direction of its familiar stable, just as Charles had known it would.

The thunder of hooves from the opposite direction caused him to fade into the grove of trees and hold perfectly still, barely breathing.

"There he goes!" someone called.

Other men shouted in triumph.

"He's mine!"

"No, he's mine. I seen him first!"

"Outta my way or I'll shoot you, instead," another yelled, cursing to punctuate the threat.

Amused and relieved, Charles remained a part of the forest until he was certain the final rider had passed, then fisted the handles of the bags, turned and cut through the trees to the river.

Chapter Ten

The Potomac flowed smoothly near the center. As the barge approached the far shore, however, the flat-bottomed craft began to list sideways and take on waves of water over the sides.

Although Johnny was still holding the nervous mare's bridle, Annabelle was glad she had dismounted. How she would get back onto the horse bothered her a lot less than the thought of falling into the river while perched atop it.

A gang of men on shore had hold of long, heavy ropes and were tugging the boat's bow closer while the keel followed the current and swung downstream on its own.

"This way," Johnny said. He was already leading the mare along the starboard side of the craft past the small, central cabin.

"How will they get all the cattle off?" Annabelle asked, hoping the men did not decide to drive the herd along the same narrow walkway she and the boy were taking.

"There. See?" He pointed.

As the stern bumped the shoreline it was efficiently secured, much to her relief. She pressed her fingertips to her throat where her white pelerine formed a collar, its long, lacy points caught by her belt in the front.

"Oh, my. That looks really dangerous."

"Not for us," Johnny remarked as casually as if he traveled by boat all the time.

There was no ramp or gangplank at the bow to facilitate their getting to shore, so the boy merely jumped, landing at the edge of the steep bank and nearly losing his balance before clambering onto the grassy verge.

Annabelle was loath to follow in spite of his urging. And the gray mare seemed to be of the same mind.

"Come," Johnny urged. "Quickly."

"I prefer to wait until I can do it without sliding around in the mud or taking a bath," she countered.

He pointed aft where a team of drovers was setting up to off-load the cattle. "If you do not jump while the cows are weighing the boat down, it will start to ride higher in the water and be farther away."

To her chagrin she had to admit he had a point. "What about the horse?"

"Get back on and ride her." Johnny had to shout to be heard above all the other noises along the shore as well as the restless bawling of the frightened cattle. "She can jump farther than you can."

Without Charles to give her a boost, remounting proved problematic. By leading the mare over to some wooden crates and climbing them like stairs, she managed to gain enough height to fit her left foot into the stirrup. Pulling herself the rest of the way into the saddle, however, was chancy.

"Stupid petticoats," Annabelle muttered, happy to be astride once again but far from comfortably settled.

Her left foot remained in one iron stirrup while she

leaned right to locate the other with the toe of her shoe. It had to be down there. If only her full skirt and petticoats were not obscuring its position, she knew she could find it.

The mare began to shift nervously and throw her heavy body back and forth as if unsure what her rider wanted or why she was so off balance.

Annabelle straightened, concerned about handling the reins and beginning to realize that the Cherokee child had been taking more charge of their prior exploits on horseback than she had imagined.

"Hold on!" he screeched in the high pitch of youth.

There was nothing to grab except the slightly raised pommel of the saddle and the gullet beneath it where the tips of her fingers curled—and no time to snatch up the reins—even if she had known how to keep control.

With three short strides the mare launched them both toward the shore just as Annabelle's toes managed to find the lost right stirrup.

The horse landed stiff-legged in the front. The initial jolt wasn't enough to unseat Annabelle completely but it did throw her onto the mare's neck where she held on for dear life.

Both of her feet came loose. Momentum raised her up as the horse shot past Johnny and broke into a run. She was upright again! "Oh, thank…"

Relief was fleeting. Annabelle was airborne by the second bounce.

The third landed her just shy of the mare's tail and as she fell backward its rear hooves barely missed hitting her!

Johnny was by her side immediately. "Are you all right?"

"I—I think so," she said, teeth chattering. "What happened?"

"You forgot to say, 'Whoa.'"

"I did, didn't I?" Relieved to be in one piece even though her pride was severely bruised, she smiled and took the boy's hand so he could help her rise.

As Annabelle straightened her dress, brushed off her skirt and looked around, she gaped in astonishment. The mare was standing nearby, calmly nibbling tufts of grass. "If I had known she was going to stop that easily I might have been able to hold on longer."

"She stopped because you fell off. Otherwise I would be chasing you down the trail."

"In that case, I guess my poor horsemanship was for the best."

She shaded her eyes from the sun and scanned the far bank, hoping against hope that Charles had eluded his erstwhile captors and found his way back to the river.

"I don't see your uncle," she told the child, her temporary burst of joy rapidly fading.

"We will meet him later." He grasped the mare's reins and began to lead her away.

"Wait! If we leave he won't be able to find us."

"Yes, he will. We will go to the inn where our party stayed the last night before entering the city."

"Is that what he told you to do?"

Her breath whooshed out in a sigh of desperation and discouragement when Johnny replied, "It is what he would want."

What was the use in arguing? Her ideas were no better than those of the Cherokee child and since he was more acquainted with his uncle's habits than she was, it made sense to let him choose their path.

If only she knew for a fact that Charles was safe, that he had escaped the posse that she had seen in pursuit, she could breathe easier. Or could she? Knowledge of his troubles would be no help at all since she was powerless to help. Not only did an entire river separate them, she had no weapons and no allies.

Yes, she did, Annabelle realized with a start. She had a wise Cherokee boy. And she had her Christian faith—a faith she shared with Charles McDonald. God was their shield and shelter from any evil that might overwhelm them.

With a glance heavenward and a prayer in her heart, she hiked her skirts above her shoe tops and stepped out, following the boy and their horse away from the Potomac.

Hatless, Charles felt only half-dressed. Still, he reasoned that the stylish top hat that had been literally shot off his head at Eaton's would have immediately marked him as not belonging in the group working along the river.

Truth to tell, his cutaway coat, vest and cravat were also not suitable attire.

Still toting Annabelle's carpetbag and the smaller sack containing the boy's things, he approached a young man who was apparently waiting in line to off-load goods into his empty farm wagon.

The brim of the fellow's brown hat drooped, partially obscuring his face, and his dark coat had seen better days. Nevertheless, he was about Charles's size and his garments seemed relatively clean and well tended.

"Good afternoon," Charles called with a wave. "Mind if I rest with you a bit?"

"Don't make me no nevermind," the freckled young man said. "C'mon up. Looks like you've had a rough time."

Charles nodded and threw the bags he'd been carrying aboard the wagon. "That, I have." He footed a front hub and hoisted himself beside the driver to share the spring seat. "It all started to go wrong when I lost my good hat."

Eyeing the floppy felt the other man was wearing he asked, "What would it take for you to part with yours?"

"My hat?"

"And your jacket, if you don't mind." Charles was shucking his cutaway coat as he spoke. "I'll give you my coat and a few extra pennies if you'll make the trade."

The youth's eyes lit with interest, yet he hesitated to agree. "Where might you be bound, mister?"

"Across the river. I won't be coming back or accusing you of cheating me, I promise. The coat is finely made and should fit you well. There's a small cut in one sleeve that can easily be mended. I can see all the young ladies appreciating you come Sunday morning church. Think how fine you'll look."

"My shirt is homespun and so are my breeches. What'd I want with a coat like yours?"

Charles laughed. "I see your point. Tell you what. I'll keep my boots but you get all the rest—except for my pocket watch."

"Well," the farmer drawled, removing his hat and combing his fingers through his long, sandy-blond hair. "My ma made all my clothes. She'd be a might put out if I was to trade 'em off without bringin' her something."

Eyes drawn to the gold watch Charles was now holding in his hand, the young man began to smile. "'Course, she'd be pleased if I brought her somethin' sparkly and pretty."

"You drive a hard bargain. All right. The watch, too." Charles cast around to make sure they weren't being observed, then climbed into the back of the high-sided wagon to change. At this point, his options were limited and his chances of getting away only temporarily better. Once the riders who had been pursuing him overtook the chestnut gelding and learned that he was no longer aboard, they were sure to return to the river and look for his trail.

As he donned the farmer's clothing he cautioned him. "There may be a few gents looking for me, so if you want to stay safe, let 'em see the light color of your hair. That way they won't make any mistakes."

"You mean think I'm you and shoot at me?"

If the young farmer had acted the least bit afraid, Charles might have felt guilty. On the contrary, he was grinning broadly and seemed to be looking forward to the possibility of a brawl.

"Don't underestimate the men who are looking for me," Charles warned. "Once they know you're not me, you should be safe enough. Just don't relax until you're sure they've realized that suit isn't mine anymore."

"Yessir." He was proudly donning the vest and trying to figure out how to tie the silk cravat while Charles was slipping his own boots back on and refilling his pockets.

"One more thing," the Cherokee said as he retrieved the traveling bags and jumped down from the wagon. "I'd be obliged if you'd tell them I went west."

"Whilst you cross the river? Glad to oblige. God be with you, sir."

"And with you," Charles said. He eyed the gold watch. "I hope your mother appreciates a fine timepiece."

"I reckon she will, if'n she learns to tell time."

Pausing just long enough to instruct the farmer about the proper care and winding of the pocket watch, Charles bid him a last farewell and started toward the shore.

The sooner he secured passage and left Washington, the better. And then he would have to buy another horse because he'd never be able to overtake Annabelle and Johnny if he walked or rode coaches.

Speaking of horses, a group of riders was cantering along the river from the northeast. He didn't have to recognize individuals to know they were the same men who had chased him through the woods less than an hour ago.

He tossed the bags onto the deck of the nearest flatboat and followed them aboard as if he belonged there. No one challenged him, nor did his movements cause interest among those folks still on shore.

With the farmer's hat pulled low over his eyes and the homespun clothing completing his disguise, he was as good as invisible.

The posse galloped closer. Charles held his breath when the riders stopped to speak to the farmer who was now wearing the Cherokee's expensive clothing.

He saw the youth stand in the wagon and point west, back toward the city, as he had promised.

Satisfied, Charles left the stern of the boat and went in search of her captain.

It was time to pay for passage into Virginia.

There were several reasons why Annabelle chose to walk from the river. One, she was stiff and sore and hoping movement would keep her muscles from tying in knots. Two, she was not ready to be thrown off the horse again. How people convinced themselves to get back on and ride after an accident such as hers was beyond comprehension.

Her small companion acted more than happy to have the mare to himself for a while. The only thing that seemed to bother him was their slow progress.

"We can go much faster if you ride," Johnny prodded.

"I know. That's the third time you've told me," Annabelle replied with a smile. "What's your hurry? Don't you want your uncle to catch up to us?"

"Of course I do."

"Then relax and enjoy the beautiful afternoon." Sun warmed her shoulders through her dress and she was thankful that her only bonnet was the small, white lace cap she nearly always wore.

Twisting his upper torso while remaining in the saddle, the boy studied the wide trail behind them, then frowned. "I am worried that someone else will come after us. We should move into the forest or stay out here and go faster."

Annabelle could not argue with such levelheaded reasoning. The neighboring woods were broken by some tilled fields and orchards but even those would have made passage difficult, particularly on horseback. Hurrying to a place of solace and safety made the most sense. And, in order to accomplish that, she would have to climb aboard the mare once again.

"All right," she said, casting about for a step on which to stand while mounting. "Find a big rock or log or something and I'll try to get back on."

Johnny beamed. "I knew you would. Tsali said you were a special woman."

That statement floored her. She gaped at the boy. "He *did*?"

Unabashed, the child nodded. "Yes. When he met us that first day, in the kitchen garden."

"He never. I heard the whole conversation."

Johnny was grinning from ear to ear and looking terribly pleased. "Some of it was in Cherokee."

"Well, yes, I guess it was, but..."

Laughing, he urged the mare closer to a rail fence and scooted forward in the saddle. "Here. Can you get on?"

Although Annabelle was still trying to come to terms with whatever Charles may have said in her regard, she nevertheless was paying attention to the child.

Hiking her skirts above her ankles, she placed one foot on the bottom rung of the fence, then climbed to the second one. Her perch was a bit precarious but suitable.

The gray mare shifted slightly. Annabelle had given one hand to the boy and had already put a foot in the left stirrup so she made a little jump and landed astride as if she had been doing so all her life. The more practice she got, the more she likened this kind of riding to her childish jaunts around a farm pasture.

"You are doing well," Johnny told her.

"Thank you. When I was a girl I used to play with an old, retired workhorse. I'd get up on a stump and she'd come over so I could ride her. I never used a saddle or bridle, though. That's why I wasn't sure how to hold the reins and such."

"Be gentle when you do," Johnny said, demonstrating. "A little pressure on one side of her neck is all you need with a well-trained horse like this. If you jerk or pull you'll hurt her mouth and then she'll be harder to handle."

"All right."

Settling into place at the rear of the saddle, Annabelle found the other stirrup, then put an arm on either side of Johnny and practiced while he guided her hands. Satisfied that she was doing well, she asked, "How do I tell her to stop?"

"A quick tug should be enough, unless she's running scared. Holler 'Whoa' at the same time you pull." He snickered. "And remember to lean back or you might lose your balance and fall off."

"Do tell." Annabelle was laughing with him.

"Are you ready to go faster?"

She nodded. "I hope so."

"Then give her a little kick. Not hard or we'll take off too fast."

"You mean like the way I left the boat?"

That seemed to amuse the boy even more because she could feel his shoulders and back shaking with barely stifled mirth.

Taking care to move slowly and deliberately, she tightened the grip of her knees, swung her feet in and nudged the mare with her heels. Soon, they were cantering smoothly, in tune with the animal's fluid movements.

"How far is it to the inn you said we should stop at?" Annabelle asked.

The Cherokee child looked to the sky. "We will be there soon."

The small boat Charles had boarded was home to a family that was preparing to leave the city for the Chesapeake. Although they had not planned a landing across the river, they were easily persuaded to put ashore by the dollar coin Charles had offered.

His landing was downstream from the place where he'd assumed Annabelle and Johnny had disembarked, yet he was satisfied he'd still be able to track them. He had to. There was no way a woman and a boy could be certain to safely make their way to Tennessee or Georgia even via the Wilderness Road forged by Daniel Boone, or later along the Federal Road. The Appalachian Mountains were rugged, the stops for weary travelers few and far between. And if they were forced to leave the marked trails there was no telling what fate might befall them.

The only horse Charles could find whose owner was willing to part with him was an animal that could very well have belonged to his grandfather—when the old man was a boy. However, its feet were sound and its temperament even, meaning it would do until he was able to trade for a better mount.

He paid the former owner, secured the bags behind the worn saddle and swung aboard. An empty rifle scabbard hung at the front.

"Where's the gun that goes in this?" Charles asked.

"Got her in my cabin," the old man said, spitting aside to punctuate his sentence.

"How much for the gun and some powder and ball?"

"How much you willin' to pay?"

In the end, the bargain was not to Charles's liking but at least he was armed again. The old muzzle-loader was ready to fire—he hoped—and he was on his way.

There was no comparison between the fine, blooded horse of Eaton's and this one, yet Charles was soon riding comfortably and making steady progress.

He looked ahead on the wide trail, wishing he could really see Annabelle instead of merely picturing her. The thought of rejoining her, and the boy, was paramount.

Nothing else mattered. Not even his own safety as long as he could insure hers.

And what then? he asked himself, remembering her beautiful blue eyes, her silky hair, the way she'd smiled at him despite their peril. Perhaps such an extraordinary woman deserved more than a Cherokee diplomat whose mother ran a Georgia plantation.

Until circumstances changed and proved to him that was so, Charles vowed to continue as Annabelle's protector and guide.

He prayed that he would not be found wanting.

Chapter Eleven

If anyone other than Johnny had advised her to stop at that rustic log cabin, Annabelle would have refused. The porch sagged, the stone chimney behind the building was leaking smoke at nearly every joint and the dwelling was so tiny she wondered if there would be room for more than a few travelers.

"Are you positive this is the right place?"

"Yes. We stayed the night when we were going up to Washington."

"All of you? Even that big man?"

"Major Ridge? Yes. He slept in the bed because he is our elder. The others put blankets on the floor."

"All right." She let Johnny slide off first to give herself more room, then leaned over the saddle and carefully swung her right leg free before kicking the left foot loose and dropping to the ground beside the mare.

"We'll need to have her fed and watered before we take care of ourselves," Annabelle said.

Johnny gave a whistle. A boy about his age, barefoot and wearing ragged clothing, ran around the cabin and took control of the horse, leading it away. He was thin and dark as Lucy, yet his eyes shone and his grin was white as snow.

"Don't we need to pay him?" Annabelle asked.

"No. He works for the innkeeper. The horse will be well cared for." The child started up the steps onto the wooden porch. "Come."

Annabelle was still put off. When Johnny pushed open the door she was more than merely hesitant, she was appalled. A single room, perhaps thirty feet long and half as wide, was already full. Men were seated on benches around a bare, plank table and stuffing themselves with what looked like lard gravy, fried back fat and biscuits, while serving girls in grimy aprons bustled around tending to their needs.

The smell of food, cheroots being smoked and the overall uncleanliness of the dwelling almost made Annabelle gag.

She froze in the doorway and stared. "No. I cannot."

Jeers and suggestive hoots from the rowdies inside were the final straw. She backed out the open door and dashed around the cabin, following the path the mare had taken.

What had she done to deserve this? Between the foul odors and lack of gentility, she may as well have been banished back to the jail. Despondent, she sank to her knees at the edge of a pile of fresh hay.

Tears dripped onto her folded hands as she prayed, "Father, why am I here? Please, please, help me."

A gentle tap on her shoulder caused her to startle and look up. Standing beside her was the painfully thin, unkempt child who had taken charge of the mare.

And the little hands were offering Annabelle a bright, red apple.

She blinked to be sure she wasn't imagining things.

The stable hand grinned. "They gets 'em for the horses but I eats 'em all the time. They're real good. Here."

Annabelle sniffled and returned the boy's smile.

Wondering if the Lord had sent this sweet albeit grimy answer to her prayers, all she could manage was a simple, heartfelt "Bless you."

The pounding of a dozen shod hooves behind him caused Charles to guide his horse off the trail into the woods. "Whoa, boy. Easy."

He waited. Listened. Heard little other than the cadence of rapidly moving horses. They were headed southwest. Groups of riders were not unusual and he would not have been bothered by their number if he weren't expecting continued pursuit.

The familiar resting place was but a short way ahead. Assuming that Annabelle and the boy had gotten this far they might soon be in added peril. There was only one thing to do. He maneuvered the horse through the thick brush and back onto the main trail, then galloped after the others.

Three lathered horses were tied to a hitching rail when Charles slowed his horse and walked it into the clearing around the so-called inn.

Dressed as he was he had no concern about being recognized—unless he was forced to speak or make eye contact with someone who might have met him before.

The old horse plodded past the others and headed for the barn, drawing no undue notice.

So far, so good, Charles thought.

He was about to dismount when he saw a familiar

mare. Annabelle was here! And if those other men were a posse, as he feared, she could be in desperate trouble.

Annabelle had retreated into the barn and hidden herself when she'd heard the approach of more travelers. The apple was gone, her hunger was sated, and all she wanted to do was rest where no one would bother her.

If Charles did arrive, she knew the Cherokee child in the inn would alert him to her presence. Other than those two—and the kind slave boy who had given her sustenance—she had no desire to speak with anyone. Truth to tell, she wasn't sure she could manage to carry on a normal conversation if her life depended upon it. All she wanted to do was curl up on the fresh hay, hug herself for warmth, and sleep for days and days.

Heavy footfalls and the snort of a horse drew her attention. Other animals in the stable began to act agitated. She knew that the stable boy had gone to fetch the mounts of newly arrived visitors but this disturbance was different. Closer. Threatening.

She cast about for a weapon, finding none until her eyes came to rest on the pitchfork the boy had been using.

"It worked for Caleb," she muttered, ruing the necessity for violence yet ready to act in her own defense if cornered.

Slowly, silently, she lifted the iron-tined tool and turned it to point upward. The notion of harming another human being was abhorrent. Standing there and letting herself be slaughtered like a sheep, however, didn't strike her as a suitable alternative.

She braced herself.

A shadowy figure darkened the doorway to the barn.

Annabelle was trembling, steeling herself for what she knew she must do and praying she wouldn't have to.

Turn around. Go back, she kept thinking, as if that, alone, would make whoever it was decide to go away.

The man-size shadow kept coming. Not only was he walking on silent feet, he seemed to be tensed like a predator ready to pounce.

He was almost there. Almost within range of the metal tines.

Her hands clamped around the wooden shaft and she felt the grain of the weathered wood. Smelled fear.

Pausing, the man seemed to be listening. Could he hear the hammering of her heart, feel the shaking of her entire body through the ground at his feet?

Tensing, crouching out of sight, she felt her muscles begin to quaver before she had held that stiff pose for more than a few seconds.

A dirty-brown hat brim masked the stranger's face, yet there was something about him that gave her pause. Made her question her decision to defend herself.

Was it the way he moved? The way his shoulders filled his coat? Or was it something else; something intangible that nevertheless drew her like a moth to a candle flame.

Annabelle waited. Prayed for wisdom. Hoped he would not spy her.

And then he turned.

"Annabelle," he whispered, and she knew.

"Charles?"

He quickly swept the hat off his head and turned toward the sound of her voice. "Yes. Are you all right?"

Instead of giving a verbal answer, she dashed into his arms and clung to him like a needy, lonely child.

To his amazement she was not weeping this time, although when he slipped a finger under her chin to lift her face and gaze into her wide, blue eyes, he did see them glistening.

She was gawking as if trying to accept what her eyes were telling her. "Those clothes. Where did you get them? I almost took a pitchfork to you."

With a smile and soft laugh he stepped back and turned to display his new outfit. "Good. If you didn't recognize me, no one else will, either."

"It is something of a shock." To his relief, Annabelle was grinning. "But I guess it's for the best." She glanced down at the burgundy day dress and brushed straw off her skirt. "I don't suppose you brought my bag?"

"Ah, but I did," he reported with a nod. "I managed to rescue your valise before I sent Eaton's horse back home on his own, as you wanted."

She clapped her hands and pressed the palms together in obvious delight. "Wonderful!"

"Where's the boy?"

Annabelle sobered and peered past him toward the rear of the inn. "He went to get something to eat. I could not bear the place so I came out here."

"He let you out of his sight?"

"Don't be angry. I was supposed to be inside with him but the odor and the press of the crowd was too much for me."

"All right. You stay here." Replacing his hat he gestured with an outstretched arm. "When the stable boy comes back, have him feed and water the big old plow horse that's tied over there."

Annabelle made a grab for his sleeve. "Wait. Where are you going?"

"To scout out the inn and rescue a certain headstrong Cherokee."

"Rescue? What do you mean?"

Although Charles would have preferred to not tell her everything, he saw no realistic alternative. If he wanted her total cooperation he'd have to provide a good enough reason.

"A group of men passed me on the trail a few minutes ago. Their horses were tied out front when I came back here and found you. I can't be positive but I think one of them looked like that stable hand you and I tied up at Eaton's."

"Caleb? Oh, no. He'll surely recognize Johnny."

"That's what I'm afraid of."

"But—" she lunged for him and grasped his arm "—you can't go in there. They'll kill you."

"Only if my disguise fails. You had trouble figuring out who I was. I have high hopes those men will be none the wiser."

"And if they do notice you? Are you armed?"

"I bought a rifle when I changed horses."

"Oh, that's wonderful," she said cynically, rolling her eyes for emphasis. "A lot of good one shot will do you against three men."

"Then you should pray I won't need to fight my way out," Charles said, hoping to distract her before she became any more overwrought.

"Prayer is always helpful," Annabelle agreed. "But God also expects us to use the good sense He gave us."

"You have a better idea?"

Her countenance fell. "No. Not yet. But I soon will. I just need a moment to think."

"We've wasted too much time already," Charles countered as he turned his back on her. "I'm going in."

For Annabelle, waiting and not knowing was worse than being involved in direct conflict. At least if she were facing their adversaries she would know, from moment to moment, that Charles and Johnny were unharmed.

When the dark-skinned stable boy returned leading three weary, lathered horses, she asked him to also care for Charles's mount.

"Yes'm. You gonna want him bedded down for the night?"

"I sincerely hope not," she said with a sigh. "Just see that he's fed soon in case we have to leave."

A seed of an idea was beginning to take root and grow. Suppose she sent this lad into the inn to fetch Johnny? No one would take notice of two children quietly leaving together—and then Charles wouldn't have to do a thing.

She gently touched the boy's arm, noting his surprise when she did so. "Please," she said. "Listen to me. I need a favor."

"Ma'am?"

The sack in her pocket rattled as she pulled it out, withdrew a coin and offered it to the child. "I know this is unusual but could you help me?"

"I don't wanna get in no trouble."

"You won't. All you have to do is go into the inn and find the boy who is traveling with me. Speak to him quietly, so no one else can hear, and tell him to come out here right away. Can you do that?" Placing the coin in his palm she folded his thin fingers around it and held them there.

"Yes, ma'am. Soon's I see to these here horses."

"No. Now. You have to go now." She reached for the bunched reins in his other hand. "I know how to feed. I'll do it for you while you're fetching my…son."

"I couldn't. This is my job, not yours."

"Then think of your errand as a new job, one for me. And while you're gone, if I happen to lead a horse or two to water, it won't hurt a thing, will it?"

"Guess not."

"Fine. Then go."

Shaking his head in obvious confusion the boy started toward the inn. Annabelle would have liked to shout at him to hurry but figured she was fortunate that he was doing her bidding at all.

As soon as she'd led the first three horses to the watering trough she fetched the one Charles had been riding and gave it a drink, too.

If she had not recognized her bag tied behind the saddle she would not have dreamed he had chosen such an unattractive animal. It had splayed hooves the size of dinner plates and a ratty mane and tail that looked as if they hadn't been combed out in years.

Nevertheless, the horse did have kind eyes and a sweet disposition, allowing her to effortlessly lead it. The moment she presented hay it began to eat hungrily.

Keeping one eye on the cabin and the other on her tasks, Annabelle realized she had inadvertently gained another advantage. If she hid Caleb's and the other men's horses, the stable boy would surely get in trouble. If she merely unsaddled them, however, it would look as if the child had simply been doing his job to make the animals comfortable. Not only would that delay their adversaries' departure when and if she, Charles and Johnny fled, it would cause confusion and provide more of a head start.

"Thank You, Jesus," she whispered, setting to work to implement her plan.

First, she would pull all the tack off the other horses, then try to bridle the gray mare. Even if she didn't succeed in saddling her it wouldn't take Charles long to do so. And then they would be on their way.

Closing her eyes for a few moments she took the time for a more formal prayer of deliverance.

Then she lifted the left stirrup on the closest horse and began to loosen the cinch.

As Charles entered the single main room of the rustic inn he was struck by the same pungent odors that had repelled Annabelle.

Not only was the place more crowded than it had been when his party had first availed themselves of its meager accommodations, the landlord had apparently found a different cook because the food was definitely less palatable this time. *Not that it had been to his liking before*.

With his hat brim pulled low, head bowed and the daylight limited inside the room, no one paid attention to his arrival. That suited Charles just fine. He had no intention of staying one second longer than absolutely necessary.

Casting around for Johnny, he was surprised to note that the boy wasn't visible. So, where had he gotten to? Since he wasn't outside and had not returned to Annabelle, what had become of him?

Charles knew that continuing to linger by the door was out of place so he ambled over to a bench in a far corner and took a seat. The meal had been served as for a large family, meaning that anyone could partake of the food on the tables while it lasted. He picked up a biscuit and tried to take a bite, never dreaming it would be almost as hard as the rocks along the trail.

Chewing carefully, he peered at the others from beneath the hat's floppy brim. If any of these men, particularly the ones from Washington City, had noticed the Indian boy, surely they would be acting excited rather than so sluggish and nonchalant.

He was about to try another bite of the hard biscuit when he felt a tap on the toe of his boot. Either the landlord's dog was scavenging under the table or someone was trying to get his attention.

Johnny? If so, how had the boy recognized him?

By his boots, of course, the only part of his costume he had not altered!

A tap of his foot on the plank floor was followed by another rap against his ankle. It had to be the boy. So, how was he going to smuggle him out? And even if they did manage to reach the door, what was to keep them from being overpowered and apprehended there?

Charles tensed, held his breath and prayed that someone or something would cause enough distraction to aid them. If not, they might as well already be in chains.

Chapter Twelve

Struggling to ready the mare, Annabelle let her guard down enough that she didn't notice a new arrival in the yard.

The gray horse, however, did, and when she turned her huge head she almost knocked Annabelle off the chunk of wood she was using as a step stool.

By hanging on to the bridle she managed to finish buckling it behind the mare's ear before jumping clear. Behind her, she heard a man's chuckle.

"Well, well, what have we here. You're a much prettier hand than old Jed usually has workin' fer him."

She considered correcting his erroneous impression, then decided against making any response. Instead, she lifted her chin, crossed her arms and faced him as if she could not believe anyone could be so ignorant.

The man's resultant guffaw was coarse, his leer suggestive. "What's the matter, girlie, you too big for your britches?" With a half-toothless grin he spread his arms like an angry bear and started to lumber toward her. "Come to Papa."

"You are drunk, sir. I suggest you go to the inn."

"After I get me a little kiss," he said, raking her with his gaze and continuing to advance.

"You'll get nothing of the kind. Leave me alone."

"Feisty little thing, ain't ya?" He spit tobacco, wiped his chin with the back of his hand and laughed. "C'mere. Give us a kiss."

The pitchfork was too far away for Annabelle to reach without turning her back on her adversary, and she doubted that a man who was already this filthy would mind being hit with a few horse leavings the way Caleb had.

The only objects close at hand were combs, brushes and the curved metal pick used to clean packed dirt and stones out of the natural depressions in the soles of hooves. The pick wasn't even sharp…but the trimmer beside it was! Hooked and bladed, that tool was meant for shaving unshod hooves to even the soles.

Annabelle spotted the makeshift weapon at the same time the stranger did. He was bigger. She was quicker. Fisting the rounded wooden handle she brandished the blade, holding it out like a knife fighter.

Rather than subdue him, her efforts merely served to amuse. She knew she would employ the weapon if she were forced to, but clearly the man did not believe she was capable of defending herself. Truth to tell, a few days ago she would have agreed with him. Now, with the grace of God, she was ready for anything.

The heavyset traveler laughed and lunged for her.

Annabelle did what she had to do. She slashed at his closest hand.

Felt contact.

Heard him bellow.

And watched him whirl and run around the side of the inn, coattails flying.

When the front door was shoved open and banged back against the wall, everyone inside the inn froze. A lone traveler stood in the doorway, holding one bloodied hand in the other and screaming unintelligibly.

Just as Charles was getting to his feet, the dusky stable boy tugged vigorously on his sleeve and pointed in the opposite direction.

"Understood." In one fluid motion the Cherokee reached under the plank table and grabbed Johnny by his sleeve.

They followed the other boy out through the rear and past a small building housing the summer kitchen. More servants were at work there but none paid undue attention to their passing.

Annabelle was standing in the open stable door. One arm was wrapped around her waist and the other was extended as if she were holding something loathsome.

The moment she spied Charles and the boys, she dropped the trimmer and called, "I—I cut him. I didn't want to. He wouldn't take no for an answer and…"

Charles was by her side in a heartbeat. "Are you all right?"

"Yes. Yes, I unsaddled the other horses but I'm too short to put the saddle back on my mare."

"I'll take care of that." Racing by, he shoved Johnny toward her. "Show him my new horse while I see to yours."

He didn't wait to see if she was obeying his orders.

Her wise foresight had equipped them for a smoother escape than he had anticipated, and as long as he took care of the final details without delay, they'd be on their way before more trouble started.

After checking the bridle to make certain it was properly fitted, he slung a pad and saddle over the mare's back, ducked to grab the girth and cinched it tight.

When he turned to call to Annabelle she was already waiting close by. "Come on. Up you go."

As soon as she was seated comfortably, both feet in the stirrup irons, he handed her the reins. "I take it you know how to handle her by now?"

"Well enough." Her wide-eyed gaze turned to the inn from which they could all hear shouting and mass confusion. "Let's get out of here."

"An excellent idea, madam," Charles said, touching the front brim of his farmer's hat in a gesture of courtesy. "I'm sorry we didn't get a chance to stay and dine."

Annabelle nudged the mare forward, following him to his own horse. "I would rather starve than be forced to eat in there."

She was making a disgusted face. He raised an eyebrow. "Prissy? You? I'd not have thought it."

"There is a big difference between wanting my food to be edible and being overly fussy," she countered.

Charles swung into his saddle and lifted the boy to ride behind him. "That there is. Ready?"

"I have never been more ready in my life," she said, grasping the reins and urging the gray mare forward.

A confused knot of men was boiling out of the inn, pushing and shoving each other. All looked armed with pistols and at least one brandished a rifle.

"Kick her and let's go!" Charles shouted, taking his own advice and putting his heels to the horse's flanks. "Ride!"

Annabelle's movements were not as well coordinated with those of the horse as she would have liked, although she did repeatedly give thanks that she was still aboard.

The sounds of shouting and cursing faded away as they galloped off. Finally, just when Annabelle was wondering if they were *ever* going to slow down, Charles reined his horse to a walk.

He swiveled in the saddle, looked at her over the top of Johnny's head and smiled. "Ah, you're still with us. Excellent."

"You did lead me on a merry chase."

"Looks as if you were up to it."

"Barely," she replied, returning his grin. "I can certainly see the advantage of men's britches when traveling this way." Her cheeks warmed unnaturally. "Not that I am suggesting such a thing for myself."

"Certainly not," Charles said, slowing to let her ride abreast and placing himself on the outside, meaning he had to duck an occasional overhanging branch.

She was thankful for his company, yet wished she were alone so she could at least loosen the strings of her corset a bit. The restrictive garment was not particularly uncomfortable as long as she had the opportunity to let her ribs breathe at night. Now, however, she yearned for a respite from being so tightly laced.

A lady would never admit that to a gentleman, of course. It wasn't seemly. Even a husband might not be privy to such personal information, or so she had been told.

It was only now that Annabelle began to realize the

complexity of her situation. She was traveling with two males, and although one was a child, that did not preclude her being thought of as a wicked woman. If she continued on like this, there was no way she could ever hope to be accepted in polite society again.

She sobered. Perhaps it was already too late, given the false charges levied against her. Once night fell and she spent it with Charles, her reputation would be well and truly ruined.

Blinking to clear her thoughts and shaking her head, she noticed that he was leaning closer, studying her. "What? Is my bonnet crooked?" She used one hand to pat the fitted white cap that covered the back of her hair and framed her face with a small ruffle.

"No. It's fine. You looked unhappy."

"Not entirely." Annabelle heaved a sigh. "It's just that I'm so unsure of my future."

"None of us can know that."

"True," she said, "but a man has more choices than a woman does. If we are questioned, what should we say? I cannot very well admit that I am a single lady traveling with an unattached gentleman."

"Scandalous."

If she had not seen his lips twitch in a repressed smile she might have been less inclined to argue. "Well, it is. To me, at least."

"What would you have me do?"

"If I knew the answer to that I would not be so perplexed," Annabelle told him.

Observing his profile as they continued down the trail, and seeing his expressions change, she decided he must be doing some deep thinking.

When he finally spoke his mind she nearly gasped.

"I suggest we travel from here on as a family." He glanced at the child before turning a steady gaze on her. "He has your eyes and all of my coloring. He could easily be our son."

"Yes, but—"

"If it comes to that, we can make it official."

Annabelle's jaw gaped. "What?"

"Marry."

"You should not joke about such things."

"Believe me, I am not joking," Charles said flatly. "It would not have to last forever if you didn't want it to. That way your reputation would be safe."

But how about my heart? she asked herself. *What will keep it safe?*

Logical answers eluded her. She could tell from Charles's sober expression that he was waiting for her reply. This was not the courtship and betrothal she had dreamed of as a girl. She was not being swept off her feet by a handsome beau. There had been no mention of love. This man hardly knew her. What would possess him to offer marriage?

She swallowed hard, looking for her voice and hoping she was about to make the right decision.

"I thank you for your kind offer," she said, speaking softly and wondering if she was going to be able to properly express everything she wanted to say. "If you are not toying with me, if you truly mean it, then my answer is yes. I will be beholden to you for such a gallant gesture."

The boy, who had been virtually ignored during their conversation, tugged on Charles's sleeve and let loose with a string of Cherokee. The tone was anxious, almost angry. And when Charles replied in kind, his communication sounded equally intense.

Annabelle did not have to understand the language to know the two were arguing, although she could not tell which one, if either, might be on her side. She supposed it didn't matter. The man had not meant for their makeshift family to endure. He had made it clear he was merely offering her the status of wife temporarily.

That was enough. It would have to be. Happiness and cottages with flowers blooming by the door were for silly dreamers. The good Lord had provided an honorable man to guide and protect her. She would not argue, nor would she complain if this man did not truly care for her.

Her teeth worried her lower lip and she let her horse fall back behind the big plow horse so Charles could not see her if she failed to curtail her tears.

Why weep? she asked herself.

The answer was as clear as if it had been shouted in her ear. *Because I will soon be the wife of a man whose heart does not belong to me—and whom I already love.*

No argument arose to contradict that conclusion.

And silent tears began to slide down her cheeks.

Darkness approached stealthily, as if the canopy of trees was absorbing all the sunlight.

Charles knew they were going to either have to spend the night in the saddle or find shelter somewhere. Given that he had had no opportunity to plan for an extended excursion, he was not properly prepared to make camp. Nevertheless, he decided it would be best for them to try to rest rather than press on when there was little moonlight to illuminate the trail.

He slowed the bay and let Annabelle's mare close

the distance between them. "I'm going to take us farther off the beaten path. You're not used to riding and we all need to rest."

"I can go on," she insisted. "You don't have to stop on my account."

Although little natural light was left, he could not miss her pained expression or the set of her jaw. She was game. And stubborn. But that did not mean she was right.

"We're going to camp for a few hours, at least, to rest the horses. I won't be able to offer you the usual comforts but I promise, as soon as we come to a settlement, I'll bargain for the proper accoutrements."

Annabelle yawned behind her hand. "Now that you have mentioned it, I believe I may be tired enough to sleep right here in the saddle."

"That won't be necessary. Just stick close to me so we don't get separated and watch for low branches. I don't want to be picking you up off the ground."

The boy, who had said little since his outburst regarding Charles's offer to marry their fair companion, suddenly began to chuckle and regale Charles with tales of Annabelle's prior adventures on horseback, particularly her embarkation from the barge on the banks of the Potomac.

Although the conversation was conducted mostly in Cherokee, Charles could tell she was getting the gist of the child's tale because she was making faces while Johnny gestured and laughed.

Gazing at her over his shoulder, Charles smiled. "I wish I had been there to see that."

"And I am delighted that you were not," she countered. "It was embarrassing enough as it was."

"No doubt. I'm glad you're a fast learner."

"So am I. And the mare seems to be getting used to me, too. It's actually quite soothing when she walks calmly like this."

"Let's hope there aren't a lot more times when we have to gallop," Charles said, making a face and elbowing Johnny when the boy made a comment in Cherokee.

Annabelle laughed. "I take it our make-believe son would be delighted to see his pretend mother flying through the air again."

"Something like that."

It didn't take Charles long to choose a suitable clearing. Dismounting after letting the boy down, he went to Annabelle, paused beside her mare and reached up.

Although she hesitated at first, she did rest her hands on his shoulders and allow him to lift her down. He set her gently at his feet. "Are you all right?"

"Fine." She smiled up at him and his heart took off like a deer being pursued by a hungry wolf.

"I was afraid you might be in pain."

"Don't be silly." She backed away, seeming a bit unsteady at first, then quickly regained her usual balance and vigor. "Where are we bedding down? And where do you want the horses?"

"Johnny can see to their needs," Charles told her. He signaled to the boy. "Let them drink all they want from the nearest stream, then hobble them where they can reach good grass but keep them close."

As soon as the boy led the animals away, Charles turned back to Annabelle. "You can use your coat as a blanket if you want. I'll cut a few tender pine boughs for your pallet."

"Just show me what to do and I'll help."

"No. You gather dry wood for a fire in case we decide to light one." He pointed. "Pile it over there."

"Won't fire make us easier to find? I mean, suppose those men we eluded back at the inn have followed us this far? They might spot flames."

"That's why I'm not sure about starting one," Charles explained. "As long as the weather holds and we can get by without it, it would be best to leave as little sign of our passing as we can."

"If you don't need a fire, I certainly don't," Annabelle vowed.

He believed her. For a woman who had been raised surrounded by luxury and with all the accoutrements of wealth, she was proving to be extremely accommodating. Of course that could change as their trek went on. Plenty of natural hazards lay ahead, not to mention the fickle weather in the Appalachians where they were bound.

It was still early enough in the year that they might encounter storms bearing freezing rain. Of all the possible risks, that was one of the worst. It made the trails slick and stung a person's face like needles being hurled by an angry porcupine.

That was why his first task must be acquiring better provisions. And, if they came to a town that had a resident preacher, he would also keep his promise to wed his traveling companion.

Such a wild notion should have caused him acute distress but it did not. Truth be known, he had surprised himself when he had offered marriage, yet the more he thought about it, the more convinced he became that it was the right thing to do.

Charles's biggest conundrum then became his own

motives. He could not help wondering if he had chosen to propose marriage for Annabelle's sake alone, or if he was merely fooling himself.

The way he viewed his actions, they felt right. Frighteningly so.

Starting into the thick forest he kept one eye on his task and the other on the lovely woman he knew he would be proud to call his wife. There was no earthly way she would have ever agreed to wed him under normal circumstances. Nor would he have asked.

The picture of their future together was so ethereal, so tenuous, he could only pray that he—that they—were following the wisest path.

Chapter Thirteen

Annabelle had been so sleepy she had almost missed getting her share of the food Johnny had purloined from the Eaton kitchen.

She dusted the biscuit crumbs off her skirt and settled comfortably onto the bed of soft branches Charles had laid for her.

Man and boy were still seated close together, talking privately. Even if they had been speaking only English she doubted she could have made out half their conversation. Nevertheless, she strained to hear bits and pieces because she was certain she had heard someone mention her name.

"Yes, I meant it," Charles grumbled.

Johnny answered in Cherokee.

"That is my business," Charles replied. "You just take care of the horses and behave yourself around her."

Annabelle didn't hear the boy say much more and assumed he was sulking the way he had been ever since Charles had mentioned possible nuptials.

Remembering her initial reaction to that conversation she felt a warmth rising in her cheeks and extending all the way to her toes. Becoming husband and wife would solve a lot of their problems for the present. What it would do to their budding relationship in the future, however, was an altogether different issue.

She shivered. Closing her eyes and tucking her heavy coat around her, she folded her hands beneath it and began to pray for divine guidance.

The next thing she knew, it was morning.

Charles apportioned the remaining biscuits carefully and warned against wastefulness as they prepared to leave camp. "I don't know when we'll find someplace where we can get decent food so make that last as long as you can. There are settlements along this road. I'm just not sure how well they'll be provisioned."

"What road is this?" Annabelle asked. "It seems to be very well traveled. Look at the wagon ruts."

"It's called the Wilderness Road. It was first designated such by Daniel Boone but the original trails were cut by the Cherokee and many other tribes."

"Is that why there are so many narrow side routes everywhere?"

"Partly. We're not the first travelers who have wished to move along without being observed." She noticed that Charles's smile had faded just before he said, "If anything should happen to me or if we get separated, stick to the main trail and you'll be fine. It would be easy to lose your way if you went off too far and couldn't see the way back."

"Don't give it another thought. You're not getting out of my sight," Annabelle promised.

She had shed her coat early and tied it on behind her saddle. Currently, the boy was riding with her and sitting on the coat, although it was clear he was not pleased with the arrangement. The few efforts she had made to speak with him had had no result other than to earn him a stern look of warning from Charles. Since she didn't want to cause trouble, she had stopped trying to exchange pleasantries.

Watching Charles's broad shoulders and straight back as he rode ahead of her, Annabelle was becoming more and more enamored of him. There was no aspect of his character that she did not admire; no element of his personality that was not pleasing. And no memory of him that was anything but uplifting. The mere thought of the sacrifices he had already made for her was enough to make her heart swell with pride and thanksgiving.

With Johnny so close by she was unwilling to pray aloud so she let her mind reach out to God and mouthed a silent "Amen."

Was the boy a Christian like Charles? she wondered. And if he was, how might she explain to him that she and his uncle were planning to pledge their troth before a man of the cloth when they might not mean it?

Worse, Annabelle realized, was how she was ever going to explain to God?

The town they encountered the following evening was small, but a white-painted spire told Charles what he needed to know. If this church had a spiritual leader in residence, rather than relying on a circuit rider, his prayers had been answered.

"You and the boy can wait for me out here," he said, stopping their party before the forest opened up fully on the settlement.

"Please, don't leave us," Annabelle begged in a tone tinged with panic.

He hesitated and studied her. It was clear she was nervous. He was at a loss to understand why they had seen no sign of their former pursuers since leaving the inn.

"I won't go far. I just want to ask around about finding a missionary or some other kind of preacher." He angled his larger horse to face her mare's tail so he could more easily take her hand, hoping a gentle touch would calm her. "We can't have the Cherokee ceremony until we have tribal support, but I thought you'd like the Christian one as soon as possible."

"Yes, of course." She shot a brief glance at the taciturn child who had already hopped down. "I simply want us all to stay together. I think that's wise, don't you?"

"Yes." Looking around and sensing no threats, he urged his horse ahead. "Come on, then. Let's go get married. Afterward, we'll visit the general store and buy whatever we need for comfort on the trail."

"We won't have to stop at any more inns like the first one, will we?" Annabelle had brought the mare even with his mount so they could converse more easily as they rode and was looking up at him expectantly, hopefully. The boy trotted alongside.

Charles smiled at her naïveté. "Not all are as atrocious as that one was, but, no, we won't be staying in any inns. Not if I can help it. I plan to continue to make camp along the trail, only with better foresight and planning than last night. That way we will be harder to track and won't have to race to stay ahead of anyone who may still be looking for us."

"Do you really think they will follow us all the way?"

"I sincerely hope not," he said. "We will leave the

horses with Johnny while we see if we can locate the preacher."

Charles's brow furrowed, his seriousness meant to make an impression on the child as he added, "You will hold our horses, watch for riders from Washington and warn us if you see anyone familiar. Is that clear?"

Although his face showed disrespect he agreed. "Yes, sir."

Dismounting in front of the tiny wooden church, Charles handed his reins to Johnny, then reached up to assist Annabelle again.

Her hands rested gently on his shoulders. He grasped her waist. Lifted. Swung her free of the saddle.

As he lowered her she landed so close, so trusting, Charles had to force himself to release her.

When she slid her hands from his shoulders, gazed up at him and smiled sweetly, he wanted to bend and kiss her so badly he almost did so.

The only thing stopping him was the realization that such an unseemly show of affection, particularly now, could frighten her. She would be much safer as his wife. Therefore, he must be careful to do nothing to dissuade or confuse her.

Perhaps later, when she began to feel comfortable with him and they were no longer together because of duress, he would ask her permission to court her properly.

The ludicrous notion almost made him laugh. He was about to *marry* the woman and here he stood, worried about how to court her!

They found the preacher's wife, Leah Hoskins, tending a garden at the rear of the church and she quickly located the clergyman for them.

It took Annabelle less than half an hour to wash, change into her Sunday dress and fix her hair. The gray frock and matching collar weren't a lot different from the burgundy day dress she had been wearing but the outfit was a sight cleaner.

Would Charles even care? She doubted it. He was approaching their wedding in the same unruffled manner that had characterized him from the start. If it had not been for the insistence of the missionary's wife that the bride would want to freshen up, he probably would have simply spoken his vows, bought supplies and headed on down the trail without delay.

"You look lovely, dear," the older woman told Annabelle.

"Thank you."

Blushing, Leah leaned closer and whispered behind her hand. "Has your mother spoken to you about wifely things?"

"I have no mother," Annabelle said sadly, not realizing to what the woman was alluding.

"Oh, my. Then I suppose…" Taking the bride by the hand she led her into a bench in a secluded corner. "Before Reverend Hoskins returns with your intended, I should warn you. Men are strange creatures."

Embarrassed and unwilling to be led into a discussion of such a personal nature, Annabelle resisted. "That won't be necessary, ma'am. Really, it won't." Wishing to begin considering her new life as reality she added, "The boy is our son."

That revelation clearly flustered and discomfited the pastor's wife because she clutched her hands together, pressed them to her ample breast and blushed. "Oh. Oh, my. I see. Well, then…"

Annabelle noticed the older woman's attention divert to the front of the tiny sanctuary. There, standing next to the gray-haired, frock-coated missionary, was the most handsome man she had ever seen.

The fancy clothing the Cherokee had been wearing when she had first laid eyes on him was no longer pertinent. Still clad in homespun and holding that ugly old hat in hand, Charles remained the best looking, most appealing man she had ever known. His long hair was slicked back, his shoulders broad, his stance imposing yet not at all off-putting.

He was the most beautiful sight she had ever beheld.

And he was smiling at her as if he actually wanted to make her his wife.

Refusing to let common sense dissuade her, Annabelle left Leah and stepped forward boldly, eager to join her groom at the altar.

If someone had asked her how she felt at that moment, she would have told them that her feet had never touched the ground.

Unsure of what amenities his new bride expected, Charles bought a pack mule, two skinning knives, powder and ball for his rifle, and enough additional supplies to take them through to Georgia without having to stop often in other towns. The way he saw it, the less they had to do with civilization on their way home to his tribe, the better their chances of eluding anyone in pursuit.

Keeping to native trails as much as possible, he headed for the Cumberland Gap.

Their first night as husband and wife was rapidly approaching and he didn't want to further frighten Annabelle by waiting until dark to pitch camp, so he found a suitable clearing and halted.

"Why are we stopping?" she asked.

"I thought we'd set up camp early since we've never done it properly before."

He swung down and ground-hitched his horse before turning to the boy. "Make sure that mule is hobbled, just like the horses, in case he takes a notion to go home, then gather some wood for a fire while I arrange the rest."

Johnny had amassed a pile of broken logs and twigs before Charles finished stringing ropes to support a canvas lean-to between a couple of pines. As long as the weather held, that kind of minimal shelter would suffice.

Since Annabelle had taken it upon herself to assist the boy, Charles went to the mule and unpacked the iron skillet and coffeepot he'd bought, plus flour, baking powder and a slab of cured meat.

"They didn't have lard so I bought some bacon," he told her. "You can use that to grease the pan."

She just stood there, cradling an armload of dead wood. Her eyes were wide, her expression one of bewilderment. "I can? Why?"

"To keep the biscuits from sticking and give them flavor. They won't be as good without lard but we won't notice after we drown them in red-eye gravy."

"Um, in what?"

"Gravy. Made from pan drippings and coffee. You said you helped the servants at Eaton's. You do know how to cook, don't you?"

"I've seen it done."

In the background, the Cherokee boy was snickering and muttering. Charles silenced him with an icy stare.

"Well, I hope you paid close attention or we'll all

starve," Charles said flatly. "Cooking is not my strongest forte."

"Nor mine," his new bride confessed.

Johnny piped up. "I helped my grandmother all the time." He was already selecting and placing rocks to form a circular cooking area. That done, he arranged dried moss and kindling in the center, struck a spark from Charles's tinder box and soon had suitable flames.

"After it dies down, we can cook," the boy said. He was looking at his adult companions and shaking his head, wordlessly chastising them.

Charles grinned. "Good thing we didn't leave him in Washington, isn't it?"

"I suppose so," Annabelle agreed, "although I feel terribly inept. My first foster mother, Myra, had started to teach me simple household chores. After she died, I did spend time with the servants and learn a few things, such as how to sew a straight seam or darn a sock. I just never did much in the kitchen except prepare the elements. You know, like peeling potatoes or gathering spices."

"I'm almost ready for the bacon," Johnny said. "And a fork if you have one."

Charles shaved off several slabs of the pungent cured pork and handed them to the boy. "That enough?"

"Yes." He was already laying it in the pan. "Did you buy anything to mix biscuits in?"

"No."

"Just give me the sack of flour, the knife and the baking powder then."

Charles turned to Annabelle. "I'll go gather pine boughs for our sleeping places if you'll stay here and make sure our cook doesn't set the woods on fire."

She was smiling as she replied, "I believe Johnny

knows what to do. He certainly seems to be more accomplished than I am."

Although Charles figured he could have muddled through and have turned out an acceptable meal, he chose to let Johnny shine. This was the first time since leaving the churchyard that the boy had spoken more than a few words. Letting him show off was for everyone's benefit, especially his.

And what about Annabelle? Could she be pretending a lack of skill for the boy's sake, too? He doubted it. Considering her usual take-charge attitude and willingness to jump in and try anything, he had to assume she truly did not know how to cook. That would not be a problem under normal circumstances because his family employed several good cooks back home. Out here, however, it would have been nice to be traveling with a party containing more than one person who knew how to make a simple biscuit.

Sighing, he took a hatchet into the woods and began to cut young, tender pine boughs.

Chapter Fourteen

It looked to Annabelle as if the boy was about to ruin their flour supply. She almost told him to stop what he was doing, then thought better of it and hunkered down to watch him work, instead.

Wielding Charles's knife he cut an X-shaped slit in the flour sack on one side, near the top, and pushed back the coarse fabric to expose some of the contents. Then he used the tip of the knife to pick up a dab of baking powder and added it to the exposed flour.

"I'll need some clean water," he told Annabelle.

Nary a please or a thank-you was offered but she complied, fetching him one of their animal-hide canteens.

Pushing a depression in the flour where he had added the baking powder, the boy poured in enough water to make a paste, stirred it slightly with the knife blade, then drizzled in a bit of the hot fat.

"Won't that cook it?" Annabelle asked.

"Not if the water was cold enough."

"Oh." She had watched Lucy make biscuits in a slightly similar fashion but seeing it done in the forest with nothing but a sack of flour and a hunting knife was rather impressive.

Finally, Johnny put his hands into the dough and worked it until it was a solid, gummy ball that he summarily handed to her.

When Annabelle stood there, just staring at the blob of dough, he said, "Break off small pieces and wrap them around a clean stick like that one." He pointed to a leftover piece of kindling. "Then hold it over the fire. Watch so it doesn't burn."

"Should I wash the stick first?"

The Cherokee child rolled his eyes. "You can if you want to. If you get it too wet the dough might slide off."

"Oh." It occurred to her that she had been promoted to kitchen helper. That was fine with her. As long as Johnny was cooking and needed to speak to her, at least she wouldn't continue to get the silent treatment.

That was what had hurt the most. Rejoining him after coming out of the chapel had resulted in one of the most difficult moments they'd shared. He had behaved as if he'd been asked to hold getaway horses for a couple of bank robbers rather than for friends and family. It was only after Charles had added the pack mule to their possessions that the boy had seemed to mellow.

Of course, he did want to ride the mule so he'd have a mount of his own and was thus being more tractable. That was a normal reaction. Annabelle didn't mind if he got his way once in a while. Children needed things of their own. Things that they did not have to share with adults.

Like my old doll, Rosie, she mused, smiling fondly. Now that they were on their way she was even gladder that she had chosen to stuff the precious relic into the bottom of her valise. It might be of no earthly use at present, but it had once meant the world to her. She could recall cuddling that doll and pretending it was her very own baby when she was little more than a babe in arms herself.

Myra had even made Annabelle and Rosie matching dresses and bonnets after embroidering AL and some floral decorations on the doll's body. How proud she had been to carry Rosie when they were dressed alike. Truth to tell, she could not remember a time when her precious doll had worn anything else.

Johnny's shout brought her back to the present.

"Hey! The biscuit."

"Oh, dear. Sorry."

She jerked the stick back. One side of the blob of dough was blackened while the other was still soft.

"You have to turn it," Johnny said, sounding astonished that she wouldn't know that.

"I wasn't thinking. Of course it needs to be turned. Do you think we can salvage this one?"

He shrugged. "Cook the other side and see."

"All right. This one will be mine, regardless."

Adding to her first attempt with a fresh glob of dough on another stick, she held them both over the fire, then eyed the taciturn six-year-old, wondering if there was some way she could let him know how deeply she commiserated.

His real problem wasn't this current situation, whether he realized it or not. She identified with Johnny because she knew what it was like to feel abandoned. The man he had counted on had first given him away, then had taken him back and let him accompany them on the trail—

only to ostensibly replace him by marrying a *woman*. And a useless one, at that.

Although that was not precisely what had happened she could see how the convoluted circumstances might easily confuse a child.

That conclusion made her give a very unladylike snort. The boy was not the only person who was totally befuddled.

She was more mystified, more lost, than she had ever been in her entire life.

Because night under the forest canopy was very dark, Charles had inclined the lean-to so that its opening faced the fire. Then, he'd banked the flames to burn slowly, less for warmth than to increase Annabelle's sense of security.

It had been all he could do to keep from laughing when she had proudly presented him with his ash-dusted supper biscuit. The memory made him smile, raise on one elbow and look over at her.

Lying between them on the bed of boughs, the boy was sound asleep.

Annabelle was not. Her head turned. "What? Is something wrong?" She sat up and clutched the coat she'd been using as a coverlet. "Did you hear something?"

"No, no. I was just checking to make sure you and Johnny were comfortable."

"As snug as a bug in a rug," she said softly, smiling. "This bed of branches is far softer than I thought it would be, especially with this new blanket thrown over it."

"Good. You haven't changed your mind about not stopping at inns?"

He saw her eyes widen. "Never. Speaking of bugs,

did I ever tell you about the cot in my jail cell?" She shivered noticeably. "It was awful. When I moved the blanket they'd given me, hundreds of black beetles scattered. And the food..."

Charles had to chuckle. "What? Didn't they give you a stick to cook with?"

"Hush." Blushing, she grinned. "I think we all did better tonight than anyone expected. After I burned the first biscuit the others turned out all right." Her eyebrows lifted. "Didn't they?"

The flickering firelight made her rosy cheeks glow and her eyes twinkle. Seeking to help her forget their true plight, Charles drawled, "Well, except for the charred outside and the uncooked part next to the stick, they were wonderful."

Annabelle made a face at him. "Thank you. I think."

Somewhere in the nearby woods there was a cracking sound, as if a dry branch had snapped. Charles froze. Put a finger to his lips. "Shush."

"What is it?" she whispered.

"I don't know. Stay still."

"You said there were lots of bears and skunks and raccoons and things like that out here. Will the fire keep them away?"

Charles nodded. It was true that the fire would repel marauding animals. It was also true that its light would attract the two-legged kind of enemy. Although he had oriented the canvas lean-to to mask their camp from the distant main road, that didn't mean there was no escaping glow.

He pulled on his boots and got to his feet, holding out his hand to signal her to stay where she was and praying she would obey.

He'd propped the muzzle loader on the ground, next to his gear, when they'd unsaddled the horses. He grasped it by the barrel and swung it across his body, ready to raise and fire if need be.

A glance back at Annabelle told him she had heeded his warning. On further examination he saw the silvery flash from a new blade, its hilt fisted in her right hand. When he had bought her a knife and sheath he had hoped she would never have to draw it. Now he was glad he'd had the foresight to arm her and that she'd been clever enough to take the weapon to bed with her.

Standing as still as one of the pines, Charles waited and listened. A slight breeze was blowing from the north. On it was carried the sound of a horse's nicker.

He saw the mule's large ears immediately swivel and settle on the direction of the sound. The old horse's head and that of the gray mare were drooping as if napping was more important to them than curiosity, so he concentrated on stopping the mule from answering the other equine's call.

At that moment, the rifle was far less important than keeping their location a secret so he laid it aside. Holding the side strap on the mule's halter he put his other hand on its nose and felt its nostrils flare, its upper lip twitch.

"Easy, boy. Easy," Charles crooned softly. "That's it. Settle down."

A distant human voice shouted something unintelligible, was answered in like manner, then faded away.

Charles didn't relax until the mule did. Even then, he waited awhile longer, just in case.

Although the mule didn't alert again, he suddenly sensed that he was not alone. Every muscle tensed. Hair on the nape of his neck prickled. Could he reach the rifle in time or should he simply whirl and face his adversary bare-handed?

Ready for battle, Charles spun around…and saw Annabelle.

He frowned and blew out the breath he'd been holding. "You scared the life out of me, woman."

"I'm sorry. When you didn't come back or make any noise to tell me you were all right, I had to see for myself."

"Well, you can put the knife away," he grumbled, still agitated and more than a little annoyed. "Whatever was out there has gone."

"Are you certain?"

"No, but the mule is and that's good enough for me."

"Oh." She nodded toward the lean-to. "Are you coming back to bed?"

He could tell that the moment she spoke, she regretted her choice of words because her face flushed. Highlighted by the glowing embers behind them, her cheeks were practically aflame.

Charles was almost as embarrassed as Annabelle, although as her legal husband he knew he should not have been.

Ah, but theirs was not a normal marriage, was it?

Facing her and hoping his expression was as guarded as he meant it to be, he simply said, "Not yet. But you'd better go back before the boy wakes and misses us. I don't want him running around in the woods playing Indian."

As he had hoped, that comment brought a smile back to her lovely face before she nodded and turned to follow his instructions.

Charles stood stock-still and watched her go. She was

graceful as well as stalwart. Pretty as well as intelligent.
Yes, she had a lot to learn and was very immature in
many ways. Cherokee girls were usually mothers by the
time they reached Annabelle's age.

But they had had the advantage of being raised in
families, with mothers and aunts to teach them, whereas
she had been passed from servant to servant like the
foundling she was.

If she proved willing in the long run, perhaps he could
give her the home she'd never known, Charles mused.
They would have to start again, from scratch, because
her presence would probably result in his being disowned by the matriarchs in his clan, but he'd gladly face
ostracism if Annabelle chose to stay with him. A bigger question was, could she stand against the animosity he knew she would be met with? Was it even fair to
ask her to?

With that disturbing conundrum tumbling around in
his brain he nevertheless managed to appear unruffled,
took a seat near the horses with his back to a pine, and
laid the rifle across his lap.

He would watch for a while longer. If he dozed there,
so much the better. The last thing he wanted to do was
go back to their shared shelter and make his bride think
he had misunderstood her faux pas and returned for the
wrong reason.

Stirring in the camp woke Annabelle at dawn. She
yawned and stretched, then realized she was the only
one still abed.

Fully clothed, she arose and stole off into the woods
for a few minutes, then rejoined her traveling companions. The fire ring had disappeared. If she had not known

better she might not have even suspected that anyone had cooked there recently.

Charles had the horses saddled and was packing the mule. He barely glanced at her as he said, "Untie the ropes holding up the canvas and bring all that to me. I need to cover the supplies."

"All right."

It was a bit puzzling to awaken to such a stern reception but since the man was under terrible pressure and had probably gotten little sleep, she was willing to let him grumble all he wanted. Particularly if that meant they would soon be underway again.

By the time she'd managed to loosen the ropes and drag the heavy canvas to the mule, Charles was ready for it.

Instead of thanking her, however, he merely accepted it and then pointed with his free hand. "See what the boy is doing? We need to scatter those branches among the natural falls in the forest to hide them."

"All right. I'll go help him."

"And when you get back, circle the clearing so you don't leave any footprints. I'll be getting rid of them while you're gone."

Hurrying to where Johnny was gathering their pine bedding she smiled at him, hoping his reaction would be more pleasant than Charles's. It was not. The boy didn't even bother to speak to her, let alone make pleasant conversation.

Annabelle was a tad miffed. They might be taciturn by nature but they had both chatted with her before, so what was wrong with them this morning?

It occurred to her to ask—at least Charles—but she quickly set that notion aside. Her ineptness regarding cooking, and then her misunderstood comment about Charles coming back to bed, were the only things she could think of that might have cost her their good graces. Did she want to learn that she had made even more mistakes? Perhaps worse ones?

No, she did not. If her traveling companions wanted to brood, or whatever they were doing, she would let them. Remaining silent would be extremely difficult for her, but she would manage to hold her tongue somehow. If nobody down here on earth wanted to talk to her she'd just converse silently with her Heavenly Father.

That thought made her smile and put a bounce back in her step. Even as a lonely child she had known God would never leave her, never abandon her. When Myra had died, Annabelle had nearly lost her faith, yet in the years following, it had not only returned, it had grown.

And now I need it more than ever, Annabelle mused. It seemed illogical to attribute her current situation to divine guidance and wisdom—unless her trust in God was complete. And so it was.

Her smile grew. That was the key, wasn't it? As long as she kept her faith and trusted her Heavenly Father, no matter what, she would eventually triumph.

Annabelle knew that was true. It was the waiting which accompanied the trusting that she found so difficult.

Stealing back through the trees as Charles had instructed, she saw him tighten the last knot on the mule's pack saddle with a jerk, then press his forehead against the side of the load as if the weight of a thousand burdens rested on his shoulders.

Poor man. Her heart clenched. She wanted to go to him, to touch his arm, perhaps tenderly rub his shoulders and assure him she knew he was doing his best to help her. To help them all.

Instead, she brought her foot down hard on a fallen branch and made it snap.

Charles jumped, immediately standing tall and acting self-possessed. In other words, he was his old, stubborn, bossy self again.

"I have the mare ready to go," he called to her. "Hurry up."

Her initial reaction was to snap back, to insist that she had been hurrying. A vivid memory of the empathy and tenderness she had felt while watching him moments before helped her quell that urge. Whatever had possessed him to bring her along on this journey, be it his sense of honor or duty or even the influence of divine providence, she was grateful beyond words.

And that was how she intended to behave, Annabelle promised herself. Neither of her companions was going to get her goat. She didn't care what they said or did, she was going to bite her tongue and respond with grace. With dignity.

And with love?

That was a whole other subject, wasn't it? One she would have to deal with on a day-by-day, hour-by-hour basis.

All of a sudden, the journey that lay ahead seemed to have grown a lot longer and far, far more hazardous.

Chapter Fifteen

"This is still the Appalachian range," Charles explained, pausing on a high ridge that looked out over a sea of green treetops. Birds soared above, wings spread, effortlessly making lazy circles above the canyons.

"It's beautiful." Annabelle's casual smile warmed him more than the noonday sun. "Is this Virginia?"

"Probably not. I'll know for sure that we're in the Carolinas when we reach the Federal Road. My people cleared and widened an old Cherokee trail for the government right after the turn of the century."

"What's the route we've been following?" She was shading her eyes with one hand, the other holding the reins.

"Daniel Boone's Wilderness Road, for the most part. I've kept to the trees as much as possible so we wouldn't be seen, but we didn't want to have to fight our way through dense forest, either."

"I understand. Will you still see me to Tennessee after we have returned the boy?"

"If you still want to go there. You hadn't mentioned

it in so long I'd thought you might have changed your mind."

"It does not weigh so heavily, that's true. However, I do want to see where I came from and try to trace my family." She began to blush. "I should say my roots."

Did she mean that she now considered him and the boy as her real family? He hoped with all his heart that she did.

Gazing at Annabelle astride the mare, he was taken with her natural beauty and the grace with which she had accepted her fate. The more time they spent together, the more he admired her. She was not only lovely on the outside she was just as exemplary to the core; gentle yet hardy, benevolent yet resolute. Charles could think of few friends he would trust as much as he now trusted Annabelle.

His Annabelle, he reminded himself. *His wife*. Not the woman his mother or tribe would have chosen for him but a perfect fit just the same.

Could it be that Annabelle was actually beginning to care for him, to think of him as her husband? Although she had not actually said anything endearing, he had caught her looking at him more than once with what he imagined could be tenderness.

At least he thought it was. Considering the befuddled condition of his mind and the way their togetherness during the trip had worn on his conscience and taxed his self-control, there was no telling how much was real and how much the wishful creation of his mind.

He didn't even have to close his eyes to see them as a family that included the boy, although Johnny had continued acting less than amiable.

Charles had allowed the child to withdraw and brood

from time to time, assuming he would eventually get over being upset. If he hadn't had such a taciturn nature to begin with, Charles would have had a better idea whether or not he had actually mellowed.

"How much farther is it to where you come from?" Annabelle asked, breaking into his thoughts.

When Charles replied, "Only two or three more days," he was astonished to see her smile fade. Might she be enjoying their sojourn? Was it possible? She had seemed to be coping well but that didn't prove anything other than that she was resilient and determined.

It occurred to him to delay their arrival in New Echota in order to eke out more time with her on the trail, but he decided that would be foolish. They had not encountered anyone who was definitively searching for them since leaving the inn that first day. To dally along the route would be to tempt the Lord their God.

That, Charles would not do. Nevertheless, he was not above asking his Savior for a blessing on his sham marriage. Only after the church ceremony had he realized fully that the vows they had taken were not just words.

They were holy.

And he wanted to honor them with every ounce of his being.

Annabelle remembered her foster father mentioning the place in Georgia called New Echota. As they'd neared the end of their journey, Charles had told her that they would go there first but he had not described the Cherokee town at any length. That was why, when she first glimpsed the settlement, she was astounded.

"Oh, my! This can't be *Indian*." As soon as she had

blurted out her candid thoughts she was embarrassed enough to blush and apologize. "I'm sorry. I didn't mean…"

"Your reaction is excusable. Most people who aren't familiar with our culture are surprised when they see our cities and our estates."

"No doubt."

Awestruck, she continued to drink in the sight. New Echota was situated on level ground and laid out in a grid, with wide streets, enormous lots for homes, and stores galore. Tall, stately buildings with real glass windows lined the main avenue. One even had a facade of Grecian columns similar to structures she'd seen back in Washington.

"I told you it was an impressive place," Charles remarked, looking proud.

"Yes, but you never said it was this *big*. What's that fancy building over there?"

"That's the council house. Next to it is the court-house and then the printing office where *The Cherokee Phoenix* is published. Remember? You saw Elias Boudinot, the editor, when our diplomatic party called on John Eaton."

"That seems like a lifetime ago," Annabelle admitted with a sigh.

Charles readily agreed. "Yes. Another life, another time. We—you—can start over here. If that's what you want."

Managing a wan smile she shook her head, considering the question and offering an honest reply. "Once, I thought I knew exactly what I wanted. Now I am not at all sure."

One of the things she had always yearned for was a home of her own and a husband who loved her. A husband, she already had. The love was another story, wasn't it? Charles had treated her with kid gloves during their travels, taking care to anticipate her needs and see to it that she was as comfortable as possible whenever they camped.

What he had not done was speak to her as his wife. On the contrary, he seemed more standoffish and grumpy since their wedding than he had before. Was he ruing his sacrifice? Did he wish they had never taken vows before the preacher's family and before God?

Annabelle's biggest problem was deciding what to do about their marriage. She no longer worried as much about her past, or possible charges against her character or truthfulness, particularly since there had been no more sign of their pursuers.

All she really cared about was learning whether or not Charles wanted her. That was it. Plain and simple. Did he or did he not wish her to continue to be his wife? And if he did, why had he not given any indication that he cherished her?

To her chagrin, he seemed to be doing his best to avoid contact of any kind, causing her to miss the gentle warmth of his hand or the simple assistance in mounting a horse that he had previously volunteered so blithely.

Annabelle urged her mare forward to closely accompany Charles into town while Johnny followed aboard the pack mule. Their arrival was creating quite a stir and she wanted to make it plain that they were together.

Heavy freight wagons crisscrossed the broad avenues, their chain traces clanking. Four-horse coaches passed, some carrying passengers and loaded with baggage, others temporarily empty.

Loose dogs barked and nipped at horses' heels or

paused to squabble over a morsel of food that had been dropped in the street.

Passing riders touched the brims of their hats in deference to Annabelle while women in fancy frocks and bonnets silently watched and assessed her from raised, board walkways.

As soon as Charles stopped at the front porch of a white-painted building, Johnny slid off the mule with a happy whoop and took off in the opposite direction.

Concerned, Annabelle looked after him. "Should we let the boy run wild like that?"

"He'll be fine. His grandmother lives just down that side street. I'm surprised he stayed with us this long."

"What about his mother? I'm ashamed that I never thought to ask."

"Long dead. That's one reason he was sent to Eaton, for a good education and to prepare him to take his place in a white man's world."

"The way you have."

"Yes. I and Elias, and many others. Although we are of mixed blood we are still considered true Cherokee."

"Really? Why?"

"Because, as I said before, inheritance comes down through our mothers. Women own the property and make all the decisions about family life."

"Then what does a chief do?"

"The chief and the councils make laws that govern the whole tribe, although lately there has been much disagreement. Some say we have too many laws and others accuse men like me of consorting with President Jackson against our tribe."

Charles swept his arm in a broad arc to encompass the neatly laid out plots in the town. "For instance, all these places were sold to the highest bidder, therefore they went to rich people. When John Ross was elected Principal Chief a couple of years ago, it caused a lot of unrest."

"Was there war?"

"No. It never went that far." Charles sobered. "White Path, Rising Fawn and others held meetings and listened to the predictions of shamans but their anger faded quickly. Various groups simply cannot agree on which laws they want and which they don't. As long as they're arguing among themselves, our elected government will suffer."

"That sounds so much like something a Washington politician would say it amazes me. Apparently, it matters little who is in charge anywhere. There will always be dissenters."

"Agreed." Charles gestured toward the porch of the newspaper office. "After you, madam."

It occurred to Annabelle to reach for his arm and slip her hand through the crook of his elbow as they had when walking together in the past. Now, however, she was no longer a damsel in distress and he was...

What was he, exactly? Stalwart? Yes. Handsome? Yes. Faithful? Of course.

And totally incomprehensible, she added, wondering if the problem was her lack of discernment or if Charles was simply acting the part of a stoic. She huffed. It was likely both.

The office of *The Phoenix* was built up off the ground on piers. A little stiff from hour upon hour in the saddle, Annabelle rested a hand on the railing and lifted her skirts to climb the steps to the porch. Her wrinkled, dusty skirts. She wished she had owned more than two dresses so she could have been more suitably clad for her introduction to Charles's friends and family.

Since she had just come from a long, trying journey she hoped everyone would forgive the dirt on her hem and cuffs, not to mention her formerly white bonnet, though she had managed to rinse it in a stream a few days ago.

Lifting her chin to display fortitude she paused on the porch while Charles opened the door.

Then, she stepped through to meet her new challenge.

Charles saw one man working alone instead of the usual crew of two or three. Dark-haired and slim, the man was wearing an ink-stained apron and was seated hunched over a slanted bench while arranging neat rows of letters cast on tiny bits of lead. He belatedly looked up, puzzled until he realized who had appeared at his door.

"Hello, Elias," Charles said.

The delight in the printer's expressive grin warmed his heart. They shook hands and clapped each other on the back as if neither had expected to meet again.

"Tsilugi!" Elias Boudinot repeated again and again. "Welcome!"

Charles was moved by the overwhelmingly exuberant greeting. "It is good to see you again, too." Clearing his throat he stepped aside to fully reveal Annabelle. "You remember this lady?"

"Of course." Although Elias looked surprised to see her, Charles was glad there was no enmity in his demeanor as he smiled, bowed and said, "Welcome to New Echota, Miss Lang."

"You may now refer to her as Mrs. McDonald," Charles explained while Annabelle was making a slight curtsy. "We were married by a missionary early in our travels."

"You were…?" Elias gaped, then recovered. "I see. Well, congratulations." A dark eyebrow arched. "Are you planning to have a Cherokee ceremony, too?"

"We have not discussed it of late," Charles said. There was no hint in Annabelle's expression to tell him what she might be thinking, let alone what her plans for the future were.

Of course his family would want to attend the Cherokee wedding if there was one. All he had to do was figure out whether or not Annabelle was willing to marry him again, Cherokee fashion, or if she was planning to abandon him as soon as she found kin in Tennessee.

Elias seemed to be waiting for her answer so Charles did the same. Finally, he was relieved to hear her say, "Perhaps. When we are both ready."

Although she had not sounded enthusiastic, Charles was willing to accept her opinion. His fondest hope was that his mother would not only approve but encourage their second wedding. There was nothing anyone could say or do that would keep him from remarrying Annabelle if she was willing, yet it would be a much more pleasant experience if his tribe was as thrilled about his bride as he was.

"Have you made arrangements for lodging?" the newspaper editor asked. He winked at the couple. "I suspect it would be best if you two didn't take up residence at Sali's. Not right away at any rate." His grin widened. "Besides, she's gone to visit one of your sisters in North Carolina."

Annabelle looked puzzled. *"Sa-li?"*

"Sally, to you," Charles explained. "My mother."

"Oh." She began brushing at her skirt as if that would somehow render it cleaner. "Your mother will not be pleased to meet me?"

"My mother is used to having her way," Charles said flatly. "Since before I came of age she has vowed that I will take a Cherokee wife."

He supposed he should have forewarned her. Then again, what would that have done other than cause her more distress? There were some opinions that could not be changed, particularly from a distance. Once his mother returned home, met and got to know Annabelle, he hoped her heart would soften. His certainly had.

"Then you will stay with us," Elias said heartily. "I'll send a boy to tell Harriet to prepare for guests."

Charles thanked him while wondering how he could tactfully explain his and Annabelle's arrangement.

"Until you decide about another ceremony, you'd best stay in separate rooms," Elias added, clapping his friend on the shoulder. "Sorry about that. You know how strong our traditions are."

Charles was greatly relieved. "I'm sure my wife will be delighted to have a room all to herself. I know she has missed the comforts of her childhood."

As his glance went to her he was not at all surprised to see a bright flush to her cheeks and lowered lashes.

The most he could hope for was that she would eventually agree to a second marriage ceremony and then begin to think of herself as his true bride.

His heart kept insisting that she would have immediately refused to consider the Cherokee ceremony if she had been planning to abandon him.

It was that supposition, and it alone, which allowed him to hope. He had been praying for this dear woman's happiness and well-being all during the trying weeks on the trail, and that had engendered a strong emotional bond. The more he grew to care for her, the harder it was to keep his distance and pretend he was merely her traveling companion and champion.

Truth to tell, he hadn't dared get too near her for fear he might say or do the wrong thing and frighten her away. Despite all her outward bravado and strength, Annabelle was still as emotionally innocent as a newborn babe.

Thinking of his outspoken mother and aunts, he gritted his teeth. It was the task of older, wise women to instruct the young wives. Unless he could figure out a way to transfer that duty to someone more sympathetic, Sali was liable to scare Annabelle so badly that she would turn tail and run before he had a chance to convince her they had a future together.

Deciding to change the subject before Elias became too forthright regarding his personal affairs, Charles said, "The boy, Johnny, came home with us. We could not leave him in Washington under the circumstances." He grinned wryly. "Besides, he wouldn't have stayed. Not after everything that has transpired."

Sobering, Elias stared out the window at the dusty street. "That is too bad."

"I will present my reasons to the chiefs. They will have to understand. With both Annabelle and I suspected of murder and she being disowned by Eaton, there was no way the child could have gotten by, let alone flourished, in such a hostile household."

"That is not what I meant," Elias explained sadly. "It is his grandmother. She died shortly after I returned from Washington. He has no close family left."

Charles felt Annabelle grasp his sleeve. Her eyes were filled with concern and empathy.

"You have to go after him. Stop him. Break the news to him gently before he finds out for himself," she insisted.

"I will," Charles told her. "But Johnny has had plenty of time to reach home and see that his grandmother is no longer there."

"Just bring him back with you? Promise?"

"I promise." He nodded toward his old friend. "Will you and Harriet look after Annabelle? I shouldn't be long."

"Of course."

As Charles turned and headed for the door he heard her lamenting, "That poor, poor little boy."

He was impressed and relieved by her sympathetic reaction. Even though Johnny had been sulking and ignoring her as much as possible during their travels, her heart was still open, still tender toward the child.

That was a good sign. A very good sign. Particularly because he was about to offer Johnny a new home with him and his family.

In Cherokee society he would have had to ask Annabelle's permission before committing himself. Since she had been raised by Eaton, her expectations would thankfully be different from those of a person like his mother.

Charles smiled. There were definite advantages to being a husband in a white man's world, weren't there?

As far as he was concerned, that male role was far more advantageous than the one he had observed while growing up.

Chapter Sixteen

The dark-haired young woman who burst through the door of the newspaper office moments after Charles's departure was balancing a curly haired toddler on one hip.

"So, this is Annabelle." She offered her hand and a smile. "I'm Harriet Boudinot. Welcome to New Echota. I have heard so much about you already."

Annabelle was overwhelmed by the warm show of hospitality. "I am very pleased to meet you, Harriet." She let her smile drift to the child. "What a beautiful baby."

"William takes after my mother," Harriet said, kissing the child's rosy cheek. "At least that's what she said when she and Father visited recently." Harriet laughed demurely. "I let her think whatever she wants as long as she accepts my family. There was a time when that was not so."

"I believe I did hear some of that story when Charles was telling me about the mission school," Annabelle said. "I'm thankful your parents forgave you."

"Was there trouble with yours when you took up with our Charles?"

Annabelle slowly shook her head and sighed. "No. I

am a foundling. I spent most of my youth in the home of John Eaton, President Jackson's secretary of war, but I am no one's daughter now."

"Ah, I see," Harriet said.

Taking Annabelle's arm, she called to her husband. "We'll be at home if anyone wants us."

Elias answered, "I'll tell Charles."

As Harriet guided Annabelle onto the porch she asked, "Where is he? I was told you rode in together."

"We did. Mr. McDonald has gone looking for Johnny."

"Who?"

"The little boy he took to Washington to give to my guardian." She sighed. "It's a long, complicated tale."

"Well, we have plenty of time. My house is just down the street. You can freshen up and then have a cup of tea while we have a nice talk. You must be very trail-weary."

That astute observation brought a wan smile. "There are times when I wonder if I can take one more step. It has been a trying journey." In more ways than she wished to enumerate.

"A journey that is over, I trust."

"God willing," Annabelle said, pausing at the hitching rail in the street. "This is my horse. Is there a place for her nearby? She's carried me faithfully and I want her to rest, too."

"We have a stable behind our house. There's plenty of room for her and for Charles's horse." She eyed the mule. "And for that beast, if you want to bring it."

"I suppose I should," Annabelle replied. "After we started letting Johnny ride, he named him Equa Gali, Golly for short. He'll want him cared for."

Harriet laughed. "That's perfect. It means big ears."

"I know. Charles finally told me—after days and days of laughing at my silly guesses."

Gathering the reins of the mare and the mule to lead them, Annabelle fell into step beside Harriet.

The wide streets were dusty and the warm, early summer air was exceedingly damp, yet she felt a sense of relief, of freedom, that reminded her of her carefree childhood.

She could not yet say that New Echota felt like home because everything was so unfamiliar. But the lightness to her step and good cheer in her heart at that moment were such unexpected blessings they brought a lump to her throat and an unshed tear to her eye.

A wizened old neighbor lady of Johnny's late grandmother had stepped in to comfort him when she had seen him racing home.

By the time Charles arrived, she and the boy were sitting in companionable silence on the porch of his grandmother's small cabin.

Johnny wasn't crying. Stoic as ever, he was merely rocking back and forth rhythmically, as if in a trance.

Recognizing Charles, the elderly woman arose and pulled a shawl tighter around her thin shoulders.

He caught her eyes and mouthed, "Thank you."

Nodding, she walked away.

The mournful child acknowledged neither her departure nor the arrival of the man with whom he had spent the past month and a half.

Wordlessly, Charles took up a place beside Johnny, sat and waited. When the boy was ready, he would speak. Until then, it was best to merely let their hearts join in shared bereavement.

Minutes ticked by. Charles didn't move. The orange sun rested low in the western sky and was about to slide below the horizon. Streaks of pink and brighter bands of golden light radiated through clouds that were dusted across the heavens like wisps of drifting fog.

Then it began, starting as a muffled moan before rising into a keening cry the likes of which he had not heard since the passing of his own father. Johnny was not weeping. Instead, he was struggling to inhale while body and soul gave voice to his anguish.

Charles reached out, put his arm around the boy's shoulders. Then gave a slight tug to urge him closer for comfort.

Instead of the resistance he had anticipated, Johnny threw himself at Charles and began to sob.

The man held him close, gently rubbed his back and prayed that the boy would accept the offer he was about to make. Because if he did not, there was a fair chance the chiefs would vote to send him back to Eaton's, regardless of the situation there.

"Hush," Charles whispered. "I know it's hard. Death always is. Your *lisi* was a Christian. You will see her again one day, in Heaven."

"I want to see her *now*," the child lamented.

"I know." Charles continued to rub his back through his jacket until his breathing began to even out. "You will come with me. I will look after you the way any good uncle would. You can become my son."

Johnny looked up through swimming eyes. "Your son?"

"Yes." He smiled benevolently. "It would be an honor to claim you as my own."

"But…what about *her*? When will she leave?"

"Annabelle?" He gave the boy an affectionate squeeze. "I'm hoping she will agree to be married in a Cherokee ceremony and stay with us always."

To Charles's dismay the child gasped, pulled away from him, ran down the porch steps and disappeared into the twilight like a frightened deer escaping a hunter.

The Boudinot home was far larger than Annabelle had expected. Not only was it two stories tall and at least forty-by-sixty-feet deep and wide, it had framed, glass windowpanes and two chimneys.

Entering the house after turning the animals over to the care of one of the Boudinot servants, Annabelle was in awe. The polished parlor floor was covered by bright Persian rugs and the room was filled with intricately carved mahogany furniture. All the place lacked to make it as fine as the sitting room at the Eaton mansion was a piano, vases of fresh flowers, and perhaps a few more crocheted lace doilies on the backs of the chairs and the tabletops.

She clasped her hands together and sighed. "Oh, my. What a lovely home you have. I never dreamed I'd find such sophistication so far from Washington City." Realizing that her comment might sound disparaging, she quickly added, "No offense intended."

Harriet laughed. "I understand perfectly. I reacted with disbelief when I first came here, too."

"You have so many nice things."

"Thank you. We order clothing, groceries, tea, paper and ink from Boston, or purchase it at the mercantile down the street. Most everything goes by steamship to Augusta and is then shipped overland. Other necessities like sugar and molasses come directly from Augusta—or sometimes Knoxville." She chuckled. "I have no problem getting whatever I need, as long as I plan ahead."

"I can't imagine having to consider all that." Annabelle averted her gaze as she confessed, "I have very little practical experience in such things."

"You'll learn. Managing a household is not as difficult as we women let our men think it is."

She gestured at a red brocade settee with scrolling across the back and delicate, arched legs. "Please. Make yourself at home."

Annabelle hesitated. "I would really rather change first and wash, if you don't mind. I wonder, might you have an old dress I can borrow while my traveling clothes are laundered? I was able to bring very little with me when I left Washington City with Mr. McDonald and the boy."

"Of course." She led the way to a staircase and started to climb. "I'll show you to your room and have one of the maids bring you a bathing tub and fill it. You can give your soiled garments to her and she'll see to them."

"I noticed that you had servants in the stable. You have them inside, too?"

Harriet nodded. "A few."

"Are they slaves?" Annabelle asked. "I didn't expect that here."

"Some are. Some are free. My cook, Fiona, is indentured from Ireland. She's a gem. We bought her debt when we were in Boston and brought her with us."

"What will you do when she's worked it off?"

"Hire her for a fair wage, I hope," Harriet said. "I don't know what I would do without her." She shook her head and sighed noisily. "As for the others, we do what we can to educate and prepare them. If the time comes when we all have to emigrate, we want our servants to be able to fend for themselves."

"Emigrate?" Coming to the upstairs room her hostess indicated, Annabelle paused in the doorway.

"Did Charles not tell you? That was one of the reasons he and the others were in Washington trying to obtain an audience with the president. The state of Georgia has declared that come June 1 of this year, all Cherokee lands belong to the state and our laws and customs are null and void."

"Oh, no! Why would they do such a thing?"

"It is a long and complicated story," Harriet told her. "Why don't you relax and take care of your ablutions now. We can talk more later."

"All right." Smiling slightly, Annabelle undid the wrinkled, fraying ribbons of her small bonnet. "I see you don't cover your hair as was the custom where I come from. I will be delighted to follow your example."

"Nor do I wear a corset," Harriet said with a giggle and a blush. "Elias was shocked at first but I see no reason to torture myself unnecessarily."

"Oh, my! Truly?" Annabelle's eyes widened. "If I had thought of being so bold, I know I would have had a much more pleasant trip."

"Consider this a revelation, then. Many of us here have foresworn tight laces for the sake of our own comfort and the health of our babies."

"Dear me." She knew her cheeks were flaming but hoped the high color was masked somewhat by the sun's previous effects on her fair skin.

The other woman's eyebrows arched. "Forgive me for being so bold. I was given to understand that you and Charles were wed."

"We—we are. It's just…"

"Ah. I think I see. The marriage is one in name only?"

"For traveling purposes," Annabelle said, wondering why she felt so embarrassed. Surely hers was not the first marriage of convenience the other woman had encountered. Would she have been accepted so readily by the Boudinots if she had traveled with Charles and the boy as a single lady? She strongly doubted it. Such things were simply not done by gentlewomen.

"Reverend Worcester will be disappointed to hear that," Harriet said. She reached out to pat Annabelle's hand. "But don't you worry. I'll intercede for you and smooth things over."

"Thank you, I think." Wondering how much the messenger boy had told her hostess, Annabelle felt obliged to add, "Charles has asked me to go through a Cherokee ceremony, as well."

"Will you?"

"I don't know. If I could be certain it was his wish, perhaps my decision would be easier."

"Why would he ask if he didn't mean it?"

"Out of honor, perhaps. Or a feeling of duty." Annabelle sighed. "I don't know. The whole situation is terribly confusing."

"And you're too weary at present to think clearly," Harriet told her. "I understand."

"I wish *I* did."

In spite of all her prior plans to break away, to strike out on her own and put all the disappointments of her past behind her, Annabelle had finally admitted, at least to herself, that leaving Charles was the last thing she wanted to do.

Was that bad? Was it weak to admit that she craved

the company of the one man who had treated her like a real lady? Was it foolish to place her trust in anyone, or had she finally found the person with whom she could build a new life?

She wasn't at all sure.

And she had no idea how to find the answers she sought.

Because he knew that Annabelle would be worried if he came back alone, Charles did his best to locate the runaway child. It took a while because this was Johnny's home territory and he had plenty of favorite hiding places.

He was about to give up searching due to the encroaching darkness when he spotted the child hunkered down behind a haystack in the barn.

Instead of berating him, he merely held out his hand and waited for Johnny to take it. "Come on. You can help me check your grandmother's chickens and see to the other livestock, in case her neighbors haven't done it yet today."

"Baby pigs were born after I left," the boy said sadly. "I saw them."

Companionable silence reigned as they fed and watered, then rode double to the Boudinot home. The mare and pack mule were already in their barn so he left his horse there, too.

Mounting the porch steps, Charles knocked. A maid wearing a bib apron over her dress answered and led him to where Harriet was seated in a rocking chair, sewing.

At her feet were three well-dressed children: baby William and two young girls in starched, ruffled dresses.

Charles bent and opened his arms.

The girls squealed and rushed to welcome him while Johnny faded into the background. "Eleanor, how you have grown! And Mary, too. Such beautiful young ladies." Grinning he nodded to their mother and said, "Hello, Harriet," as his eyes swept the otherwise empty room.

The young matron laughed demurely. "Don't look so worried. Your wife is upstairs bathing."

"Good. The journey was wearing on all of us, especially her. We could have ridden a stagecoach part of the time but there were mercenaries, bounty hunters abroad, seeking to do us harm, and we didn't dare travel in the open."

Harriet laid aside her needle and thread, taking care to keep them from the baby. "Have they stopped looking for you?"

"I don't know. We saw no clear signs of pursuit after the first encounter. Now that we are on Cherokee land, we should be safe enough."

"While we still *have* land," Harriet said. She leaned to peer at the boy standing in Charles's shadow. "I'm relieved to see that you've returned with one of our gifts. I had strongly protested the notion of giving away a person in the first place. That is hardly the way to convince Washington that we are civilized."

"It all worked out for the best," Charles replied. "If you have no objections, I'll share a room with Johnny and let Annabelle have private quarters."

"She has explained a little about your arrangement," Harriet said. "It is too bad you two cannot exchange letters the way Elias and I did when we were getting to know each other."

She paused, apparently choosing her words carefully.

"Be gentle with her, Charles, and I think all will be well. She is younger than I was when I chose to marry and seems to have been overprotected."

He nodded. "I suspect it is more a case of neglect than coddling. If it is not too much imposition I would prefer that she stay here with you rather than accompany me when I eventually go to my mother's."

That brought a return of Harriet's smile. "I would not wish a visit to your Sali on my worst enemy. Annabelle may lodge with us for as long as need be. And so may you and the boy, if that's what you choose."

"Thank you. I don't know how long it will take word of my homecoming to reach my mother. Once she hears and returns to New Echota, Johnny and I will probably move in there with her."

"And leave Annabelle here? A wise decision. She will need to be schooled in the proper way to behave before you expose her to the older, traditional Cherokee women like your mother."

"I agree. Can I count on you to educate her?"

"As well as I can," Harriet said, lifting her youngest into her lap and cuddling him. "You are very fortunate that your children will now be considered Cherokee instead of the way it was when the Ridges married a few years ago."

"We have you and Elias to thank for that, too," Charles said.

"And the tribal elders." She patted the baby's back. "The only natural inheritance I could provide for my children was one that they will find useless as long as we remain among the Cherokee. Now that they can also claim their father's tribal connections they will be fine."

Charles understood what she was saying all too well.

Since clan membership passed only through the mother's line, children with non-Indian mothers had been considered nobodies. Without a clan and therefore without identity. But all that had recently changed, much to the relief of John Ridge, Major Ridge's son, who had married Sarah Northrop, and, of course, Elias and Harriet Boudinot.

What about his future children—if there were any? Charles wondered at this point if he should even think about offspring. He saw himself as fully wed but his bride did not seem to share his views.

They had both sworn in front of their Christian God to be faithful, to love and honor each other. What kind of future could either of them expect if they chose to dishonor those vows?

More than that, Charles concluded soberly, if Annabelle decided to leave him, to go her own way, would he ever be able to feel whole again?

Yes, he had his tribe, his kin, his Cherokee heritage. Yet when he pictured himself without the wife he already loved with all his heart, he felt totally alone.

Understanding dawned. That was *exactly* the way Johnny must currently be feeling.

Although his prayers for the love of his wife had not been answered the way he had hoped, it looked as if his pleas for the boy's sake were starting to have an effect.

He and Johnny were more alike than he had thought. Both craved love and acceptance.

And both were unsure of where to find it. Or how to keep it from vanishing like a will-o'-the-wisp.

Chapter Seventeen

The light cotton frock one of Harriet's maids had laid out for Annabelle while she was bathing was much nicer than she had expected—so lovely she was hesitant to wear it. It was a pale-blue-and-indigo-gingham print with piped bodice seams and very loose sleeves gathered into cuffs at the wrists. There was a matching belt that fit her so perfectly, even without a corset, that she was amazed. The separate collar was ample enough to almost form a cape and was fastened at the front of the neck with pins and a blue satin bow.

"Thank you. I can dress myself," Annabelle told the wiry, middle-aged maid.

"Yes, ma'am. I've unpacked for you."

"There was little left in my valise that did not need washing, I'm afraid."

"Where shall I put the doll?" the maid asked, cradling it as if it were a real baby.

"Just lay it on the bed."

"Yes'm."

Standing there in a clean chemise after the maid left, Annabelle marveled at the gown she had been given to wear. The Boudinots must be quite wealthy if this garment was any indication. Come to think of it, Harriet and the children were also clad lavishly, particularly since they lived on what Annabelle considered the frontier.

Growing up in rural Tennessee, she had taken Eaton's farmland and servants for granted, only learning how rich he was compared to others after they'd taken up residence in the Capitol.

The differences in status there, however, had not been nearly the shock that seeing this Cherokee civilization was. These Indians had modern homes and servants and all the refinements she had noticed in Washington City. They were, for all their strangeness of speech and custom, very like the privileged classes of people among which she had grown up.

She slipped the dress over her head and threaded her arms into the sleeves as she continued to ponder. Where she had expected to encounter simple country folk, she'd found culture and elegance.

That discovery might have suited most women but realizing what it meant made Annabelle tremble. If she stayed, if Charles still wanted her, he would have to make allowances for her sketchy background. It was obvious that the Cherokees held great store by their ancestry. And hers was beyond unknown. She had been a homeless, orphaned waif when Myra Eaton had taken her in all those years ago.

A knock at the door startled her out of her reverie.

"Yes?"

"Will you be wanting me to dress your hair for you, missus?" a young voice called.

"No. No, thank you. I can manage."

"It's no trouble."

Annabelle opened the door to a maid she had not seen before. "That's very kind of you—what is your name?"

The girl curtsyed. "Madi, missus. That's Martha in English"

"All right, Martha. I'm afraid I've done all I can with my hair when it's so damp. Perhaps you can help me dry it a bit more and then we can pin it up."

"Yes'm. I can fetch some pretty combs if you'd like."

"That would be lovely."

The girl hid her grin behind a thin hand. "Do you be Mr. Charlie's wife?"

"Yes, I guess I am." Watching the maid giggle was a bit off-putting. "What's so funny?"

"Nothing," Martha said, struggling to regain her lost composure. "We just never figured he'd pick him a girl from far away."

"You mean you thought he'd marry a Cherokee?"

"Yes'm."

Annabelle sighed and smoothed the pleated, voluminous skirt of the dress. "I suppose everyone is surprised." She managed a smile. "Perhaps me, most of all."

The parlor was buzzing with activity by the time Martha finished dressing Annabelle's hair and pronounced it perfect.

Descending the stairs in the crisp, calico gown, Annabelle almost stopped, turned around and went back to her room. If she had not spied Charles, she might have done so. To her relief and delight, Johnny was by his side.

The man's immediate smile of recognition warmed her far more than the close quarters in Harriet's home. Elias and other gentlemen stood in groups, talking and smoking, while a few women who were clad much as she was occupied the chairs and settee. Besides Johnny, there were at least five children racing in and out among the adults.

Harriet came forward and clasped her hand when she reached the bottom of the stairway. "You look beautiful, my dear. Please, come meet a few of my friends."

All Annabelle really wanted was to quietly rejoin Charles and ask him the details of finding Johnny but it looked as if she was not going to get her wish.

Man and boy stood side by side, once again attired in similar fine suits and looking as if they had been cut from the same cloth. Charles was hatless and had slicked back his thick, dark hair, making him look even more handsome, if that were possible.

Every time Annabelle let her gaze stray in his direction, she found him watching her. Was he judging her ability to conform to his society? she wondered. Or was he perhaps lamenting the sacrifice he had made when he'd agreed to marry her to protect her reputation? If she could go back, do everything again, would she allow him to forfeit his freedom for her sake? Annabelle was not sure.

Harriet's grip on her arm tightened to draw her attention. "This is Reverend Samuel Worcester and his wife, Ann," she said, introducing a tall, lean, frock-coated gentleman and a contrastingly tiny woman. "Samuel has been sent by the mission board to help Elias with Bible translations for *The Phoenix* and for separate books in Cherokee. He's quite the linguist."

"My pleasure to meet you both," Annabelle said, with a slight curtsy. "I seem to recall having heard your name somewhere."

"Probably due to my speaking out against some foolish law or other depriving the Cherokees of their rightful lands and possessions." A smile softened his otherwise severe-looking features. "I have done my best to write the truth and have it published in *The Phoenix* as well as in many eastern papers."

"Surely that was it," Annabelle said. She had sensed an undercurrent of unrest in the room and until the missionary had spoken she had assumed the tension was due to her unexpected presence. Now she could see that there were plenty of other reasons for friction.

As Harriet led her from person to person, Annabelle spoke quietly aside. "I shall need to brush up on my local politics, I fear. Will you help me keep from putting my foot in my mouth?"

"As much as I can," the other woman vowed. "Even among friends and family there can be serious disagreements. Some people want to take the tribe forward into a white man's world while others see no advantage to doing so. No sooner is one treaty ratified than the government in Washington finds a reason to nullify it and declare it against the law."

When she looked suddenly contrite, Annabelle was quick to reassure her. "I understand and commiserate. Really I do. Remember, it was that same unbending rule of law that sent me into exile."

"I trust you did nothing to warrant it?"

"No. Nothing. But that did not keep me from being arrested and thrown in jail." She pressed her lips tightly together before deciding to reveal more. "I thought my foster father would champion my cause but he failed me. Charles was right. We had no choice but to flee or face punishment we did not deserve."

"Then I'm glad the Good Lord guided you here, to us," Harriet told her. "Finding a friend like you will be akin to adding a fragrant rose to an already beautiful garden."

Annabelle's eyes misted. "I don't know how to thank you—for everything."

"Just be kind and follow your heart," the older woman said. "That's all the thanks I need or want."

Charles had not argued with Johnny or berated him while they had cared for his late grandmother's livestock. Now that he had had time to ponder the situation further, it had occurred to him that perhaps the answer to some of his prayers had already arrived—in the form of an empty house, furnishings and animals that needed looking after.

Clearly, the child was distressed, although Charles wasn't certain whether he was mostly mourning or more out of sorts about being hauled back to Boudinot's and made to dress in fancy clothing again.

When there was a lull in the parlor conversation he took Johnny by the hand and led him outside.

"I have been thinking," Charles said as soon as they were alone.

The child kicked the toe of his boot into the dust and didn't look at him.

"What would you say to staying in your *lisi*'s home for a while?"

Wide-eyed, the boy stared. "Me?"

"Us. I would be with you," Charles said. "Since there are no women left to claim the land we should have no trouble." He arched a brow and smiled. "If you were a girl, there would be no question of ownership. Since you are not, I think we should plan to stay there only as long as your distant kin allow."

With a sly look and a quirky smile, the boy said, "You do not wish to return to your mother's estate?"

The truth made Charles chuckle wryly. "I always knew you were smart. No, I do not wish to live at my old home. And I prefer to not cause Mrs. Boudinot any trouble by staying here with her family." A sardonic grin spread. "It is better to have my mother and my aunts upset with me than with my friends."

"What about the woman?"

"You can call her Annabelle, you know. You once did."

"That was before, when she was *oginalii.*"

"She's still your friend, Johnny. Remember how she cared for you and defended you?" His smile faded, his countenance darkening. "If she had not been trying to protect you, she would not have been down by the Potomac that night when she got into so much trouble."

"It was you she was helping. So was I. If we had not, you might be dead."

"Or, I might have gotten the better of the thugs and walked away without anyone ever being the wiser," Charles countered. "The point is, she was there because of her concern for you."

"And you," the child insisted.

"We will talk about that some other time. Right now, I want you to go upstairs to our room, pack our things and take them to the stable. We'll leave right after we eat."

"Can I take Golly?" His enthusiasm was evident.

"Yes. You can take him. He will be yours from now on and I will expect you to see to all his needs, just like you did on the trail."

The child was fidgeting. "Can I go now?"

Charles laughed. "Yes. Go. But no racing through the

house and disturbing other guests." He reached for his pocket watch out of habit before he remembered it was long gone. "I suspect you will be fed in the kitchen with the rest of the children. Behave yourself, eat politely and report to me as soon as you see that the adults are finished with their meal."

"Yes, sir!" he said, and then he was off.

Straightening, Charles was still smiling at the boy's enthusiasm when he sensed something amiss.

He froze.

Listened.

Let his heightened senses explore his surroundings without giving any sign that he was more alert than normal.

Nothing out of the ordinary came to him, nor did he continue to feel threatened after a few minutes had passed.

Figuring he was merely more sensitive because of his conversation about Annabelle, he shrugged, turned and rejoined the others in the parlor.

Seated at dinner between Charles and the missionary's wife, Annabelle had such a pounding headache she could barely force down any food.

The cook had prepared a meat stew with fresh carrots and potatoes. Side dishes were boiled greens, cornbread, beans and coffee that was so strong and bitter she pushed it away after the first sip.

"They love it with chicory," the missionary, Ann, whispered behind her hand just for Annabelle's ears. "I prefer sweet tea or lemonade."

"That would be nice," Annabelle replied, watching

as the tiny woman signaled to a servant and ordered replacement drinks for them both.

"So, tell me about your wedding. Was it a large affair?"

"Um…" Annabelle nearly choked on a bite of stew.

Leaning forward to speak around her, Charles said, "It was, of necessity, rather hurried." His smile seemed to soften his words when he added, "Since we were running for our lives at the time."

"Oh, dear me." The older woman fanned herself rapidly with an open hand. "I see. How tragic."

"Only if we had not survived," Charles said. "Since we are home and safe now, I think it's time to thank the Lord, don't you?"

"Absolutely. I will add you both to my daily devotions," the missionary's wife vowed. She patted Annabelle's hand. "You must have been so frightened."

"Perhaps at first," she admitted quietly. "The rest of our trip was quite enjoyable. The wild country between Washington and here is breathtaking."

"Were you able to find suitable accommodations? When Samuel and I made the trip from Boston, we were appalled by many of the so-called inns."

"As was I," Annabelle told her. "That's why Mr. McDonald made camp for us every evening. Except for swarms of insects near some of the rivers and lakes, we had a very pleasant journey."

"Well, I never." Eyeing her own husband, Ann rolled her eyes. "I certainly do not understand these younger generations."

Annabelle was relieved to see the usually somber older man smile as he patted his wife's wrist. "Nor did your parents understand us," he said. "So it always is."

"I suppose you are right, dear."

Worcester focused on Charles. "I would be delighted to perform a proper ceremony."

Annabelle choked again. She pressed her linen napkin over her mouth and coughed into it. If Charles had not made her angry by laughing softly, she might have had more trouble regaining her composure.

"I think my wife is satisfied with our first marriage," he said, grinning and giving her a wink. "If we decide on a Cherokee ceremony, however, we would be honored to have you as our guests."

Having garnered undue notice, he raised his voice and gestured casually around the table. "All of you."

Annabelle wished she dared slip from her chair and duck under the table. Anything but have to sit there and be the center of everyone's attention. Her pounding pulse was worsening her headache and her breathing was shallow and rapid despite the lack of a tight corset.

Light from the kerosene lamps arrayed in sconces along the walls cast flickering shadows that made her head swim and her vision dance.

She was so weary, so confused by her conflicting emotions, she feared she might swoon for the second time in her life. If she had not felt so dizzy she might have jumped up and run from the room.

Before she could make up her mind what to do, Charles was at her side, pulling her chair away from the table, taking her arm and steadying her as he helped her stand. "I see my wife is not well. It has been a difficult day."

"Really, I…"

"Are you arguing with me?"

"No." Annabelle's breath hitched, partly from his

nearness and partly from the turbulence of her buried emotions.

She glanced at her hostess. "Please, excuse me?"

Harriet didn't hesitate. On her feet in a trice, she bustled around the table and took Annabelle's other arm. "Of course, dear. I kept this group small but I should have realized you'd need more time to rest before I entertained. It's all my fault. I'll help you up to your room."

Although Annabelle knew the other woman was merely being supportive, she was reluctant to have anyone take Charles's place. Truth to tell, she had not expected him to recognize her distress, let alone offer solace, and was still laboring to accept his solicitous behavior.

Together, the three paused at the base of the stairs.

Harriet ignored Annabelle and spoke to Charles. "I can take her from here. There's no need for you to go up."

As he started to step away, Annabelle raised her eyes to meet his gaze and saw both concern and hurt. His conduct had always been that of a perfect gentleman, so why was Harriet so intent on keeping him from escorting her upstairs?

Did the other woman know something Annabelle did not? The Boudinots had been friends with Charles and his family for years. Had he confided his aversion to his bride to them? Or was Harriet merely trying to protect him from further involvement with a person of questionable lineage, such as herself?

It didn't really matter, did it? Annabelle mused. Her head was splitting, her stomach was upset and the room continued to spin, faster and faster, as she pondered the untenable situation.

Voices around her echoed, faded, thrummed in her temples like a swarm of angry bees.

She thought she heard Charles say something like, "Look out," as her knees folded and her eyes closed.

The world tilted. She felt strong arms encircle her, lift her, hold her close and begin to carry her up the stairway.

Laying her cheek against his chest, Annabelle listened to the strong beat of Charles's heart and realized one of her prayers had just been answered.

She was back in his embrace.

Chapter Eighteen

Harriet and one of the maids had taken over once Charles had laid his wife on the quilted coverlet atop the canopied bed in her room.

It should have been easy for him to walk off, to leave her to their tender ministrations, yet he could barely tear himself away.

A tug on his coattails finally broke in on his reverie. It was Johnny.

"Can we go now?" the boy asked.

One more moment, one last look at the wife he cherished, was all Charles permitted himself before turning to the child. "Wait for me in the stables. I need to tell Elias what we're planning to do before we leave."

"But…"

Inclining his head and frowning, Charles silenced Johnny's protests with a stern look and sent him on his way.

Resting his hand on the edge of the doorjamb he stood, waiting and watching for long seconds, until Annabelle begin to stir.

Relief flooded over and through him, made him so

thankful that a flash of gratitude to God brought immediate, fervent, silent prayer.

Harriet bustled across the room toward him and started to close him out. "She's fine. You should go."

"Tell her…" Charles peered past the printer's wife and saw the maid placing a damp compress on Annabelle's forehead. She was in good hands. He could leave her. He just didn't want to.

"Well?" Harriet was still acting the sentry and holding firm to the edge of the half-open door.

"Tell her the boy and I will be staying at his grandmother's old place for a while." When she looked puzzled he added, "For Johnny's sake. He needs to be in a familiar home, and if I accompany him, there will be less trouble in the future."

"I take it you mean less trouble from your kin."

"Yes. It's for the best. For everyone."

Harriet stepped into the hallway, closed the door on Annabelle and laid her hand gently on his sleeve. "For everyone? Are you certain?"

"Truthfully? No." He tellingly eyed the door. "I just don't want her to feel pressured. You saw tonight how fragile she is."

"I wonder. I understand she did very well on the way here. And from what Elias has told me about your adventures in Washington, she was far from a helpless victim."

Charles's frown deepened. "Then what's the matter with her now?"

"I suspect she's simply come to the end of her rope and needs rest more than anything," Harriet told him. She smiled and patted his arm. "I will take good care of her. You just be careful out there."

"Careful?"

She nodded. "Yes. One of the guests mentioned a couple of strangers hanging around town recently."

"New Echota is the center of tribal government. Strangers are not unusual. Besides, I've only just arrived so they can't have trailed me."

"Still…whoever was pursuing you might have anticipated your destination and come straight here while you were working your way through the back country."

Although he had considered that possibility, hearing it voiced was unsettling. "All right. I'll be watchful. Knowing Annabelle is safe with you, I won't worry."

"She will be fine—as long as you do not stay away too long. I truly believe she cares for you, Charles."

If only he could accept that conclusion. His heart yearned to, but his mind kept insisting that she never would have agreed to become his bride if she had had any other workable option.

Without reply, he turned on his heel and started downstairs, bound for the stable.

Truth to tell, he would not have chosen to marry her, either, at that particular juncture. Now, however, he was more than willing to make her his wife again. The tricky parts would be convincing his clan to accept her as well as convincing Annabelle that she truly belonged among his people.

With him. Forever.

When Annabelle awoke, she thought the only light in her room came from a guttering candle flame. Then, she raised on one elbow to look out the window and realized what had roused her. There was a storm brewing.

Spring and summertime thunder and lightning had been so prevalent in Tennessee when she was a girl she wasn't surprised to see that same kind of wild weather occurring here in Georgia.

As a child, she had quaked from the rumbles and crashes as bright bolts zigzagged across the sky. Then, as she'd matured, she'd come to appreciate the majesty of the Lord's works, even though rapid weather changes were often heralded by the kind of debilitating headache that had laid her so low the previous evening.

She swung her bare feet to the floor, leaned to blow out the candle, then padded to the window to watch the grandeur unfold. God's power was truly amazing.

Gray and black clouds billowed against a night sky, lighting it as if a thousand candles suddenly glowed behind them, then vanishing in a blur. The flashes were so frequent and bright she could tell that the wind was moving everything rapidly, propelling rain and threatening to flatten some of the crops in nearby fields.

Annabelle wrapped her arms around herself and shivered, thinking of the nights she, Charles and Johnny had spent on the trail and thanking God that, although they had experienced some rain, they had not been caught in this kind of maelstrom.

She realized she was secure here. And the horses were bedded down in the Boudinot stables, as well. So why did she keep getting a niggling sense of doom? Of something very, very wrong? Was this the kind of foreboding Johnny had experienced when they had followed Charles to the banks of the Potomac?

Annabelle shook herself and turned from the window. Imagining trouble where there was none was more than foolish, it was a sin. Besides, she trusted the Lord now more than ever. He had brought her little party through the wilderness unscathed and she'd given Him thanks again and again.

Since she'd trusted her faith in the worst of times, she reasoned, there was no excuse for doubting God when things were going well. Unless, of course, the Lord was trying to tell her something important and she was too blind and deaf to see or hear the warning.

That thought took her aback. What was she missing? She closed her eyes and folded her hands right where she stood.

"What is it, Father? What do you want me to do?"

Could it be she was meant to go comfort the boy?

That notion was summarily banished. Charles was with Johnny so she dared not approach their room lest her efforts be misinterpreted. If the child needed solace the man would provide it, just as he had during their journey.

Nevertheless, Annabelle could not rest. Waiting for repeated flashes from the storm to guide her steps in the unfamiliar bedroom, she haltingly made her way to the armoire, found her long wrapper where one of the maids had hung it after it was washed and dried, and donned it for modesty's sake.

"If no one is up and about, there will be no harm done," she told herself as she headed for the hallway. "And if there truly is something wrong, I will soon find out what it is."

Her heart also hoped she would encounter Charles. The last time she had looked upon his handsome face was when she had swooned, and his expression had been filled with concern. With compassion. And, perhaps, a little affection, unless her imagination was playing tricks on her.

"That's probably what's going on right now, too," Annabelle whispered to herself. "I'm being a silly goose."

Well, too bad. If she explored the house and found nothing amiss, she would be delighted. If, however, her nighttime wanderings showed her a need that she could meet, she was more than ready to do so.

In spite of the erroneous opinion that her momentary physical weakness may have caused during Harriet's dinner party, she was strong and healthy, and willing to step into the fray for the sake of good whenever necessary.

"Just as I did for Johnny back in Washington," she murmured, realizing for perhaps the first time that that one simple act of kindness toward a child had changed her life completely.

Charles had wrapped himself in a blanket and found a comfortable place to rest without actually getting undressed and going to bed in the cabin. He'd seen no threats during or after their pilgrimage to the old woman's home, yet Harriet's warning continued to echo in his thoughts.

There had been many times when he had wondered why their pursuers had apparently given up so easily. Even amateur bounty hunters would be driven to continue because of the potential for reward. So where were the men from Eaton's or the inn? Why had there been no inkling of their presence since the confrontation at the inn? Had he been that clever? Or had they circumvented his plans and merely guessed where he and his party would eventually surface?

Like it or not, the latter was more than possible. It was probable. It was what he would have done if following directly had proved too difficult. Once the posse had caught and saddled their horses behind the inn, the most sensible course would have been to head straight down the trail.

Since he had led Annabelle and the boy via side routes, the others might have overtaken and passed them quickly, leaving no clue behind.

Eaton knew where the Cherokee delegation had come from, Charles reminded himself. What was to say he had not dispatched another group—or added more men to the first—to hunt them down?

That thought ran through him like icy water from a mountain stream. Unable to relax enough to close his eyes, he threw off the blanket and wandered to the window to check the progress of the storm.

Lightning was flashing so frequently it was almost bright as midday. Trees bent low, their branches thrashing from the force of the gale. New, green leaves that were meant to last all summer were being torn loose to tumble away with the old, dry ones.

Charles froze, wondering if his mind was playing tricks on him.

There. Again. He *had* seen something. Or someone.

Instead of pausing whenever the sky lit up, a solitary figure boldly continued to work its way around the house. The prowler was on foot. And apparently not unduly worried about being noticed.

A brace of pistols was one of the only items of value that Charles had retained after his ill-fated sojourn in Washington. Now that he was back home and in need of such protection, he was glad his chiefs had forbidden the carrying of firearms while on their diplomatic mission.

Otherwise, he would not have left his guns at Elias's for safekeeping and therefore have them now.

He strapped on the belt with the double holsters, stood in the shadows beside the window, and waited.

If they came for him, or for the boy, he would be ready.

And if they did not, he would start at first light and track them down himself.

Annabelle crept down the stairs barefoot, taking care to step as silently as possible. The storm kept her progress fairly well illuminated until she reached the ground floor and realized there was a steady light streaming from the direction of the kitchen.

A reddish-haired, well-endowed, middle-aged woman looked up when she entered the warm room. "Mornin', ma'am."

"Good morning. You certainly rise early," Annabelle said pleasantly.

"A-fore dawn, if you must know. There's no other way to get the stove hot and breakfast ready by the time the mister and missus want it." She wiped her hands on her apron and bent to stir the coals in the firebox with a poker.

"You must be Fiona. I've heard you're a wonder in the kitchen."

"Thank you, ma'am. Are you feelin' better today?"

Nodding, Annabelle wasn't at all surprised to find that the servants were well-informed. The ones at the Eatons' had known plenty about the inner workings of the family.

"Yes, thanks." She pressed her fingertips to her temples and massaged in tiny circles, relieved when there was no pain beyond a dull twinge. "I sometimes get terrible headaches when there's a storm brewing."

"You were certainly right about that happening," Fiona said with a smile. "'Tis right nasty out there."

Agreeing with a nod, Annabelle looked around for something to occupy her. "I don't really know much about cooking but I sometimes used to help in the kitchen at home," she said. "Is there some way I can assist you?"

The astonishment on the woman's face took her aback, made her realize belatedly that she was no longer being viewed as the social equal of a servant. Yet, in her heart, that was exactly how she felt. She had grown up relying on the kindness of both servants and outright slaves. They had been her substitute family for so long she had taken her status among them for granted.

"I have a girl that helps me when I need her," Fiona said flatly. "There's no need for a lady like you to get her hands dirty."

Annabelle smiled slightly before she said, "I think I should explain. I'm an orphan. I was never a fine lady like your mistress."

"Still…"

She shook her head. "I learned my place early in life, Fiona. I don't belong in a drawing room, doing embroidery or sewing fine garments the way some highborn women do." She gestured at the table where the cook had begun to assemble the makings of a sumptuous breakfast. "I belong right here. I may be free to do as I wish but this kind of life is what gives me comfort." Her smile bloomed. "Please? May I assist you somehow?"

"Well, all right, but if Miz Harriet gets upset, you'll have to promise to tell her it was your idea."

"Gladly," Annabelle said. "Perhaps you could teach me how to bake an acceptable biscuit." She started to push up the sleeves of her wrapper, then decided to run back upstairs and dress first. "I'll be back in a jiffy."

She could hear the cook mumbling to herself as she dashed from the kitchen and up the stairs, only slowing to tiptoe when she passed the closed door to the room Charles and Johnny had been given.

It was going to feel good to be of use again, to provide for others the way she used to while growing up. Perhaps many women in her place would have reveled in being coddled but Annabelle did not. She never had as a little girl in Tennessee, either.

Thinking fondly of Myra, she realized that a strong work ethic had been one of the strengths the first Mrs. Eaton had imparted to her. So had an abiding faith in God and a love for her fellow human beings. That included everyone, all the Fionas and the Marthas and especially the innocent little children of the world.

Which was probably why she didn't look down on the Cherokees, either, she mused. They were just as dear to her as Myra had been.

And a couple of them especially so, Annabelle thought, blushing and picturing Charles McDonald with the child she had grown to love.

As I love the man, she admitted to herself without reservation. His gallantry had won her respect; his compassion, her heart. That was a given.

What she would do about her feelings was a different question altogether. If his background was that of wealth and privilege as she suspected, there was no way she could bring herself up to his level. Not in a million years. He would not want to include a homeless waif in his family any more than Margaret and John Eaton had.

Dressing quickly, Annabelle used two of the combs from the evening before to secure the sides of her long hair, lifting the locks at the temples and leaving the rest loose to drape over her shoulders and down her back rather than take the time to pin it all up. The blue ribbon that had been fastened at her neck before was perfect to gather long tresses at her nape.

Satisfied and eager to be of use, to somehow fit in, she pulled up clean stockings, slipped her feet into her shoes and hurried back to the kitchen.

No stirrings came from the room occupied by her traveling companions as she passed their closed door, but she wasn't worried. She had retired early and was thus well rested. By the time Charles and Johnny came down to breakfast she would have proven her worth and perhaps even have learned how to make good biscuits.

Her fondest hope was to make an ally of Fiona without disappointing Harriet.

The world between master and servant was her bailiwick. It might be a mystery to most folks, but it was where she belonged.

Chapter Nineteen

The brunt of the storm seemed to pass as Charles watched through the cabin windows. There had been no more suspicious activity in the yard since his first sighting, making him relax and doubt he had seen anything other than a helpful neighbor checking on the livestock.

Dawn was muted by lingering clouds that scudded across the sky. Distant thunder accompanied a glow from lightning that was now jumping from cloud to cloud without going to ground.

Nothing about the storm had sounded nearby for the past hour, nor had he lit a fire in the stove, so he was incredulous when he began to smell a hint of smoke.

Clapping the farmer's hat on his head, Charles shrugged into the coarse jacket and stepped outside.

The narrow covered porch, like the rest of the old woman's home, was run-down and weathered. A rocking chair sat to one side, its cane seat broken and sagging. Wild morning glory vines climbed strings stretched from the ground to the overhang on the east side. Rain had washed dust from the leaves and flowers, leaving twinkling droplets of freshness behind.

A cloud of what Charles initially assumed was fog lay in the direction of the barn.

He started down the porch steps.

The odor got stronger.

Starting to run, he rounded the corner and saw everything clearly.

The old barn was on fire!

For Annabelle, being helpful in the kitchen was akin to coming home. Even when Harriet bustled in and caught her, she couldn't help grinning.

"Don't be cross with Fiona," Annabelle pleaded. "This was my idea. She's going to teach me how to cook." Drying her hands she poured two cups of hot coffee and urged Harriet to join her at the table. "Please. Sit and talk with me for a bit so I can explain?"

"All right."

Annabelle could tell that the slightly older woman was flabbergasted so she hurried her explanation. "I told you I was a foundling. Well, there's more. You see, Myra Eaton took me in after my grandmother died when I was very young. Barely three years old, she said. She's the only mother I remember ever having and when she passed away at a young age, it was the household servants who stepped in and raised me, who became my family."

"This was where? In Tennessee?"

"Yes. John Eaton, Myra's widower, moved his household to Washington when he was elected to Congress. Then, about a year ago, he married a widow, Margaret Timberlake. She wasn't thrilled having me underfoot and I found that I was happiest being among the servants—so there I stayed."

"Eaton is an important man."

"True. And Margaret is a special friend of President Jackson. I fear I did not fit into her social circles."

Falling silent, Annabelle watched her hostess assimilate all she had imparted. There was more to consider, of course. There was Charles McDonald's family. Until she knew more about his background she dared not hope or plan beyond current circumstances.

Harriet took a cautious sip of her coffee and nodded. "I see. Have you ever tried to trace your family?"

"Not lately. When Myra died, I was so bereaved I thought of little else, but John refused to discuss it. Then, as time went by and I realized the impossibility of learning the truth, I settled into the routine that was my life, until I met Charles and we were unjustly blamed for killing a ruffian."

"He told me as much. Stepping forward to help him was very brave of you."

"It was right. I could not just stand there and see him overpowered." She focused on her cup. "Or worse."

Harriet patted her hand. "Nevertheless, I am grateful."

Still thinking of her unknown background, Annabelle said, "Charles has promised to guide me to Tennessee to see if I can find out more about my family."

"Is that what you want?"

Annabelle sighed noisily. "I thought it was. Now, I am not so sure. I wish I could predict what we'd find. I fear uncovering bad news that will make me an even less suitable mate. I really know very little about my husband's past."

She paused, hoping Harriet would provide details about him.

When she did not, Annabelle asked, "What was his upbringing like? He speaks and writes very well. Did he go to school with your husband?"

"Only for a short time. Elias graduated from the Cornwall Foreign Mission School in Connecticut. My parents were connected to the school. That's where we first met. Then, after Cornwall closed, Elias continued his studies at Andover Theological Seminary while Charles came home to work with John Ridge and his father, Major Ridge, on political matters."

"I was very disappointed when Charles told me the Cornwall school had closed. I was hoping to be sent there."

Astonishment colored Harriet's expression and she carefully placed her cup on the table before speaking. "What made you think that?"

"I can't remember how the notion began, other than to recall Myra and John discussing it while she was so ill. She seemed to believe he would keep his promise to send me to study there when I was older. Now, of course, it's too late." She smiled wistfully. "Why do you ask?"

"Because, dear heart," Harriet said, reaching for Annabelle's hand and grasping it firmly, "that school was created to educate Indians. Only Indians. If the Eatons were going to send you to Cornwall, they must have known you have mixed blood."

"Charles suggested the same when we discussed it. But look at me. My eyes are blue and my hair is lighter than that of most European dignitaries who visited the Eaton home. How can I possibly be?" Annabelle held her breath. Was that why she had felt such strong affinity for Johnny and the others? Was her heart remembering that which had long ago faded from memory?

"Nevertheless, it is a distinct possibility," Harriet insisted gently. "Elias and I would have had far less opposition to our marriage if I could have said the same of myself."

"How—how would I tell? Is there some secret way? Something no one has ever told me?"

"I'm afraid not—unless you can get information from your foster father. Judging by the tales I've heard about him—and his new wife—that will not be easy."

"If I returned to Washington City to see him, I would undoubtedly be arrested, maybe even hanged. I cannot risk that. I suppose I could write him a letter."

"Do you believe he'd answer it?"

Annabelle shook her head. "No."

"Then think. Is there nothing of significance you recall from your childhood? Some long-forgotten detail? Some memento? Anything at all?"

"All I have left is Rosie, a china doll that Myra gave me when I was very young."

"I saw her on your bed when we took you to your room last night. I'm afraid she does not look a bit like a Cherokee."

"Or any other tribe."

"All right. Who else from your early life might you ask?"

"I had planned to question the Eaton cook and valet but Charles and I were forced to flee before I had a chance to speak with either of them in private." Another sigh. "I suppose there's no harm done if I never find out for sure."

"On the contrary," Harriet said soberly. "There is a Cherokee taboo against marrying within your mother's clan. If your mother happened to be from the Wolf Clan, you will be strictly forbidden by tribal law from ever marrying Charles."

"And if I don't know?"

Harriet got to her feet and silently carried both their cups to the sink. When she finally turned and spoke there were unshed tears misting her eyes.

"I'm not sure," she said sadly. "But this lack of information will certainly complicate your meeting with Charles's kin."

"I wondered how things could get any worse," Annabelle said with a heavy sigh. "Now I know."

A rider arrived at the Boudinot house just as the adults in the family were sitting down to breakfast in the dining room.

Annabelle had begged off and stayed in the kitchen with Fiona, the children and their nanny, hoping to think through her latest dilemma before discussing the possibilities with Charles.

When the horseman burst through the front door, he let it slam behind him.

Hearing him shouting the word "Fire," Annabelle and Fiona looked at each other in fright and decided to eavesdrop without need of discussion.

Most of the messenger's conversation was taking place in rapid Cherokee, making it impossible to follow. If it had not been for his frantic gesticulating and raised voice, Annabelle would not have been nearly so worried.

She turned to Fiona. "What is he saying?"

"Bless me if I know," the cook replied, "but he surely does seem upset."

"There's a fire outside town at one of the old farms," Elias explained as he stood and looked at his wife. "I'll take a few of the servants with me. You women and children stay here."

"I can help," Harriet said, noting Annabelle and Fiona peeking from the doorway. "We'll bring a wagon with water and provisions for the workers."

"No!" Elias's shout made his wife plop backward into her chair as if pushed. "It's at Johnny's grandmother's place."

Annabelle's fingertips pressed to her lips. *Oh, how sad for the poor little boy.*

When Harriet rounded the dining table and hurried to her side to slip an arm around her waist, she was a bit surprised by the maternal gesture, though not put off.

Shock started to set in, however, as soon as the other woman blurted, "That's where Charles and the boy went."

Annabelle stared at her, eyes wide, jaw gaping. "They're upstairs, aren't they? I thought they were just sleeping late."

"No." Harriet was shaking her head. "They went to Johnny's grandmother's house after supper. Charles thought it would be best for the boy." Her voice shook. "They were out there all night."

"Then I have to go!" Annabelle could tell that her outburst was frightening the nearby children so she sought to control herself—with minimal success.

"No. You mustn't. You heard Elias."

"I'm going, with or without you."

"You don't even know where that farm is. I'll have to come along." Harriet motioned to Fiona. "See that the children are looked after, then prepare crocks of water. And send someone out to hitch up a wagon."

Annabelle had already gone to the closest window and was staring into the distance.

She was not going to need a guide to find the fire. It had lit up the sky more brightly than a summer sun at noon.

All at once, she ran for the stables.

Charles's first task was saving the larger animals. He looped a rope around his old plow horse's neck and coaxed it out of its stall in spite of its panic.

Before he could go back for the mule, Johnny appeared, running toward the conflagration and screaming, "Golly! He'll burn."

Charles snagged him by his sleeve, fisted the rope he'd been using and shoved it at the boy. "Hold on to this one for me. I'll go fetch the mule."

The child was openly weeping and trembling so badly Charles wondered if he would obey but there was no time to argue.

Leaving him holding the big gelding, he pulled off his coat as he ran back into the burning barn. Smarter than horses by far, mules were also harder to handle in tense situations. Although he suspected that Golly would find his way to safety if he were loose, Charles was not going to take any chances that the animal might panic and run back into the fire, instead.

He grabbed the mule's halter to pull its head down, then threw his jacket over its eyes.

That was not enough to calm it completely but it helped. Fisting the arms of the coat under the animal's throat he pulled him forward until they had traveled far enough in the right direction, then slapped him on the rump to drive him out through the open door.

Chickens scattered ahead of the pounding hooves. The goat and litter of half-grown piglets easily found their way outside, too, squealing as they ran.

Neighbors were beginning to arrive to help fight the fire. Men yelled. Horses snorted and whinnied.

Spotting his larger horse, Charles was relieved to see that Johnny had followed instructions. Not only was he still restraining the riding horse, he also had hold of the mule's halter.

"He came right to me," the boy shouted. "He's all right."

"Good. Take them farther away so we can work," Charles called back. He didn't see any way that the group of willing hands was going to be able to quench the barn fire. At this point, all he could hope for was that the house would be spared.

The nearby live trees and weathered logs of the cabin had been soaked by the storm and a fine mist was still falling. That was a plus. So was the southeast wind that was carrying glowing orange embers away from the structure.

Lightning was a common foe of farmers and city dwellers alike. Charles had had no time to investigate where the bolts had struck or see what other damage they might have done besides kindle this fire. All he'd cared about was saving the living creatures.

The crackling of the flames, shouting of men and noise from frightened animals muted a startling bang.

Barn wood above Charles's head splintered.

He ducked.

Then whirled and faced the yard in a crouch, searching for the source of the threat.

Everyone else seemed too busy to have noticed the

shot but Charles had no doubt. Someone had just taken aim at him. And they had only missed by a few inches.

For the first time since he'd seen smoke, he began to wonder if the fire had truly been an accident of nature or if it had been lit to draw him out of the house.

During the course of their journey from Washington City, Annabelle had learned how to ready her mare by herself. It wasn't easy because of her height. But having succeeded once, she had insisted on taking care of the mare herself from then on.

Now that pandemonium reigned in the Boudinot stable, she was glad she was so accomplished. While several servants saddled horses for Elias and his men, she bridled her mare.

"Get back in the house with Harriet," Elias shouted when he noticed her. "We'll take care of this."

Annabelle wanted to scream at him, to insist that she was going to Charles whether anyone approved or not, but she saw little advantage in such a confrontation so she merely led the mare aside and waited, fidgeting, during the few minutes before the printer and a few of his servants mounted up and rode away.

The morning air was cool, the ground outside muddy. Patches of fog lay in pockets, intensifying the mist that had already dampened Annabelle's hair and dress. If she had not been so consumed by fear for her loved ones, she might have taken the time to return to the house for her coat.

Casting any thought of personal comfort aside, she stood on a box to place the saddle, tightened the cinch and mounted. The mare was almost as ready to go as Annabelle was.

Someone shouted, "Wait for me!"

Annabelle belatedly recognized Harriet's voice. She whirled the mare to face her. "No. There's no time."

"What can you do? Let the men handle it."

"You don't understand. I have to go. I have to."

"Why?"

Unwilling to answer so publicly, Annabelle reined the horse in the direction of the fire's glow, hung on tight and gave her a kick in the sides.

The gray leaped forward, almost unseating her as they passed through the stable doors.

Annabelle instinctively leaned forward and rode as if she'd been born in the saddle. She'd had enough recent riding practice that her body took over naturally when her frenzied thoughts failed her.

Rambling, prayerful pleas for Charles, and for Johnny, were the best she could do.

"Father, please? Please help them. And me. I—I have to see him."

Her mind instantly provided a crystal clear image of her Cherokee husband. So dear. So special she had no words to describe how much she cherished him.

"Let him be all right? Please? And forgive me for being afraid to tell him how I feel."

Wind whipped her loose, damp hair across her face, stinging her cheeks, as she washed her conscience clean with her tears.

Chapter Twenty

"Back off! Let it burn," Charles shouted in an attempt to protect his friends and neighbors from whoever was shooting at them.

There was so much pandemonium around him that the warning was virtually ignored.

Staying low, he tried to decide if one of the men he could see might have fired. Nobody looked guilty. They were all busy pulling tools out of the barn or setting up a bucket brigade from the watering troughs in the yard. That water wouldn't last long at the rate it was being used. Besides, the worst of the flames were coming from the hayloft and were therefore out of reach.

A couple of young men were struggling to get the old sow away from her pen and into the open. While he was watching them, Charles caught another movement out of the corner of his eye.

Someone else was in the barn.

"Hey, get out of there," he yelled, stepping through the wide-open door.

The figure stopped and turned.

Billows of smoke kept Charles from identifying anyone. He waved his arms. "Get out. The animals are safe."

Instead of complying, the man stood stock-still. Except for his right hand. That, he raised.

A pistol pointed directly at Charles.

In the second it took him to realize what was happening, flint hit steel, a spark was generated, the powder ignited and the lead ball was on its way.

Had all that occurred instantaneously, Charles would not have stood a chance of evading the bullet. The slight delay between the pulling of the trigger and the actual shot gave him just enough time to dive for cover.

The closer Annabelle rode, the worse the conflagration appeared. She had seen buildings burn before. This fire seemed to have a life of its own.

As the flames flowed out under the eaves they wrapped around the roof like giant, cupped hands, then rose into the dawn as if drawn upward by a thousand invisible threads. The roar of combustion was so loud it drowned out the rush of her pulse and stole her breath.

Chaos ruled the farmyard. Men and boys ran from place to place, seemingly without reason, while others filled and passed water buckets down a line toward the fire. There were also some bystanders who seemed less inclined to pitch in, although she supposed there was only so much that could be done.

Spotting Golly's big ears, she hurried her mare in that direction, hoping she would see Charles. Instead, she found Johnny. He was staring, wide-eyed and disbelieving, at the increasing destruction.

Annabelle kicked loose from her stirrups and slid to the ground beside him. Her dress was so damp the skirt hung limp. Curls of wet hair were plastered to her forehead. She brushed them away with one hand while she touched his shoulder with the other. "What happened? Where's your uncle?"

The boy merely pointed to the barn.

And to the fire, which by now had crept down the side walls and nearly reached the floor.

"He's in there? He can't be. Look at it!"

Still, the child continued to point. That was when she saw a shadow moving inside the barn. Whoever it was seemed to be staggering. Was that Charles? Was he hurt?

"Stay here," she ordered, handing her reins to the child.

He didn't try to stop her. No one did. The others were all too busy to notice a lone woman running through the billowing smoke toward the barn. Toward her husband. To the man she loved and now feared she might lose.

Please, Lord, let me find him. Let me tell him how I feel. Please? Before it's too late?

The shape she had seen from a distance was no longer visible but she knew approximately where he should be. That was where she headed.

Creaking of the overhead beams sounded ominous. Annabelle stopped at the door and shielded her face by raising her arms, glad the weather had soaked her clothing so advantageously.

"Charles!" she shouted. "Where are you?"

He didn't answer. No one did. The heat from the fire turned some of the moisture in her dress to steam, scalding her and bringing fresh tears to her eyes. Tears of physical pain and emotional loss.

"Charles!" The heat forced her back. One step. Two

steps. If he was in there she could not leave him. She simply could not.

"Charles!"

Silhouetted by the fire behind and partially masked by that in front, a man's form arose.

Annabelle gasped.

She reached out to him.

He seemed to be reaching back to her.

Her breathing was ragged, painful. "Charles?"

A creaking, snapping sound, so loud it temporarily blotted out everything else, split the morning air.

Annabelle screamed.

The second story loft support had burned through.

And the man she had been calling to disappeared into the inferno as it failed and fell.

Charles had ducked outside to escape his assailant and didn't see Annabelle standing in the doorway with her hands in front of her face, until the sound of the building's interior collapse drew his attention.

"Annabelle!" His shout was so filled with agony it became a mournful wail.

Racing toward her, he prayed he'd be in time.

What was wrong with her? Why didn't she fall back? Why didn't she turn and run? Couldn't she see the danger?

Burning, glowing embers rode up and spiraled around her like tiny tornados of fire and rose into the dawn sky. The walls of the structure were starting to tilt now that there was no center support.

The whole barn began to cant to one side. Everything was happening in slow motion except for the one man who was running toward the inferno with every ounce of strength he could muster.

Charles saw the frame around the door start to come loose. Knew that Annabelle was too close. There was no time left.

Smoke burned his lungs and stole his breath. He gasped. Coughed. Made one final heroic effort to reach her in time.

When Annabelle saw the loft fall on the man inside the burning barn, her heart had split asunder. She'd lost the only person who loved her. She feared that all hope had died with him.

Numbed by her apparent loss, she simply stood there, staring, unable to move and not conscious of the terrible heat from the flames.

If her dress had not been wet she would have already joined Charles in death, she thought, wondering why she had been spared when God had just called him home.

No longer able to breathe, let alone scream his name one more time, she simply froze in place with her hands pressed over her face, closed her eyes and waited for the end. Hers was not a conscious wish for death. It was simply a yielding to the fate she thought was inevitable.

Charles tackled her as he passed, not stopping but simply sweeping her off her feet and letting his momentum carry them away.

Behind him, the walls of the barn finished their downward plunge, landing in the already burning straw and refuse with a whoosh that shot more clouds of glowing embers into the yard.

Charles did not stop running until he knew they were safe. Then he set Annabelle on her feet and embraced her as if she were the most important person in his life.

At that moment, he realized she *was*. Gone were his worries about her motives, or his tribe, or their tenuous future. All that mattered was Annabelle. Safe. In his arms.

Gasping and weeping she clung to him for long moments before she tried to speak. And then all she did was whisper his name.

"Charles..."

"I'm here. I've got you. You're safe."

Raising her gaze to his she stared as if unsure he was real. "I saw... I thought... In the barn. That wasn't you?"

He drew her even closer and threaded his fingers through her damp hair as she laid her head on his chest. "No. That was someone who had hoped to kill me when I came out to fight the fire."

"Oh, Charles. Are you sure?"

"Positive. If the barn door was not gone I could find the ball and prove it to you. The bullet barely missed me."

"Then that man died in the fire. I saw..."

"I know." Fighting to control the quaver in his voice he asked, "Why didn't you run when you saw the place collapsing?"

He felt her shoulders trembling. Her arms around his waist tightened. Then she said words he had only dreamed of hearing.

"Because I was afraid I had lost the only man I had ever loved."

No longer hesitant, Charles slipped a finger under her chin, lifted her face and gently kissed away her tears.

* * *

A small group of bystanders, including Harriet Boudinot, had gathered their wagons aside and were ministering to the smoky, sweaty, exhausted men who had already worked so hard.

Annabelle would have stayed in her husband's embrace for hours if he had not led her over to the other women and insisted she be looked after properly.

She snatched his hand to stop him from leaving her. "Wait. There's nothing more to be done. Stay with me?"

"I need to see to Johnny and the livestock," he explained tenderly. "I won't go far. I promise."

When Harriet's arm slipped around her shoulders, Annabelle reluctantly released him. It occurred to her as they parted that although one nemesis was dead, there could still be others lurking about.

She scanned the crowd. Everyone there was a stranger to her except for the Boudinots and their servants.

"Charles thinks the fire was set to ambush him," Annabelle breathlessly explained to Harriet. "We must be very vigilant in case there are more assailants about."

"I did pass two strange riders leaving in a hurry as I arrived. Let's hope they're long gone."

"I pray so," Annabelle replied. Her eyes were stinging and watering and she gladly accepted the wet wash rag that was offered and wiped her face before turning to assess the cabin.

"It looks like they'll be able to save the house," Harriet said. "That's a relief. Johnny will have a home. For a while, at least."

Annabelle's brows knit. She continued to blot her face. "What do you mean? Isn't he the only family member left?"

"Yes, but he's male. Inheritance passes only through the mother's lineage. It will be up to his distant female relatives whether or not he's allowed to live there."

Noting Annabelle's surprise, Harriet added, "I know. It takes a lot of getting used to."

"I'll say. Tell me more. How about Charles's mother? What's her situation?"

"She owns and runs what Northerners call a plantation. They grow cotton and tobacco. The cotton is a fairly recent crop since England kept it from us for so long, but it's doing amazingly well here."

"So, they're wealthy?"

"Oh, yes." Harriet rolled her eyes. "You should see the gowns from Paris that Sali wears, even for day dresses."

"That's what I was afraid of."

Harriet patted her hand. "Don't let her intimidate you, dear. She may have money and fancy things, but you have Charles's heart."

That comment made Annabelle blush. "It does seem so, doesn't it?"

"Yes, and I think the same goes for you. You love him."

"Very much."

"And you have told him?"

Annabelle had to chuckle, which brought on a spate of coughing. As soon as she could speak clearly she said, "I think so. Truth to tell, I am not certain. Everything happened so fast and was so confusing, I may not have made my feelings clear."

"Judging by the way I saw him kissing you I would say you managed to get your point across," Harriet teased. "Later today, when we're back home and have had a chance to recover, I will begin to tell you what you need to know to prepare for the Cherokee wedding ceremony."

"Assuming the tribe thinks I qualify. That's what scares me," Annabelle admitted aside. "I want to do what's right for Charles. Suppose I am Cherokee and from the wrong clan or something. What can I do about that?"

"We will cross that bridge when we come to it," her companion said. "In the meantime, it won't hurt for you to learn a bit about being a Cherokee wife. It took Elias's people a while to accept me, but the same goes for him and my family back in Connecticut." She huffed.

"All right. I will write to John Eaton, as you suggested," Annabelle vowed. "All he can do is refuse to answer me."

"We can send your letter via steamboat. That way it will be harder for him or anyone else to trace you."

Sobering, Annabelle gazed at the smoldering ruins of the barn. "I suspect that doesn't matter. Unless the bounty hunters who were chasing us give up after this, I'm afraid we can expect more of the same."

"Is there a reward offered for you?"

"I'm not sure about myself but we know there is one on Charles. We learned of it when we were still in Washington, which is why we left in such a hurry. A posse followed us partway here."

"Because he was with Major Ridge's party, they came here to look for you?"

"Apparently. It did not take a genius to figure out where we were probably bound."

Harriet seemed deep in thought before she finally began to smile. "Then perhaps it is time to not only change your names but to emigrate."

"How would that help?"

"It would give you both a new start in a new land. Some of our people have already moved west and settled there. They say the country in Arkansas holds great promise and the tribe is also free to govern itself there."

"But Charles's family and his work are here."

"For now they are." She sobered, shaking her head. "However, if the federal government keeps siding with the Georgia legislature, there may soon be no secure home for the eastern band of the Cherokee here."

Pondering Harriet's words, Annabelle began to think of a new life in a new place. Was it possible to begin again?

She had no ties to anyone else, but her husband did. Would it be fair to ask him to pull up stakes and make a move? Or would he resent her for suggesting it?

There was only one way to find out. She would have to ask for his opinion. Later. When the fire was out and their life settled down. If it ever did.

In the meantime, she would heed Harriet and learn the ways of the Cherokee enough to participate in a native ceremony, if that was what Charles wished.

Their Christian wedding had been rushed, yet she remembered it fondly. Perhaps the tribal wedding would bring the peace she craved and strengthen the bond she and her Cherokee groom already shared.

First, however, she would consult with Samuel Worcester, the reverend she had recently met, to make sure it was not contradictory to the teachings of Christianity. Then, if he approved, she would gladly take part in whatever ceremony was needed to bring her closer to the man she loved with all her heart and soul.

The thought of spending the rest of her days with

Charles McDonald was so amazing, so exhilarating, it lifted her mood and made her number him as first among the most incredible blessings of her entire life.

Chapter Twenty-One

When Charles finished finding temporary homes for the displaced livestock from the farm, he hurried to rejoin his wife in New Echota. They had had so little time together during and after the crisis that he had begun to question whether Annabelle's reactions had been overly influenced by the trauma or if she did, truly, love him.

Would he have to ask? he wondered. Hopefully not. He was already wearing his heart on his sleeve. If she had rethought her response to him saving her life during the fire, he didn't know how he was going to cope.

What he wanted to do was race back to the Boudinots', leap from his horse and sweep her off her feet and into his arms the same way he had when she'd strayed too close to the flames.

Instead, he paced himself so the boy and mule could keep up, alert in case of another ambush.

None came, and Charles returned to thinking of Annabelle. Picturing her lovely face. Seeing the delight in her sky-blue eyes. The softness of her lips.

The memory of their earnest embrace left his heart pounding and stole his breath. Oh, how he loved that woman. Any lingering doubts had vanished in the moments when he'd feared she would be killed. Why her dress did not burst into flames from the searing heat was a wonderment in itself.

He stopped at the stables behind the printer's house and spoke to Johnny. "You stay here with the horses. I have some business to take care of that needs to be private. Understand?"

"Yes, sir. Can we go back to Lisi's tonight?"

"Probably in a few days," Charles replied. "Some of the neighbors have offered to rebuild the barn. We'll definitely go back then, if not before."

The boy pouted but didn't argue.

Pausing to rinse his sooty face and hands at the pump in the courtyard, Charles raked his fingers through his hair and pronounced himself ready. There were many other niceties he could have employed but time was wasting. He had to see Annabelle again. He simply had to.

He stomped and scraped mud off his boots at the kitchen door, then entered. As he had hoped, the women were gathered there, soaking up warmth from the cookstove.

Everyone looked up. One person jumped to her feet and flew into his arms. Holding tight. Reminding him of their meeting by the fiery barn.

"Annabelle." Her name was all he could manage right then. His entire being was filled to overflowing with love and thankfulness. Clearly, she did *not* regret her earlier expression of affection. As a matter of fact, considering she was willing to express those same feelings in front of everyone in the room, she must have had a serious change of heart since their time on the trail.

Eyes bright with unshed tears, cheeks rosy, lips lifted

by a smile, she met his gaze. "I have missed you, husband."

Charles didn't know whether to laugh or cry. Or both. Instead, he lifted her feet off the ground and swung her around in a circle before giving her the second kiss of their married life.

"I have something to talk to you about," Annabelle told him after they strolled out onto the porch to be alone. She kept hold of his hand, imparting her love while also drawing on his strength.

"Whatever you say will suit me," Charles replied.

"Perhaps." She indicated a wooden swing and seated herself so there would be plenty of room for him to join her. When he did, she pushed her feet against the porch floor to set the swing in motion and took a few moments to gather her thoughts. "I wish to discuss my background."

"None of that matters to me," he assured her. "I don't care where you came from. All I care about is the future we will have together."

"That is the problem," she said slowly as she watched his expression for any sign of disapproval. "Harriet thinks I may have Indian ancestors."

"So?" A grin lit his handsome face. "I have those, too. I told you I had already suspected as much."

"But you know who yours are. I don't."

"I still don't understand. What bothers you about it?"

"I came to the Eatons in Tennessee. I know there were some other tribes around there as well as yours, but what if I am part Cherokee?"

"All the better."

"Only if I am not Wolf clan."

She saw the slightest shift of his shoulders, the tiniest flash of worry in his eyes.

"There are seven clans, Annabelle. Why would you think you were part of mine?"

"I don't. I simply have no idea and Harriet says that can keep us from taking part in the Cherokee ceremony."

"Then we won't do it." Charles slipped an arm around her shoulders and tucked her in beside him. "We're already married in the sight of our Christian God. We don't need anything else."

"What about your mother? Your other kin? And what will that do to your place in the tribe? Major Ridge and Elias and many others were married twice."

"That doesn't matter."

"Yes, it does. How will I be able to face your mother if I'm the reason you can't take part in customary rites?"

"Sali will come around. Eventually. And even if she doesn't, you'll still have me."

Cuddling closer, she rested her head against his chest, listening to his strong heart beat and hearing it echo her own. "And Johnny? Will we be able to make him part of our family if it isn't traditional?"

Charles's concerned expression countered his words as he said, "Of course we will."

When Annabelle had earlier posed that same question to Harriet, however, the answer had been negative. As kin to Chief John Ross, the boy was special. It would be up to the council of chiefs, including Ross, to decide his ultimate fate, just as they had when they had sent him to Washington to be a human peace offering.

She chose to sit quietly beside her husband on the swing and let him puzzle it out for himself. Yes, she was happy. And, yes, she knew they shared a mutual love.

But what would happen to their feelings for each other if her background kept them from having a full life?

According to Harriet, Charles had promised to make the boy his son. If he had to break that promise he would never forgive her, nor would she be able to forgive herself.

Therefore, the first thing she must do is write to John H. Eaton and beg him to tell her all he knew about her past, her lineage. Even if he claimed to know nothing, that would be better than making a terrible mistake and finding out too late.

As she pondered her childhood, two other faces appeared in her thoughts. Adams had been with Eaton for as long as Annabelle could remember, but without being able to see his face and decide on his allegiance as she pled her case, it might be foolish to write to him. That left Lucy. Was there some way she could get a letter past Margaret and Adams and into the hands of the faithful cook? There must be, but how?

Suddenly, she sat up and swiveled to face Charles. "When will the next Cherokee delegation be going to Washington? Soon?"

"Probably. Since our mission was cut short, I suspect the chiefs will send others before long. Why?"

"Because I will need someone to act as my messenger and take a letter to one of the Eaton servants."

"Why? I thought you had talked to them."

"No. I never had time. Adams, Father's valet, may be able to tell me about my lineage but I'm not sure I can fully trust him. Lucy is sympathetic to our plight. The trouble is, I don't know if she can read."

"Adams can read the letter to her."

"No. He might tell Father."

"I don't think you have to worry about that," Charles assured her. "Adams was the one who helped me escape from the Eaton estate the day we left Washington."

"Adams? Are you sure?"

"Positive. He disarmed a man with a knife so I could get to a horse and told me to go and take care of you." Charles's smile grew and he pulled her close once again. "I think you have more friends in Washington than you know."

"Do I?"

Recalling instances when Adams had looked after her best interests, Annabelle began to realize Charles was right. She sighed, relieved and gladdened. So, there was hope, after all. Hope of learning who she was and from whence she had come.

The only scary part was the slim chance that her origins might preclude being happily married.

Still, she insisted, not knowing and worrying was far worse. To start a new life she had to know more about her old one. Even if the news was bad.

Charles was still in New Echota when a messenger brought news that Sali McDonald had returned to her estate. Charles sent the servant back to her with affirmation that he would visit the following day.

He went to break the news to Annabelle the moment he knew and found her in the Boudinot kitchen with Fiona.

The wide smile with which she greeted him made his heart rejoice. "I'm glad to see you're none the worse for wear after the fire."

"Thank you. I thought Martha would never get the smell of smoke out of my hair." As Annabelle spoke she drew the back of her wrist across her forehead to push aside damp ringlets.

"Careful," Charles teased, "or Martha will be washing globs of flour out of your hair."

Annabelle beamed. "I'm learning to make biscuits."

Her enthusiasm and joy made him chuckle. "Better than the ones you helped Johnny with on the trail, I hope."

"Much better. There are no open fires or sticks involved."

"That's good to know."

Fiona had been standing back, listening, and laughed, too. "Annabelle tells me you were quite the hunter during your travels. The next time you shoot a deer, I wish you'd bring us some of the meat. Mr. Elias is not very good with a rifle."

"Ah, but he is quite accomplished with the pen," Charles countered.

That comment made the slightly portly cook grin. "True. Except we'd all starve to death if that was our only source of food."

"Harriet keeps a wonderful vegetable garden," Annabelle commented. "It's much bigger and grander than the Eatons ever had."

Charles, who had been looking for an easy way to broach the touchy subject, decided that this moment would suffice. "Speaking of gardens, I just got word that my mother is back home. You'll have to come with me and let her show you how well she's managing the estate."

Her floury hands stilled. Annabelle stared. "Me? Go see her? Aren't you going to break the news to her first?"

"I suppose I could, if that's what you want, but I'm

certain she already knows. When she got word that I was back, she undoubtedly also heard that you were with me."

Waiting for his announcement to sink in, Charles bided his time and studied the woman he loved. Annabelle had changed back into the burgundy dress in which she had traveled, thankfully putting an apron over it to keep it clean this time. There was a light dusting of flour on her cuffs but she was otherwise more than presentable.

Wide-eyed and obviously concerned, she asked, "When did you want to go?"

"I sent word that we will visit tomorrow."

"So soon?"

Charles smiled in the hopes it would comfort her. If the cook had not been present he might have slipped his arm around Annabelle then and there. "When you have a dose of bitter medicine to swallow, isn't it better to hold your nose, open your mouth and get it over with?"

To his relief, a smile did start to illuminate her sweet face. "I will have to be bribed to keep from telling your dear mother that you consider her a bitter pill to swallow," she gibed.

At that, Fiona cackled like a hen on a nest.

Annabelle giggled.

Charles regarded them both with mock seriousness. "I strongly advise against being too candid with Sali. She is used to having her way and she's very good at managing the farm. After my father died and she took over everything, production doubled."

"Then she is to be commended," Annabelle said. "Perhaps she and I will get along better than you imagine."

"*Anything* will be better than I imagine," Charles said wryly. "I'm going to go check on Johnny and make sure he's staying out of trouble." He nodded and touched a finger to his forehead in place of tipping a hat. "Ladies."

If he were to describe his mood as he left the kitchen, Charles would have had to be ambiguous. On one hand he was looking forward to arranging a Cherokee ceremony so he and Annabelle could start their new life together with the blessings of his family and tribe. On the other hand, he was very concerned that Sali's strong will might clash with Annabelle's and cause unnecessary conflict.

He supposed the most sensible thing for him to do was pay an early visit to his mother and warn her off. Not that that would have much effect. Still, he could try.

Then again, if he was too forceful he might bias her against Annabelle before the two ever met.

He loved Sali—as much as her stolid character would allow. She had never been a nurturer, not even to his sisters. It simply was not her way. But she was strong and honest and faithful to her family and to the tribe and Wolf clan. The perfect Cherokee woman.

And Annabelle? She was just as strong and brave and quick-witted. But she was far more sensitive, partly due to her upbringing, he had decided. What kind of person she would have become if Myra Eaton had lived longer was a moot point. Annabelle was who she was. Period.

And he loved her. Sali would have to understand that, above all.

He wished they had had time to send those letters to Eaton's old retainers and receive replies before he had to try to explain the situation to his clan.

Charles sighed deeply, poignantly, as he made his way

to the stable to look for Johnny. Where the mule was, he could usually find the boy. This time was no different.

Johnny beamed when he saw the man, ran to him and threw his arms around his torso. "He's hardly burned at all. Just some of the long hairs on the end of his tail."

"That's good to hear." Charles took him by the hand and led him back to Golly's stall.

"I have arranged for us to move back into our old room in this house for a few days. We'll sleep here and spend our days at your *lisi*'s, cleaning up the mess and salvaging what we can from the old barn. Then we'll put out the word and let the neighbors help us build a new one."

"But, why can't we sleep out there?"

Charles didn't want to tell the boy it wasn't safe, yet he also didn't want him to think the decision had been made on a whim.

"We will. Soon. A lot of smoke blew into the cabin so we'll have some cleaning and airing to do. You can help me take the rugs and the furniture out into the sun."

The child pulled a face. "If we had servants we wouldn't have to work so hard."

"Speaking of that kind of thing, I'll be gone tomorrow and I'll want you to stay here," Charles said.

"Why? Where are you going?"

"Home. But only for a visit."

The boy's expression darkened even more. "What about her?"

"Annabelle is going with me."

"Then why can't I go?"

"Because I need you to stay here."

"But…"

"No arguments," Charles said flatly. "Annabelle

and I will leave in the morning and return before dark. While we are away I want you to behave yourself. Understand?"

Although Johnny did nod, Charles wasn't totally convinced he would do as he was told.

On the other hand, how much trouble could a Cherokee child get into when every member of the tribe was considered his family? He arched an eyebrow. Studied the boy's face.

How much trouble? Maybe a lot.

Chapter Twenty-Two

For her first meeting with Sali, Annabelle chose to don the modest gray dress in which she had been married. The small white cap that she had worn all the time in Washington was in such a poor state of repair she decided against adding it to her outfit.

Atop the gray mare, she rode beside Charles. He had borrowed a sleek gelding from Elias and looked much more appropriate mounted thus. As a matter of fact, he looked so elegant, so perfect, her heart galloped whenever she gazed at him.

A breeze ruffled her hair and threatened to loosen the combs Martha had placed so carefully to lift her tresses. She fingered the sausage curls that had been set with sugar water and arranged to hang beside her cheeks.

"Your hair looks fine," Charles volunteered.

"It's not that," Annabelle confessed. "I don't have a proper bonnet to complement my gown."

"Then I shall send for one."

"Thank you, but the need is now, before I meet your mother."

"Oh. Did you think to ask Harriet about borrowing a hat?"

With a sigh, Annabelle nodded. "Yes. She had a nice brown bonnet but it was wrong for this dress. If your mother is as fashionable as I have heard, it is better to meet her with no bonnet than with the wrong one."

"If you say so."

She pulled a face. "Stop laughing at me, Mr. McDonald. Such things may not matter to you but they are important to women."

"So I have heard."

He straightened his tailored jacket over his vest and squared his top hat, then held out his hand. She took it gladly and threaded her fingers between his. As long as both horses kept walking close together she was just able to reach.

"Tell me about your home?"

"In what way?"

"Its history, perhaps? And that of your mother?"

"All right."

Annabelle watched him gather his thoughts and wondered if he was ever going to speak. Patience might be a godly virtue but it was, unfortunately, not one of hers.

"My grandfather was a fur trapper," he began. "That's where the Scottish name came from. He married a woman from the Blue clan and moved into her village, as tradition dictates."

"You said there are seven clans?"

"Yes. Our legends tell of more in the distant past. Some, who would not obey Cherokee laws and customs were expelled. Those people supposedly became the Erie, Mohawk, Onandaga, Cayuga, Seneca, Oneida and

Chickamauga. That left seven. Those are the clans that continue today."

"How interesting. But if he married into the Blue clan, why are you Wolf?"

"Because no man is allowed to marry within his mother's clan. That meant that when my father grew up he had to choose a bride from one of the other six."

"He kept his father's surname and his mother's clan?"

"Until he married Sali. Then he became Wolf."

"It seems very complicated."

"Not to those of us who grew up knowing it. Where you come from, everything is traced through the men and the women are ignored. You're used to that system so it seems right. Ours makes perfect sense to us, particularly since the Cherokee are not as numerous as they once were."

"Really? Is that because of wars?"

"Some. Our men fought beside federal troops in 1812. That's where Major Ridge got his name. He adopted the rank he was given after a battle as his actual first name. Many of us change names for various reasons."

"That's amazing. Was yours always Charles?"

"Yes, but Elias Boudinot was born Galagina Oowatie. When he was about fifteen, a war hero who had no sons adopted him and asked him to take his name to carry on the Boudinot legacy."

"Oh, like Sequoya is also called George Guess."

"Exactly. Although Sequoya is so famous among the Cherokee for inventing our alphabet he seldom uses any other name."

Annabelle heaved a sigh and shook her head. "I fear I will never be able to keep it all straight."

"I'll help you."

She squeezed his fingers and released his hand. "Thank you. Is that your home place over there, through those trees?"

"No." Charles was grinning. "Those are some of the homes we built for our servants and slaves. Follow me."

He gave the borrowed horse a kick to hurry its pace so Annabelle did the same. They rounded a bend lush with vegetation and stopped in the middle of a broad avenue that seemed to appear out of nowhere.

Rows of stately oak and hickory trees lined the road and canopied the approach to a magnificent mansion. It was at least three stories high with gabled windows facing the front along the steep roof. Fluted, Grecian-type columns supported second-story balconies. Sunlight glinted off tall glass windows, more windows than Annabelle had ever seen in any dwelling except that of President Jackson.

Her jaw dropped. She gaped. "Oh, my word."

"Impressive, isn't it?"

"Very." Her brow furrowed. This was worse than she had imagined. Charles's family must be almost as rich as King Solomon in the Bible. How awful!

"Wait till you see the land to the north. The back of the house faces a branch of the Chattahoochee and has a magnificent view. Mother still owns the ferry business my father started, and one of the main crossings is just upstream a ways. You can see for miles from the porches on that side, particularly up on the balconies. That's by design."

Annabelle was speechless. Charles came from so much wealth and privilege he *must* think her beneath him. So why had he volunteered to marry her in the first place, let alone want to perpetuate that mistake by asking for a Cherokee ceremony? Yes, it was possible that he loved her, yet it was also possible he felt obligated merely because she had helped save his life by the Potomac and was now alone in the world.

Riding in silence, she let her horse lag behind his until she was following him rather than keeping abreast.

She huffed. A suitable bonnet was the least of her worries.

A suitable life history, which she could not possibly attain in a million years, was what she really needed.

Charles dismounted first and paused to assist his wife while a stable boy took charge of their horses.

When Annabelle stood stock-still and acted as if she were about to bolt, he gently took her hand, placed it in the crook of his arm and held it there. "Come on. No sense putting this off."

"Oh, I don't know. How about if I go with the horses and you visit your mother without me?"

"The fearless Annabelle McDonald cannot be afraid of one old woman. Not when she's faced armed attackers and fought her way out of Washington practically bare-handed." He chuckled softly. "Except for a little horse manure."

The teasing had the effect he had hoped. Annabelle used her free hand to playfully smack his arm through the sleeve of his jacket.

"Shush. It's bad enough that I don't know who my parents were. Don't make it worse by inferring I have the manners of a street urchin."

Charles laughed quietly as they mounted the stone steps to the covered porch. "Of course not. Their manners are *much* better."

The door opened before he had a chance to say more.

The liveried butler who greeted them was as tall and stately as Charles, with white hair and gleaming teeth that contrasted the darkness of his skin when he smiled.

His pose did not alter when he saw who had arrived, but his grin was wide and his dark eyes gleamed. "Master Charles. Welcome home."

"Thank you, David. Is my mother receiving?"

The butler bowed. "Yes, sir. This way."

Charles could tell that his bride, who had proved so fearless when defending him or Johnny against formidable dangers, was petrified about meeting his mother. He supposed that was to be expected considering Sali's reputation with other mixed-bloods. Although she, herself, had married thus, she treated everyone else who was not pure Cherokee as a lesser being.

The butler opened a door and stepped aside as soon as he had announced them.

Charles walked boldly forward, practically having to drag Annabelle along.

His mother's face brightened. She began to smile. Then, as if a cloud had passed across her face, she focused her attention on Annabelle and scowled.

"Mother," he said, "I'd like to present my wife, Annabelle."

The older woman's otherwise quite acceptable face screwed into a grimace. She looked straight at her son and said, "What have you *done*?"

If Annabelle could have dropped through a hole in the floor she would have gladly done so. Anything she may have heard about this woman's haughty attitudes had clearly been understated. Not only was she rich, she had a mean streak as wide as the road leading up to her mansion.

I will not cry, Annabelle told herself, biting the inside of her cheek for distraction. *She can do or say whatever she wants to me but I will not give her the satisfaction of weeping.*

Lifting her chin, she met Sali's steady, critical gaze with a show of inner strength she had not imagined she might possess.

Rather than cringe and retreat, Annabelle let go of Charles's arm and offered her hand to the other woman with a smile. A smile that took every ounce of courage she possessed.

Sali ignored her.

Annabelle was not to be deterred. She stepped closer to the other woman, reached for her bejeweled hand and clasped it firmly. "I am delighted to finally meet you," she said.

If she had not been so intent on making a good impression, she might have giggled at Sali's shocked expression. Considering that she was Charles's mother, the woman was remarkably well preserved. Her hair was dark and shiny, her eyes bright. And her skin showed far fewer wrinkles than Margaret Eaton's had.

And her gown! Annabelle had instantly marveled at its cut and the drape of the fine fabric. It must be of silk, she reasoned, the most beautiful example of weaving she had ever seen, even in the most posh Washington drawing rooms.

"You have a lovely home," Annabelle added before releasing Sali's hand.

"Yes, well, it suits us."

"Quite well, I can see." Searching her memory for

details she had amassed when Margaret had redecorated the Eaton home, she scanned the room, settling on a few items whose origin seemed assured. "That rug is the most beautiful Persian carpet I have ever seen."

"Why, thank you. I picked it up in New York."

"And the Hepplewhite chairs? I think they're much more practical than Chippendale, don't you?"

"Really, I..."

Annabelle sauntered across the expensive imported carpet to admire the marble-cased clock on the mantel. "I believe there is one just like this in the White House. I'm almost certain of it."

"Then come and sit by me while we have tea," Sali said, taking a seat on the settee and patting the cushion beside her. "I want you to tell me all about Washington City. My son has been there several times but he never notices the important things. What kind of bonnets are they wearing there now?"

Reminded of her bare head, Annabelle nervously touched her hair. "The brims are a bit larger this season, perhaps, and there is a lot of velvet. They're still worn over the common white lace cap, of course." She shyly lowered her gaze. "Alas, mine suffered during our journey and I have had no chance to replace it."

"We don't follow all the fashion trends here in Georgia, anyway," Sali said. "Our summer is too warm for such foolishness." She motioned toward a doorway and a servant delivered a tea service much more ornate than the one Margaret Eaton had been so impressed to receive.

When Annabelle looked up at Charles and saw his mouth hanging open in astonishment, she almost giggled.

* * *

Listening to his mother and his wife chatting was akin to hearing the babble of a brook. The sound was not too strident but neither was it informative. Of all the questions he had expected Sali to fire at Annabelle, ones about fashion and furniture had not even occurred to him.

Happily, Annabelle seemed to be holding her own. She had evidently picked up useful knowledge while remaining in the background of her foster father's life.

Charles had relaxed as much as he could in one of the dainty chairs the women had been talking about with such enthusiasm. He didn't know one seat from another except to notice which ones looked too spindly to support a grown man's weight. Speaking of size, now that he could see his mother and Annabelle so close together he suspected that his wife had lost a little weight on the trail. Either that or his mother had become more portly, a possibility he would not have mentioned if his life had depended upon it.

The Cherokee women he had known did seem to have a tendency to gain, probably because the ones who traveled in his circles all had servants. People who did their own work seemed to stay more fit, like their ancestors.

"So, enough about Washington," Sali finally said, sipping her tea from a delicate porcelain cup. "Tell me about yourself. Who are your people? I heard something about an important man. John H. Eaton?"

Nodding, Annabelle set her cup on the tray to mask the fact that her hands had begun to tremble. "He was my guardian."

"Guardian? You are not his true daughter?"

"No." Annabelle shook her head, then squared her

shoulders and faced the woman who was technically already her mother-in-law. "I was taken in by the Eatons when I was three years old. I don't remember who my real parents were, and no one seems to be able to tell me."

"I see." Sali's eyebrows arched, accentuating her high cheekbones and imperious attitude.

"There is a good chance Annabelle has Indian blood," Charles interjected.

Annabelle could have smacked him. Just when she was starting to get along with his mother he had to go and stir the kettle.

Sali gracefully put down her cup and saucer. "Really? What makes you think so?"

Annabelle tried to explain. "Before my first foster mother died, I heard her and John Eaton talking about sending me to the Cornwall school as soon as I was old enough."

"Did you go there?"

"No." She shook her head sadly, soberly. "After Myra passed away there was no more mention of school for me. I taught myself to read and write."

"You had no nursemaid? No nanny?" The older woman snorted delicately. "That is scandalous."

"Nevertheless," Annabelle replied, "it is the truth. I plan to write to some of the old retainers in my father's employ and ask if they know more, but it could take months to hear back from them."

"Well, until then you are wise to have kept to yourselves," Sali said, acting as if she was giving them a compliment rather than condemning them to live apart. "That is our way, as Charles well knows."

"But...we were married in the church," Annabelle

offered, realizing too late that making that particular confession was not in her favor.

Stone-faced, Sali arose. "I think we have discussed this more than enough," she said as she glided toward the doorway to the foyer. "When you have learned who you really are, perhaps you'll visit again and we can continue our conversation. In the meantime, Charles can have his former room back. I'll see that it's readied."

Left openmouthed, Annabelle watched her go. "Did I just get thrown out?"

He was slowly shaking his head as he took her hands and helped her to her feet. "In a manner of speaking, yes. What my mother doesn't realize is that I will not be staying here. It's too far away from you."

"She will be annoyed."

He laughed so heartily it brought David peeking in to see what was amiss.

Charles waved him off and took Annabelle's arm to escort her outside. "Woman, you have an amazing way of understating the obvious. My mother will not be annoyed. She will be *furious*."

Chapter Twenty-Three

Expecting to find Johnny where he had left him, Charles went straight to the Boudinot stables with the horses while Annabelle chose to seek out Harriet. He could understand her need to speak to a woman who properly commiserated. If anyone understood what it meant to step into a role in Cherokee society, Harriet did. If she had not had the heart of a missionary and a love for native people to start with, he didn't know how she would have coped when her family in Connecticut had initially disowned her.

Entering the barns, Charles called, "Johnny? *Uwetsi?* Son?"

It was becoming more and more natural to refer to the boy as his kin in either language. The warm feeling made Charles smile. His mood plummeted, however, when he noted that Golly was missing. That was not a good sign.

None of the workers in the Boudinot stable or yard claimed to have noticed the boy. Hurrying into the house, Charles found Harriet and Annabelle seated together at the kitchen table. Not only were they crying, so was Fiona.

Frustrated and growing short tempered, he ignored their tears and simply announced, "I can't find Johnny. The mule is gone, too."

Chastened, Annabelle realized that she had been thinking only of herself. Charles must also be suffering from his mother's unreasonableness. And poor Johnny had no one left now that his grandmother was gone. No wonder he had run away.

She whisked at her tears and jumped up, sniffling a little but ready to go. "Where should we look first?"

"I don't know. He was mad because I didn't take him to Mother's with us and told him we'd be staying here for a few nights. He probably went back to his grandmother's place to sulk. I hope so because if he's not there he could be anywhere."

"I'll go get Elias," Harriet said.

Charles stopped her. "No. He has a paper to print and a deadline. I'll go out alone."

"You may be going, but not alone," Annabelle insisted, fully expecting him to argue. When he merely wheeled and headed back to the stable, she followed.

They stopped the grooms from stabling their horses, remounted and headed north.

"Why would he run away when he knew we were coming back?" Annabelle asked, then answered her own question. "Wait. I get it. He figured you'd stay with your mother and I'd come back to New Echota alone. Isn't that right?"

"Possibly. Probably."

Charles was leaning to one side, studying the road.

"Check on your right and look for the mule's unshod hoofprints."

Complying, she used that quiet time for contemplation. Not only did Sali reject her, so did Johnny, in spite of their tenuous camaraderie during their cross-country travels. Apparently the boy thought she was fine as a companion but not as a member of his clan or family. That attitude should not have surprised her, yet it did. Moreover, it emphasized the wide gulf between Cherokee culture and her own upbringing.

Another thought struck her in the conscience and left a theoretical wound. She had rejected John Eaton's choice of Margaret Timberlake in exactly the same manner.

"But Margaret was wicked and sinful," Annabelle muttered, convinced that her own motives had been pure while arguing that she had merely been concerned for her foster father's happiness. That was true. She had. And the times when she had tried to be friendly to Margaret, her overtures had been summarily rejected. Nevertheless, the woman was John's wife, and as such, should have been treated with at least a modicum of respect.

Charles straightened. "See anything?"

"No. Just lots of overlapping prints and mud."

"We have that storm to thank for saving the house," Charles said. "I thought the barn fire was caused by lightning until the man you saw in there shot at me."

"Well, at least the others left."

He grabbed her wrist. "What?"

"Harriet said two strangers rode past her, going the other way, while she was on her way to help."

"Why didn't you say something sooner?"

"She didn't tell me about it until we were back in town. I guess I hadn't recovered from thinking I'd watched you die." Annabelle knew there was an angry edge to her tone but couldn't help it. "There were dozens of locals there. Harriet can't possibly know everybody. Besides, there's no proof that the men she saw were up to no good. They may have been going to fetch more help."

"What did she say they looked like?"

"People. Men. I may have passed them, too, and not noticed."

"What made you finally remember to tell me?"

She shrugged. "I really don't know. The memory just popped into my head."

Charles released her abruptly as if throwing a bone to hungry dogs. "Go back. Now, while we're not far from town. I don't want you out here."

"What about what I want? I love Johnny, too."

"Then act like it and take care of yourself. If something happens to me, you may be able to convince Elias to help you stay in town to look after the boy, even if it's only as his guardian."

"Wait a minute. What are you saying?"

"That if the man who died in the fire was not alone, there's a good chance his partners are waiting where they found me before. If Johnny has wandered into a trap, there's no way I can look after you, as well. Now, go."

With logic so irrefutable, Annabelle was forced to listen. "All right. I'll turn back to Harriet's and bring help. Will you wait?"

"Not when the boy may be in mortal danger."

"I understand. At least promise me you'll be very, very careful?"

"Always."

She held her excited mare in check as Charles gave his horse a kick and galloped away. Watching him go gave her pangs of heartache.

The full effects of isolation now that he had gone heaped a huge dose of fright atop her already shaky mountain of emotions. Nothing seemed amiss in field or forest, yet she imagined all sorts of menace.

That was more than enough to make her urge the mare into a gallop and race back to New Echota.

To sanctuary. To home.

The ruins of the barn were still smoldering when Charles arrived, sending tiny fingers of smoke wafting skyward whenever a breeze stirred the last embers beneath the deep bed of ashes.

He noted Johnny's mule, standing with its reins looped over the hitching rail, and patted it on the neck in passing. He was going to give that boy a good talking-to when he found him. Leaving any animal tied without food or water, let alone under saddle, was unforgivable—unless there were extenuating circumstances.

Charles checked his surroundings, was satisfied things were quiet, then began to climb the steps to the porch. One. Two. Three, and he was at the door.

It hung misaligned with the frame rather than closed as it should have been.

Alerted, he hesitated. Hair at the nape of his neck prickled. Behind him, the mule brayed.

Whirling, he saw nothing until he looked in the direction Golly's long ears were pointing. The mule may as well have had hands to show him the threat.

Johnny was being toted off, thrown over a man's shoulder like a sack of flour.

Charles shouted, "Stop!" Reached for one of his pistols. Took aim.

The kidnapper not only failed to slow, a second man showed himself and fired. Charles shot back. Both missed.

A muffled cry of "Tsali!" tied his gut in knots. He took cover and watched as the men disappeared around what was left of the burned barn.

It took Annabelle little time to arrive back at Harriet's and pass the word to Elias and other available men. She never said that Charles had sent her for help, nor did she infer he was in trouble. Bare facts were enough encouragement. A group of five men mounted up and rode hard for Johnny's *lisi*'s former home. Staying to the rear of the pack where she wouldn't be noticed, Annabelle followed along. This time, nobody bothered to order otherwise.

One thing she wished she had was a rifle. Charles had given her firearms instructions during their travels and had even let her shoot his pistols as soon as she had demonstrated proficiency reloading. Although he had not said so, she assumed the lessons were less for her amusement than they were to prepare her to assist him if they were attacked.

Worse, since she had dressed up to visit Sali's she had not stuck her hunting knife beneath her sash the way she had while on the trail. Disgusted, Annabelle realized Charles had been right to send her back to New Echota. Given the possibly dangerous situation and her ineptitude regarding self-defense, she was no asset. She was a hindrance.

Starting to slow the mare and let the posse pull ahead, Annabelle rued her penchant for going off half-cocked like a faulty flintlock. She'd been acting foolishly and she was penitent.

"I should go back," she told herself. "I should obey my husband and wait for him at the Boudinots'."

The old Annabelle Lang would have listened to those sage notions. This Annabelle thought of her grandmother and of Myra and of Charles's imperious mother, Sali; strong women, all of them. She pointed the horse toward Johnny's *lisi*'s house, leaned forward, planted her heels in the mare's sides and shouted, "Yah!" at the top of her lungs.

Charles followed the boy's captors immediately instead of pausing to reload. By the time he reached the place where he had last seen them they had disappeared despite his quick action.

He froze in place. Listened. Heard rustling ahead. They were either in what was left of the rear of the barn or outside behind it. He chose to sneak up on the outside. A prickling sense came too late to effectively warn him.

Intense pain sent Charles crashing to the dirt before he could react. Lights flashed in his eyes. The back of his head throbbed. He landed face-first.

Someone shouted in triumph. Another person laughed coarsely. "Woo-hoo. *That's* better. Get his pistols while I drag him inside."

"Ain't you gonna finish him?"

"Not until I figure out how to prove he's dead and get my money," the first man replied.

Through the fog of his injury, Charles thought he recognized the voice of Caleb, one of John Eaton's stable hands.

Lying still, he feigned unconsciousness as his senses

began to slowly return. The only blessing to this entire fiasco was that he had left Annabelle behind where she would be safe. Chances were good that these men had no interest in her.

"I told ya' grabbin' the kid'd bring him to us," the second man said. "What'd I tell you? Huh?"

"Yeah, yeah. Shut up and let me think. We can't haul his dead body all the way back to Washington. The flies'd drive us crazy before we got there, 'specially in the summer."

"We could take him back alive. Keep him shackled and make him work for us." He guffawed. "We'd have our own Injun slave!"

Given the choices, Charles would have gladly volunteered to become their slave—until such time as he could make his escape. Since they thought he was still unconscious, however, he decided to keep his opinions to himself.

The way he had it figured, the longer they argued, the more alert he'd become and the better his chances of winning a fair fight.

He'd have felt a lot more positive about his survival if they hadn't disarmed him. He could see the brace of pistols where the thugs had thrown them aside. One was loaded, one was not. If they got careless and he could manage to reach the loaded one, he might have a chance.

If he picked up the wrong one and aimed it, however, he'd be dead before he even realized his mistake.

By the time Annabelle reached the burned-out barn the men from New Echota had it surrounded and were shouting at whoever was holed up inside. She left her mare beside the house and circled in the opposite direction. She had no plan, nor was she acting irrationally, given the group of armed men on her side. She was simply curious and unwilling to stand by and wonder.

The first Cherokee she came to filled her in. "We got a pair of bounty hunters trapped back there in what's left of the old barn. It's a standoff. They're holding McDonald and the boy."

"What are you going to do?"

"Wait for Elias to decide, I reckon. I'm supposed to stop 'em if they try to get by me."

Annabelle backed away, torn. She knew she should keep her distance and fully intended to—until she heard a thud and a sharp cry of pain. *Charles!* They were hurting him. And these men were just standing there, letting him be abused. Or worse.

Visualizing the structure the last time she'd seen it, she had trouble imagining that anything substantial enough to hide four people had survived. There was part of a rear wall with deep piles of ruins jumbled in front of it. Perhaps a portion of the loft remained, making a barrier that hid the bounty hunters and her loved ones.

The sun was setting. Soon the men who had captured Charles would have the advantage of darkness. That would never do.

She edged away until she was hidden from the posse members by a portion of the dilapidated chicken house. The hens had roosted for the night and were quiet, so she took pains to keep from disturbing them and thus giving away her presence.

She didn't have to tiptoe to keep her soft shoes from making noise. Creeping closer to the remnants of the barn, she heard voices. Men talking. But not Charles's voice. If she had not heard him cry out she might have suspected they had lied about taking him prisoner.

One peek between warped boards and she knew the worst. Charles lay on the floor, unmoving, while his captors argued about how to save their own necks.

"I told ya we shouldn't mess with the Indians in their own town, but did you listen to me? No. You had to bull your way through. We wouldn't have lost Patrick in the fire if you'd taken your time."

"Bah! He knew the risks. We all did. The reward was worth takin' a few chances. You're just sore 'cause we got surrounded."

Annabelle hardly dared breathe for fear they'd sense her presence.

Back away. Run, her brain shouted.

Find an answer and act, countered her heart.

Moving her head from side to side gave her a wider view of the scene. Charles's pistols lay in the ash and dirt mere inches from the partial wall she was hiding behind. To reach them, however, she'd have to show herself and move very surely. Quickly. And be ready to fire as soon as her hands closed around the guns.

It would be doubly tricky to handle both because they were heavy, so she opted to grab just one and fire only if she were forced to.

Whispering a plea to Jesus for help and strength, she started to rise.

The men were so engrossed in their argument they didn't notice her until she had grasped the pistol in both hands, raised the barrel and pulled the hammer back with her thumbs. It made a clicking noise that was unmistakable.

All conversation ceased.

Annabelle froze with her finger on the trigger.

One shot, Charles had taught her. *You only have one shot, so make it count*.

Both men turned and lunged for her.

She pulled the trigger.

Nothing happened!

A large hand fisted on the pistol barrel, jerking it forward as Annabelle made a frantic attempt to hang on.

Her index finger tightened. Pulled the trigger again in the hopes the failure had been a misfire and it would work this time.

It didn't.

Annabelle screamed.

After that, everything happened so fast she only caught brief glimpses of the action.

A charred piece of wood arced through the air. Hit on the side of his head beside his eye, one of the men dropped like a marionette whose strings had been snipped.

The thug who had disarmed her was left holding and pointing a useless pistol.

Charles rolled to the side, still on the floor, and reached his second gun. He fired from there, mortally wounding the remaining miscreant.

Annabelle pressed her fingertips to her lips to squelch the screams still locked inside her.

In seconds she realized Charles was not only alive, he was getting to his feet and starting to check on the two men while Johnny stood over one with the piece of wood he had thrown as accurately as a spear, ready to deliver another blow.

Shouts from outside preceded the arrival of the five

from the impromptu posse. Charles stood and waved the empty pistol announcing, "It's over. They're both down."

Annabelle hurried to him, slipping her arms around his waist and holding tight. "When I saw you on the floor I thought…"

"I was playing possum." He held her away and scowled. "What are you doing here? I told you to go home."

"I did. These friends of yours came to the rescue because I alerted them."

"And you had to guide them back here?" An eyebrow arched and he gave her a stern look.

"Maybe."

"Then why didn't you stay outside with them?" He frowned at her, then began to smile in spite of himself. "I know. Don't tell me. You thought only you could save me."

"Not exactly." Blushing, she eyed the men from town. "When I gave the alarm I wasn't even sure you were in trouble. Not directly, anyway. It was like when Johnny and I followed you to the river. He said he just knew you were in trouble. It was the same for me tonight."

She noticed him swaying slightly. "Are you all right?"

"I will be," Charles said. "but I suspect I'll have a headache like the ones you get when the weather changes."

"I sincerely hope not," she said, steadying him. "Those are awful." Her gaze traveled to Johnny. "I'm glad he was able to help, too."

"Yes. He's resourceful. Like you. Although I have high hopes we won't have need to test either of you further." He eyed the bounty hunters as his friends carried their limp bodies out into the yard. "Hopefully, this will put an end to the vendetta."

"And if not?"

He tucked her into the crook of his arm and pulled her closer, making Annabelle feel more loved than ever before. "If not, we may choose to take Elias's advice, change our names and emigrate. I had considered it in the past, before Chief John Ross convinced me to join him as an emissary to the federal government."

"Why? What's the advantage to moving to a new place when you don't have to?"

"Getting choice of the best available land, for one. And escaping the tribal political disagreements here. There is already a large contingent of Cherokees in Arkansas and Oklahoma. We wouldn't be going into uncharted territory."

"But, this is your home," Annabelle reminded him.

Charles shook his head. "My home is wherever my family is. Wherever you and Johnny are. That's all that matters."

Annabelle had absolutely no urge to argue so she emulated Naomi in the Book of Ruth and said, "Wherever you go, I will go. Your people shall be my people."

Chapter Twenty-Four

Charles's announcement that they were planning to leave New Echota for good stirred up a hornet's nest. His mother blamed Annabelle no matter how often he tried to explain. Elias and Harriet argued about whether or not they would be safer among trusted friends in Georgia. Chief John Ross accused Charles of abdicating his responsibility to the tribe. And Johnny stopped speaking to everybody as soon as he realized Charles and Annabelle intended to try to take him with them as their adopted son.

Frustrated by his lack of success convincing anybody he was doing the sensible thing, he went looking for Annabelle and found her upstairs in Harriet's room. The women were sorting through clothing while Harriet tried to gift his bride with a suitable wardrobe.

"I traveled from Washington with a mere two dresses," Annabelle was arguing as he knocked on the open door. Her instant expression of delight at seeing him warmed his heart.

"Good morning, ladies."

"Charles!" She looked past him. "Is Johnny with you?"

"No. Sadly."

He took Annabelle's hand and held it gently while adding, "I did all I could. The council refuses to let us take him when we are not an official man and wife."

"They'd rather place him with someone like John and Margaret Eaton? That's ridiculous."

"Nevertheless..." Seeking to distract her, he gestured toward the pile of clothing arrayed on the bed. "If you are planning to take all that with you we will have to travel by wagon."

"It's my fault," Harried chimed in. "I want her to be the best dressed new arrival in Arkansas."

Chuckling, he gestured toward the pillow where Rosie lay. "I suppose you'll insist on taking that, too."

"Of course." Annabelle released his hand and scooped up the precious memento, cradling the way she had as a child. "Rosie has been with me for as long as I remember. She even has my initials embroidered on her."

Harriet joined her. "You've told me that before. Let me see."

Charles paid little attention to the two women fussing over a doll until he saw Harriet's eyes widen.

"What?" Annabelle asked.

Instead of answering directly, Harriet said, "Charles. Come here. Look at this."

He waved her off. Men did not concern themselves with childish women's toys.

Harriet was not to be deterred. She bustled over to him, grabbed his sleeve and practically dragged him to Annabelle and the doll.

At first, all he saw was lettering. It was when he

began to study the leafy floral pattern surrounding the initials that he saw what the other woman did.

His jaw dropped. He looked from the doll to Annabelle and back to the doll. "Where did you get this?"

"I told you. Myra repaired it for me when I was very young and embroidered it so I would know it was mine."

"She told you to keep it, always, didn't she?"

Annabelle was frowning, looking puzzled by all the fuss. "I suppose she did. All I can remember is being positive Rosie was mine and would always be with me."

The thrill he felt was indescribable. Not only was the design familiar, the seamstress had added enough detail to remove all doubt. This was a wild potato vine, a symbol of a Cherokee clan. They finally knew they were free to marry!

Leading Annabelle to a boudoir chair and urging her to be seated, Charles dropped to one knee in front of her. He knew there were unshed tears in his eyes and blinked them away as he took her hands. The precious doll lay between them in her lap.

"There is no need to wait for letters from the Eaton servants who knew you long ago," he said tenderly. "You are from the Wild Potato clan. Nothing stands between us anymore. We can be married in a Cherokee ceremony."

"What?"

"It's all right there, on your doll. Your initials and the insignia of your clan."

"I—I thought that was just pretty decoration."

"As would most people," Charles explained. "Carrying your heritage with you that way kept you safe as well as identifying you when you needed to know. Myra was a wise woman."

"She loved me very much," Annabelle told him as she began to weep silently. "Are you sure this is enough proof?"

"It is for me. I will present the information to the council. I am virtually certain they will approve."

He picked up the doll and drew Annabelle to her feet to stand with him. His voice lowered, softened. "Will you marry me again? Be my Cherokee wife?"

A nod was enough. He sealed their pact with a kiss.

Annabelle could hardly catch her breath. She paced the porch and fussed until she saw Charles galloping toward the house. He reined in his horse and leaped to the ground. The doll was clutched in his gloved hand.

She met him at the steps. "Well?"

"You are Cherokee."

Annabelle threw herself at him and wrapped her arms around his neck. "I am so glad."

Lifting her face to him she accepted his thrilling kiss. When he ended it and set her away she was confused. "Where are you going?"

Charles grinned broadly. All he said was, "Hunting," but thanks to the lessons Harriet had been giving her, Annabelle knew exactly what that meant. She, too, had preparations to make.

They met in the council house seven days later.

Dressed in simple calico, Annabelle entered the room with a group of unmarried women, plus Harriet who would act in place of her mother, and Elias who would take the part of a brother. Together, they approached the fire to be blessed by the priest along with all the wedding guests, including Reverend Worcester and his wife.

Charles wore a customary ribboned shirt. Sali, clad simply instead of in white man's finery, approached Charles on the side of the room where the men had gathered and handed him the venison roast and a new blanket.

Although she knew what was supposed to happen next, Annabelle was so nervous she was afraid she would drop the special gifts Harriet was about to give her for the exchange: an ear of corn and another blanket.

Everyone else returned to their places.

Annabelle held tight to her blanket and corn. When the room quieted and she saw Charles start to walk slowly toward her, she stepped out, too.

This day had been so long in coming she wanted to run to him, to throw herself into his strong arms and never let go.

Meeting his intense gaze she was nearly overcome. No matter how many times he expressed his love, this was the moment she would remember best.

Mouthing a soundless, "I love you," Annabelle joined him, took his folded blanket and laid it with her own, then handed him the corn.

Smiling gently, he gave her the roast.

Blue blankets were draped over each of them and singing began. They shared a simultaneous drink from a special wedding vessel. Then the first blankets were removed by the priest and replaced with a single one that was white. He raised his hand as if bestowing a Christian benediction and proclaimed, "The blankets are joined."

The room erupted into a shouting, cheering celebration.

Annabelle and Charles were deaf to the commotion. They only had eyes, and hearts, for each other.

They joined hands and threaded their way through the throng. Johnny was waiting aside for them. His expression seemed less guarded than before so she assumed he was growing to accept her. At least she hoped so, since he was to become their son as if he had been born thus.

Charles approached with Annabelle and knelt down to face the boy on his level. "You have a Cherokee mother and father now. Why are you acting sad."

Johnny averted his gaze.

Charles objected. "We will have none of that, son. When your mother or I ask you a question, you will answer."

The child's blue gaze darted to her before returning to Charles.

"I mean it. We are married. Twice. And we are your parents. You will answer me."

Tears filled the child's eyes and overflowed, making Annabelle wish she could intervene, dry his cheeks and give him a mother's hug for comfort. As he finally began to speak, however, it was all she could do to subdue her bubbling humor and keep from embarrassing them all.

"I don't want to be a potato," Johnny whined loudly. "I want to be a *wolf*."

Charles began to chuckle, then laugh, then roar. All around them, members of the other clans who had overheard the boy joined in.

That was too much for Annabelle and she, too, laughed until she cried. Sali, who had been wiping a different kind of tears from her eyes, was hiding her amusement behind a handkerchief and clearly enjoying the moment as much as they all were.

Charles stood, drew both mother and wife to him and kissed each on the brow. "I, too, have enjoyed being in the Wolf clan but I will make this sacrifice for my Wild Potato clan wife."

Filled with joy, yet barely recovered from the tension leading up to the ceremony, Annabelle allowed her spirits to soar and replied, "I suggest you stop worrying about the potato part and start paying closer attention to the *wild*."

Sali patted Charles's cheek, then smiled over at Annabelle and said, "Welcome to the tribe, daughter. You will do well."

Annabelle had no doubt she was right. God had answered her prayers with more blessings than she had dared dream. She didn't have to go to Tennessee or wait for answers to her letters to find out who she really was. Right here, right now, she had a family, friends and relatives who cared about her.

She belonged.

Finally.

* * * * *

Dear Reader,

This story takes place before the disastrous Trail of Tears, as the forced removal has come to be known. Instead of being a single event, however, it took place over time, ending with a final push in 1838 to oust those individuals and tribes who had refused to migrate west.

To make matters worse, there were warring factions among the Cherokee that each claimed authority to legally sign treaties and make promises on behalf of all. Both sides resorted to violence. The result was a painful split in the tribe and a loss of credibility in Washington.

I now live in the part of Arkansas that one of the routes, Benge's Trail, passed through. That's what caused me to begin this book and travel to visit the Cherokee Museum in North Carolina. I highly recommend it (Cherokeemuseum.org).

Almost all the characters in this story are actual historical figures, including the boy Johnny and the way he arrived in Washington. I have fictionalized his life, and those of others, while keeping the basic facts as true to the written record as possible.

Blessings from the Ozarks,

Valerie Hansen